# REDUNDANCY PAY

# REDUNDANCY PAY

by

## J. R. L. ANDERSON

LONDON
VICTOR GOLLANCZ LTD
1976

© J. R. L. Anderson 1976

ISBN 0 575 02083 0

MADE AND PRINTED IN GREAT BRITAIN BY
THE GARDEN CITY PRESS LIMITED
LETCHWORTH, HERTFORDSHIRE SG6 1JS

# CONTENTS

## AUTHOR'S NOTE

The bones of the land and seascape in this story are real enough, but the flesh is largely imagined—there is no River Fin rising on Dartmoor, and thus no little fishing port called Finmouth where it meets the sea.

I have rendered the speech of South Devon fishermen in more or less standard English, because unless you attempt the precision of a phonetic dictionary—which may be useful linguistically but is typographically horrible—it has always seemed to me merely irritating to try to convey dialect by malforming ordinary words and phrases. But read it, please, with the ear as well as with the eye, to hear the slight broadening of vowels, and the softening of "s"—not quite to the "z" of Somerset, but to something a little nearer "z" than you get in common English —that make the Devon tongue so kindly and attractive.

Collectively, in their strength, independence and generosity, my fishing folk are real, but individually all the characters in my tale are wholly imagined.

# I

## *Point of Departure*

"WHAT YOU NEED, David, is a good, stiff gin," Louise said, adding her tinkly little laugh, which once he had found so enticing but which now was merely irritating.

"There isn't any gin," he said.

"What do you mean, 'There isn't any gin'?"

"Well, you poured yourself a drink before I came in, and that finished the bottle. There isn't another one."

"But you pass the wine shop on your way home, and there's no problem of parking in the evening. Why didn't you get some more?"

"Because I can't afford it."

Louise got up, walked round the room, and stamped her foot.

"David, I'm getting absolutely fed up with you," she said. "I daresay you have been made redundant, but you're supposed to be a good accountant, and you can easily get another job if you try. Why, Stephen was on the phone this afternoon—I'd have told you before if you hadn't been so bad-tempered. He wants you to go to see him, to talk about a job at Peerage Investments."

"I don't want a job at Peerage Investments. I've been made redundant, and as far as I can see that's precisely what I am— redundant. I've been well educated and highly trained—and all I've done is to make paper money. Now the paper's rotting away. I want to do something useful."

"What do you suppose you can do?"

"I can catch lobsters."

Again the tinkly laugh. "What a baby you are! Because you used to go fishing with your father, you think you're the world's great fisherman. How many years is it since you've caught a lobster—if you ever have? And if you do go lobster-fishing, what am I supposed to do? Boil the bloody things?"

9

"At least you'd be helping to produce food."

"You make me sick. Pull yourself together, slip out to the wine shop and get some more gin."

"I am not going to the wine shop."

"What are you going to do, then?"

"Well, I'd hoped we could have a sensible talk about things. Since obviously we can't, I think I'll go away."

"When?"

"I don't suppose you've cooked any supper, so I might as well go now."

"I had lunch with Gwen and afterwards we went to Harrods, so I haven't had time to cook. I thought we'd go out to that new restaurant—you know, the one in Kentish Town."

"You can go if you like. I'm not going, because we can't afford it. I'm going away."

"David, are you really leaving me?"

"Yes."

"How absolutely fascinating!"

The row between them ended with Louise making a skirt-swirling exit, slamming the door of the sitting-room, and going out in her own car. David remained in a state of frozen misery until he heard the car drive off. Then he went to the spare room where he was allowed to store what Louise called his "junk", and hunted at the back of a cupboard for a rucksack that he had once owned, and believed he still had. After some rummaging, he found it. Was he really going to leave Louise? Had he meant to? Was this final? His frozen state passed off, and he tried to think about things clearly.

At thirty-one, David Grendon was a profoundly unhappy man. Until last week, his life had been what most people would have called a success story. He had come down from Cambridge with a good degree in maths, qualified as an accountant, and developed a shrewd ability as a tax consultant, particularly in the property market. He joined Main Street Holdings, the big consortium specialising in the development of shop and office property, and a year ago had been appointed Chief Accountant. Then came the crash: property values fell, and Main Street's large borrowings were no longer covered by the underlying value of its assets. The concern held too much money invested by insurance companies and pension funds to be allowed to go under, a rescue operation was mounted by the banks, and liquidation arrested. But the price was a virtual take-over by other groups; all but two of Main Street's board had to go, and most of the company's chief officers were sacked with them. David, perhaps, need not have gone: his reputation was good, he had seen the crash coming, he had done what he could to warn the board, and in the resulting reconstruction much of his advice was taken by the rescuing banks. But he was sickened by the whole business, and as the terms of the final merger called for heavy redundancies among Main Street's senior staff he took his notice with his colleagues. His period of notice was now ending: and at the end of the week he would be out of a job. There would be a bit of redundancy pay, but he had been with the firm only for three years, and that was that.

For months he had been trying to get Louise to accept that their financial future was extremely precarious, but she refused to contemplate any change in their style of living, arguing simply that all David had to do was to get another job. David, having experienced the collapse of Main Street Holdings and living from day to day in the ominous depression of the City, was less sanguine—if he took the job that he could probably get in Peerage Investments they, too, might be on the rocks in a few months. But there was a deeper reason for his unhappiness —he was wholly disenchanted with what he had come to call "the paper-money chase", which seemed an abject waste of life. His and Louise's financial improvidence now shocked him. He had been earning quite a lot of money, but had nothing real to show for it: their nice house in Highgate had been bought with a huge mortgage; they spent his salary as it came in.

He had married Louise three years ago, when he got his job with Main Street. As the wife of a rising young business man, she was near perfection—but he had slowly come to realise that he had never been able to talk to her about anything that really mattered. David was a fair-minded person, and he did not blame her—she was what she was, extremely pretty, but she wanted a lot from life. Why not? But David felt more and more deeply that most of the things she wanted were not worth having, and that the things she *didn't* want meant a great deal. She did not want children—and David, privately, longed to start a family. As long as shops would give credit, she simply did not care how the bills were to be met. She liked London parties and smart

11

restaurants: the idea of living and working anywhere out of London appalled her. If there was blame, David thought, it rested on him—he should never have wanted to marry her. But considerations of blame were futile—the one vital question was whether their life together could go on. The events of that evening seemed decisive—it could not. David had little idea of what would become of him, but he was fairly certain that Louise would fall on her feet. She was still only twenty-five—better make a break now and give her a chance to team up with someone else, than drag on into a future that seemed all too likely to drag them both down.

The hunt for the rucksack manifested an overpowering longing that had suddenly come upon him—to get clear away from London and live somewhere in the open air. In his Cambridge days he'd been keen on rock-climbing, and until he and Louise were married he'd kept it up a bit. Marriage had put paid to all that—Louise regarded such activities as plain idiocy. He'd kept some kit, though—the rucksack, a small bivouac tent, some camping equipment. He collected them now, and packed them with a minimum of personal belongings—a couple of spare shirts, pullover, socks and shaving things. Then he changed from his City suit into old trousers, thick jersey and boots. Taking nothing that he could not carry on his back, he went out of the house. He left his latchkey on the hall table: once he had shut himself outside the door, he could not get back into the house.

Grendon is a place-name on Dartmoor, and the Grendons were a Devon family. David's father had been a rather prosperous solicitor, but his grandfather—and his forbears for as long as anybody knew—had been boatbuilders on the South Devon coast. The traditional sailing fishing-boats they built belonged to history, and after his grandfather's death the boatbuilding business was no more—apart from a little repair work, it had barely existed for some years before he died. The old man, however, had taught David to sail, and there was nothing his father liked better than to abandon his busy practice for a holiday with his parents. Lobster-fishing was his speciality, and David's earliest memories were of going out before dawn to get to the lobster-pots at first light. He thought vaguely now

12

that if he could get some sort of job with an inshore fishing-boat he could perhaps earn a living from it—and he wanted more than anything else at the moment to feel that he *could* earn a living by doing something with his hands, in the open air.

Until he walked out of his house that evening he had not given conscious thought to making plans. Unconsciously his mind must have been busily planning, for once he had decided to act he found that he had a clear idea of at least his immediate actions. First, he must return his car, which was a company car. It would have to go back at the end of the week, anyway, and he could leave a note on the steering wheel to say that he was turning it in, and turning himself out, a couple of days in advance. Main Street's successors had already moved into the grandiose Main Street building in the City. There was privileged parking space there for the senior staff, and he drove the car to the bay that, for two days longer, was still his. Having written a brief note on a page of his loose-leaf notebook, he tore it out, attached it to the wheel, and left.

He was now on his own. It was nearly nine o'clock and the City was deserted, but he could get to Paddington on the Metropolitan line, and there were plenty of small eating-places around Paddington where he could get some sort of meal. He did not consciously decide to make for Paddington—it just seemed the obvious place to go. He could get a train from there to the West Country, and the automatic part of him had already decided to go there.

In a little side-street off the main road outside Paddington station he found a coffee-bar, went in and bought a plate of bacon, chips and egg. He was surprised to find how hungry he was, and after the meal he felt better. Over a second cup of coffee he considered what to do next.

He had on him in cash £25 in notes and a few coins. There were a number of small hotels in the area, and he debated whether to get a room for the night and go on to Devon in the morning, or whether to travel by the midnight mail train. The advantages all seemed to be with the night journey. First, it would conserve his cash, and secondly it would get him to Devon with the whole day before him. He finished his coffee, humped his pack, walked across to Paddington station and bought a single ticket for Totnes.

The train was not crowded, and sitting in a corner-seat he

felt relaxed and comfortable. He had to make an effort to think of Louise; already she seemed to belong to another world. Was he treating her badly in running away? Was he running away? Yes and no to both. Louise would be all right. She might be a bit put out because he'd actually gone off, but he doubted if she would even miss him much: he was no use to her without a fat City job. He'd paid £200 into her personal bank account last week, so she was all right for money for the moment. After that she had her father who was—on paper, anyway—a well-off stockbroker. If he went bust it might make Louise start to think, but he had not gone bust yet. The old boy would probably be quite pleased to have Louise keep home for him for a bit, until she found a replacement husband. They were the same sort of people, and got on well together. Thinking of Louise's father turned his thoughts to his own father. He and his mother had died within six months of each other in his last year at Cambridge. That was nearly ten years ago—how old he was getting! And he still missed his father. He was the only child and he had been close to both his parents, but particularly to his father. His father had never known Louise—he wondered what he would have made of her. Would he approve of his running away from her? Probably not, for he had a strict family code. But his father would have understood; he would not have tried to persuade him to go back. And was he running away? In one sense, obviously, but he didn't feel like running away— he felt more as if he was setting out to look for something. Oh, well, it was done now, and regret was the most futile of all emotions. He supposed that he'd have to write to Louise—he had nothing to say to her, but it would be tidier to write, and when she wanted a divorce she could show the letter to her lawyer. But he wasn't going to try to write in the train. He felt pleasantly sleepy, and soon after the train had stopped at Reading he drifted off to sleep.

He slept through to Exeter, where a particularly loud clatter of milk cans or something woke him up. It was just on 5 a.m. Exeter to Totnes was about an hour's run, and although it was early he thought he'd better use the lavatory on the train to wash and shave, for he didn't know where or when he'd get another chance.

Shaved and refreshed both by the wash and his sleep, he spent the last half hour of the journey in planning the immediate future. He would shop for supplies in Totnes, and then make for Dartmoor, where he would pitch his tent. That was as far ahead as he thought it worth planning for the moment.

The train got to Totnes a few minutes after six. It wasn't a bad morning, grey, but fine, and it would have been pleasant to set off walking at once, but it wouldn't do because although he had his tent and things, he had no food, and needed paraffin and methylated spirit for his Primus. So he would have to stay in Totnes until the shops opened. With his kit he had a small writing-case that his mother had given him when he was at school, and which he always travelled with. He went into the station waiting-room, took his writing-case from the rucksack, and wrote his letter to Louise. It took only a few minutes. He wrote simply that he was sorry that things had turned out as they had, that he was sure she would be happier to be free of him, that he couldn't give an address because he intended to tramp on Dartmoor for a bit, but that he would let his only relative—a cousin, married to a doctor in Edinburgh—know where he was from time to time, and if for any legal reason Louise might want to get in touch with him, she could do so through his cousin. When he had written his letter, it seemed a sadly arid ending to a marriage, and he wondered briefly whether he ought to add anything in the way of sentiment. He decided not to: it wouldn't mean anything to Louise, who was not a sentimental person, and it would be wholly insincere. He had a stamp in his wallet, and there was a pillar-box just outside the station. He posted the letter, and felt better.

Next he contemplated his finances. After paying for his ticket and his supper, he had just over £17. That would be enough for food for some time, and he didn't think he would need much else. He still had about £120 in his current account at the bank, and just over £700 on deposit. He also owned the house in Exeter which his father had left him, but that was let, and as he was unlikely to be able to get a possession order against the tenants even if he wanted to—which he didn't, because they were very decent people—it was not an easily negotiable asset. There remained further about £6,000 invested in two building societies, the balance of his father's legacy, most of which had gone into the Highgate house. He was, therefore, not exactly penniless, but he didn't want to touch any money apart from the cash he had with him. If Louise decided to divorce him

15

—and he was sure that she would—he would have to pay the legal costs, and he'd need money in hand for that. More important, though, was his determination to make a living somehow, a *real* living as distinct from the paper-money chase. The £17 he had with him would have to do until he could earn some more.

Totnes station in the early morning began to seem rather tedious. There was still more than an hour before he could hope to find any shops open, he was quite hungry, and briefly he considered going to a hotel for some breakfast. He put that idea out of his mind as soon as he thought of it—it would make far too big a hole in his available capital. So he left his pack in the waiting-room, and went for a walk instead.

When the shops did open he made his food purchases— porridge oats, sugar, tinned milk, a small packet of salt, rye biscuits, cheese and a pound of sausages. As a luxury he allowed himself a half-pound tin of ground coffee. Paraffin was rather a problem, because he had no container, but after two unsuccessful efforts he found a garage which let him have an empty one-gallon oil tin. A gallon of paraffin was more weight than he wanted to carry, but the tin was the best he could do, and at least it would last for some time.

Having done his shopping he went back to the station, collected his pack, and arranged his load. It seemed horribly heavy. Five years ago, when he was more in training, it would not have bothered him, but now, he was shocked to discover, it did. However, there was nothing to be done about it, and he hoped he would soon get back into condition. He shouldered his pack and set off for South Brent, about six miles out of Totnes.

On the way out of the town he passed a shop which had "For Sale" notices on it, and which was being used temporarily to sell second-hand goods in aid of a charity. On the pavement outside stood an elderly bicycle, offered for £6. He stopped to have a look at it—old, certainly, but it seemed in fair condition, and it had a carrier at the back. Six pounds would be a severe strain on what was left of his money after shopping, but the bicycle seemed quite a bargain, and it would undoubtedly be useful. He went in and bought it, tied his pack to the carrier, and rode on. The bicycle made his load much lighter, and his spirits rose as he began to leave the town behind him.

A bicycle had not figured in his earlier planning, but now that he had one he wondered why he had not thought of it before. It called for a bit more capital expenditure though—it would be useless to have a bicycle if he couldn't blow up the tyres, or mend a puncture. Well, that couldn't be helped. He stopped at a garage which also had a sort of general shop and bought a pump, repair outfit, and a torch-battery cycle lamp. He had no other means of lighting, and the lamp could be used for general purposes, as well as on the bicycle. Having bought it, he decided that he had better get a spare battery as well. After these purchases, he had just £4 left.

Shopping, and the excitements of the bicycle, had taken his mind off breakfast, but two or three miles out of Totnes he began to feel very empty indeed. He had left the main road at Fork Cross and was following the valley of the Barbourne River. There was a pleasant spot by the bank of the stream, and here he stopped for a meal of rye biscuits and cheese. Although he had no appointment to keep, and it mattered to nobody where he went, or when he got there, he felt curiously guilty about stopping, and as soon as he had eaten he mounted the bicycle again, and went on. After crossing the busy road to Ivybridge and Plymouth, the high ground of Brent Moor and Ugborough Moor began to seem quite close, Brent Moor to the north-west, Ugborough Moor due west. It was a countryside that he had known as a boy, and although the moors can often seem grim and forbidding they appeared almost to be beckoning to him now.

He decided to make for Ugborough Moor, and a mile or so after passing South Brent he left the road for a track that more or less followed the Glaze Brook. He could ride for a bit, but when the track became rough grass and started to climb steeply he had to get off and walk. But he was still glad of the bicycle—it was much easier to push his load on wheels than it would have been to carry it.

Near the summit of the moor, a quarter of a mile or so to his left, rose a hillock, crowned with what, from a distance, looked like a ruined castle. He knew that there was no castle there, and that the "ruins" were simply outcrops of rock, though some of them may indeed have formed dwellings in Neolithic times, 4,000 or 5,000 years ago. There was no direct path to the hillock, but the ground was firm, and the going just about good enough

17

to wheel his bicycle. He left the track, and made his way to the rocks. When he got there he saw that some of them formed rough circles, the so-called "hut-circles" that are fairly common in this part of Dartmoor, suggesting a prehistoric population a good deal larger than the moor supports now. One of these circles, a little below the top of the hillock, and sheltered by a curve in the hillside from west through north to east, seemed ideally suitable as a site for his tent. There was a leaning stone which was nearly as good as a shed for his bicycle and a flat patch of grass offering a splendid floor—and a reasonably soft bed—for his living quarters. He unpacked, and put up the tent. "Neolithic Villa seems all right," he said to himself.

It was a still day, and he could hear the trickle of water not far away. He made towards the sound, and about 100 yards below the hilltop found a stream splashing over some big stones. The water was beautifully clear, and, cupping his hands, he gave himself a long, cool drink. Never, he thought, had water tasted so good. This was not the beastly, chlorinated stuff of towns, but natural, living water—just such water, he thought, as must have come from the rock when Moses struck it.

He had two water bottles, filled them both, and went back to his camp. Then he got the Primus going, cooked three of his sausages, and ate them on rye biscuits with deep contentment. He wound up his meal with a pan of coffee.

There was no habitation in sight, but he had passed a farm shortly before he left the track, and it could not be more than half a mile away. He thought that later on he would see if he could get some eggs there. But not today. For the moment he wanted nothing but the peace and sense of space of the moor and sky. It pleased him to feel that he had pitched his tent perhaps where some family had lived two thousand years before anyone had heard of money. They had got a living somehow, and he would, too. Not on the moor, for short of sheep-stealing, which he didn't propose to go in for, he doubted if soft twentieth-century hands—weak twentieth-century spirit, rather —could scrape a living from the moor any longer. He could live on the moor for a bit, though—Neolithic Villa was rent-free. The bicycle had widened greatly his range of possible activity, and tomorrow he would have a look at the coast. The whole of Bigbury Bay would be within reasonable cycling reach, within a radius of ten to fifteen miles. He would see if there was any chance of a job at Finmouth, mostly holiday resort now, but still a fishing village at heart. He must be somewhere near the headwaters of the Fin River—perhaps the brook that he drank from ran into it.

It was barely evening, but he had been awake since five, and for all that the bicycle had made it easier to carry his load, unaccustomed cycling had been quite hard work. The sleeping-bag in his low, bivouac tent was inviting. He got into it, and left the flap of the tent open, so that he could see the sky. It was still light enough to read—but he had nothing to read. Or—it was just possible that he had. He searched in one of the little pockets of his rucksack. . . . Yes, it was still there, a little paper-back collection of some of the English metaphysical poets. He remembered taking it to the Italian Alps, five, six, it must have been seven years ago. It was like meeting a long-lost friend. He opened it at random, and the page gave him Henry Vaughan's lovely poem,

> I saw Eternity the other night
> Like a great ring of pure and endless light
> All calm as it was bright . . .

## II

# *The Combe Dean Chalice*

DETECTIVE SERGEANT John Blundell felt sorry for the distracted young woman in his office, but somehow he had to get a coherent story from her. He knew Elizabeth Danvers slightly; at least he knew her by sight as the daughter of the Rector of Combe Dean, a small village in the large area in which he was supposed to keep crime in check.

"Can you give me any idea, Miss Danvers, when the chalice was last seen?" he asked.

"But that's just what we can't do! You see, it was much too valuable to use. And now it's gone. I think it will kill Daddy if you can't get it back."

Sergeant Blundell sighed. In the days—he supposed there were once such days—when men feared the wrath of God it would have been unthinkable for a chalice to be stolen. But only last week he had been called to a church where an offertory box had been forced open with a crowbar for the gain of $7\frac{1}{2}$p. He had caught the louts who did it, and they had complained of the meagre return for their effort. The Combe Dean chalice was worth—he did not know what, but certainly a great deal of money. "Tell me," he said gently, "just how your father discovered that it was missing."

The girl tried to collect herself. "It was after lunch," she said. "We don't often have people to lunch—we usually have just bread and cheese ourselves—but today we had Sir George Dorrance, a friend of Daddy's from Oxford, and a photographer friend of his, a woman called Sue Grainger. Sir George is writing a book on sixteenth-century gold plate, and naturally he wanted to write about the chalice, and to have a photograph of it. They didn't arrive until just after one o'clock, so we thought we'd have lunch first. After lunch I gave them coffee, and Daddy went across to the church to get the chalice. He came back a minute or two later and just said, 'It isn't there'. So we all went to the church with him. The safe in the vestry was open, and the chalice wasn't there."

"Was the safe open when your father got there, or did he open it?"

"Daddy thinks he opened it with his key. But he isn't absolutely sure. He is very upset."

"Well, I'd better get out there straight away. Why didn't you telephone instead of coming all the way to Ivybridge?"

"I wanted to telephone, but Daddy said it would be better if I came to see you to tell you about it. I think he felt that I would be doing something—oh, I can't explain."

"I can understand that, Miss Danvers. Try not to worry too much." Blundell felt how stilted the words were, and wished he could say something more adequate to comfort her. "Would you like to come with me, or will you drive back in your own car?"

"I'd better take our car home. We're awfully stuck without it."

"You go on then, and I'll follow." The elderly Mini was parked near the police station. Blundell opened the door for her, and watched her drive off. His police car would be a good deal faster, and he did not want to be on her tail through the twisty lanes to Combe Dean. So he gave her a few minutes start, and then set off after her.

There are two Combes, nestling on the southern edge of Dartmoor, neither quite on the moor, but both, in a sense, of it. One is Combe Dean, the other Combe Episcopi and both are related to the bishopric of Exeter, their produce once bespoken by the Dean and Bishop respectively. Combe Dean is slightly the larger of the two, but the parishes are now combined, and the living is that of Dean cum Episcopi. It could not, Blundell reflected, be a particularly rich living—Miss Danvers' remark about the bread and cheese lunches stayed in his mind. He knew her slightly, at any rate by sight, for the Combes were in his district, and Canon Danvers had been rector of Combe for ages, and both the rector and his daughter were respected and well-liked. He thought over what he knew about them. The Canon must have been at Combe for something like thirty years. Elizabeth—his only child—was born a few years after he came, which would make her around twenty-six or twenty-seven. Her mother had been killed in a road accident getting on for ten years ago, and since then Elizabeth had looked after her father and run the rectory. Rather a trap, Blundell thought, for the girl, but she seemed to find plenty to do. Whenever anything took him to the Combes—through them rather than to them, for they were generally law-abiding villages—he nearly always met her Mini somewhere on the road. There were a number of outlying farms in the parish, and she was always about the place, driving her father to visit somebody, delivering parish magazines, doing something or other for the Women's Institute. Her load of unpaid work was huge.

And the Canon? Blundell had seen him less often than his daughter, but there was no difficulty about recognising him for he was exceptionally tall and thin, with a deeply-lined face and a head of silvery-white hair, no trace of baldness for all that he couldn't be much under seventy. "He looks as if he ought to have a halo," somebody had once said, and indeed he had a reputation for saintliness. He was also reputed to be a scholar, and the local people were proud of him, though nobody seemed quite sure in what field his scholarship lay. In fact— though Blundell did not know this—Canon Danvers was a world authority on the Hittites, those strange, virile people who once rivalled the power of the Egyptian Pharaohs and then disappeared from history until their ancient capital in what is now Turkey was excavated early in the twentieth century.

Blundell had never seen the Combe Dean chalice, although he had, of course, heard of it, for it was among the most precious church possessions in Devonshire. It was reputed to have been presented to the church at Combe Dean—whose then rector was a friend of his—by Sir Francis Drake, on his return from his famous voyage in the *Golden Hind*. It was said to have been made from gold captured from the Spaniards during the voyage, and was a magnificent example of sixteenth-century craftsmanship. Its theft—if it was stolen—would create a stir. Blundell sighed. If it was stolen, it was likely to be a highly-specialised theft, not in any way local, the sort of crime that is exceedingly hard to unravel. And unless it had been taken by someone who wanted to gloat on it in secret, it seemed a fairly pointless theft, for although the chalice was immensely valuable it was in all the reference books, and would certainly be recognised if it came up for sale. Of course, it might have been taken by vandals simply to be melted down. Blundell sighed again.

The destruction of the chalice would be an outrage greater than its theft, and unless it could be traced it was obviously in risk of damage or destruction. That meant he would have to act quickly.

The Mini got to the rectory a couple of minutes before Blundell, and Miss Danvers and the rector were waiting for him on the steps of the still elegant, though sadly dilapidated, eighteenth-century portico. Blundell was shocked by the rector's appearance; he looked like a man stricken by some dreadful illness. But he spoke with an old-fashioned courtesy, somehow in keeping with the eighteenth-century rectory. "It is good of you to have come so quickly. I fear I have put you to much trouble," he said.

"Who knows that the chalice is missing?" Blundell asked.

"So far only myself and my daughter, Sir George Dorrance, Mrs Grainger, and you—and, of course, whoever may have taken it. I shall have to report the loss to the churchwardens and to the Bishop, but I thought it right to wait until you came."

"That is wise, I think. Can you show me the safe where it was kept?"

"It is in the vestry. Let us go across to the church."

The walled garden of the rectory adjoined the churchyard, and a door in the wall led to a path to the church. When the rector opened the church door Blundell observed that it was not locked.

"Is this door normally locked?" he asked.

"No. God's house is never locked," the rector said. The vestry was a small room opening from the west end of the nave. A row of cassocks and surplices for the choir hung along one wall, and in a corner opposite was a big early-Victorian safe. It was clearly of immense weight, for the sturdy oak trestle on which it stood was bowed. The rector opened the safe with a key from a small bunch which he carried in his trouser pocket, the key-ring on a chain attached to a trouser button. The heavy door swung easily. The safe was divided by a shelf into two compartments. The bottom was stacked with parish registers, and on the shelf were a silver chalice and patten and a bottle of Sacrament wine.

"This is the chalice we use. The gold chalice should be on the shelf beside it. It is gone," the rector said.

Blundell was appalled. "Do you mean that the Combe Dean chalice was kept in this safe in an unlocked church?" he asked.

"Of course. Where else should it be kept? It belongs to the church. It has been here for 300 years."

The vestry was poorly lighted by one small window of heavily-leaded panes of glass and most of such light as might have come through them was obscured by a creeper on the outside wall. There was one electric light bulb but it was not very bright. Blundell took a torch from his bag and studied the safe. It was really a museum-piece, he thought. The main protection it offered was simply its weight, for he reckoned that the lock could probably be opened in a few minutes with modern tools. There were fingerprints on the rim of the inside shelf, and also on the door. They would have to be photographed, but he doubted if they would yield much—they would probably turn out to be the rector's own, or maybe the churchwardens'. The safe itself could be sent for expert examination at the forensic laboratory, which would show whether the lock had been tampered with, or opened with a key. That was necessary routine, but whether it would do anything towards finding the thief was another matter. And there was a lot more routine work to be set in motion as soon as possible—house-to-house inquiries in the village to ask whether any strangers or strange cars had been seen in the vicinity, the antiques' trade and bullion dealers would have to be notified, and so would the Customs and numerous other authorities; and there would have to be a detailed examination of the church itself and its surroundings.

"There's not much more we can do here at the moment but there is a great deal of investigating to be done," Blundell said. "Can you please lock the vestry and the church until I can get the safe photographed and taken away for examination? And may I use your telephone?"

"Of course. We'll go back to the rectory. I can lock the vestry, but I don't know about the church—I'm not at all sure that I can find the key."

"I know where the key is, Daddy. It's on a hook on the wall near the font," Elizabeth Danvers said.

"Thank you, Elizabeth. Perhaps you would get it for us. I hate leaving the church locked, even temporarily, but in the circumstances I suppose it will have to be done. Are you ready to return to the rectory, Sergeant Blundell?"

\* \* \*

24

When he got to the telephone Blundell first rang his own police station and asked for a photographer, for a lorry and a crew of four men to move the safe, and for a constable to help him in his house-to-house inquiries. Then he reported to his immediate superior in Plymouth, who understood at once the importance and the implications of the case. He told Blundell that he would get in touch with the headquarters of the CID at Exeter, and asked him if he could stay at the rectory for a bit in case one of the high-ups from Exeter wanted to come down himself. Blundell had expected this. He wanted to get on with his own inquiries in the village, so he said that he couldn't guarantee to be at the rectory, but he would be in the village, and that he would make sure that the rector or his daughter knew where he was.

The telephoning over, his next job was to try to establish when the chalice had been taken. This was not easy. There had been the customary eight o'clock Communion service on Sunday, and the rector had opened the safe then to get the silver chalice and patten that were normally used. He could not swear that the gold chalice had been in the safe then because he had no reason to look specially for it, but he felt sure that he would have noticed if it had been missing. Blundell thought this reasonable, and concluded that the chalice was probably in the safe on Sunday. But today was Thursday—could the rector narrow the gap in any way? The rector did not think he could. Blundell went on with patient questioning. Had he been to the vestry at all between Sunday and today? Yes, several times. Was it locked each time? Well, it was supposed to be kept locked but he could not be sure that it always was. "I know it was locked on Tuesday," said his daughter, "because of the choir practice." She explained that she played the organ in the church and had to go to the vestry on Tuesday evening to get some music for the choir practice. She had tried the door, found it locked, and had to go back to the house to ask her father for the key. Had she locked up afterwards? Yes, she was sure she had. The rector confirmed this: he had been to the vestry on Wednesday morning to look at the parish register, and he remembered having to unlock it. Was the register in the safe? Yes, all the registers were kept in the safe. So he had opened the safe again on Wednesday?

"I had forgotten about the register," the rector said, "but of course I must have opened the safe to get it. I had a visit from a man who was staying in Plymouth. He was an American, over here on holiday. He believed that his great-grandfather had been born at Combe, and he asked if I could find any records of the family. I told him that the registers are remarkably complete from early in the eighteenth century, and that we have some going back well into the seventeenth century. If his great-grandfather had been baptised at Combe there would almost certainly be a record of it. He came over to the church with me, and I got out several volumes of the register. His great-grandfather had died about 1900, but he did not know his age, though he thought he had been an elderly man. That did not mean much—he might have been born at any time between 1820 and 1850, with the probability, perhaps, tending towards the 1830s or 1840s. Unhappily, there must have been some mistake, for I could find no one of the name. He was much disappointed."

"Did you notice the chalice?"

"I can't say that I noticed it, but I think I would have noticed if it had not been there." He passed his hand wearily across his forehead. "It is so difficult, you see. The chalice has always been there—I have known it for thirty years. I *think* I would have noticed if it had not been in its place—I think I should have *felt* that something was wrong. I knew at once today, as soon as I opened the safe. But you are asking about yesterday. I can say only what I *think*—I cannot be quite sure."

"You must have been in the vestry a considerable time while looking up the registers."

"Yes, we were there at least an hour. I remember it was close on one o'clock when we left. I felt guilty about not offering my visitor some lunch—he was distressed at not learning anything about his ancestor. But in these days you will understand—it would not have been fair to Elizabeth. We eat little ourselves, and there is not much for unexpected guests."

"Did the man help you at all with the registers? Did he hand them to you to put back in the safe, or help you get them out?"

"We studied them on the vestry-table. Yes, he was well-mannered. They are quite heavy volumes, and I'm sure he helped me handle them."

"What was his name?"

"His great-grandfather's name was Layton, he believed James

26

or John Layton, but he was not certain which. But that was his mother's grandfather, so the surname was not his. His own name? Wait—he gave me a card, and it must still be in my pocket."

The rector felt in several pockets and finally produced a visiting-card. It read "Wilbur S. Platt" with an address at Old Colony Avenue, Boston, Massachusetts. "But he said he was staying in Plymouth," the rector said.

"Did he say where?"

"No. But I assumed it was at a hotel. I don't know why—he *looked* as if he would be staying at a hotel. He was well-dressed, and he seemed quite prosperous. He asked if I should be paid anything for showing him the registers. I said that there was no need to pay me, but that if he cared to put a contribution in the offertory box in the church, it would be welcome. I think he did drop in an offering as we went out."

"We must try to get hold of Mr Platt," Blundell said. "It is possible that he may have noticed the chalice—if so, it would confirm that it was still there yesterday morning. Since we don't know where he is staying I shall have to ask Plymouth police to make inquiries. We'll need a description of him, too. What sort of age, height—how would you describe him?"

The rector could have given an admirable description of a Hittite inscription, but he was much less observant of yesterday's visitor. "I didn't really notice him very much," he said apologetically. "I think he was wearing a darkish suit—dark brown perhaps. He had glasses, horn-rimmed glasses. I don't think he was particularly tall, or particularly short, for that matter. Age? Oh dear, I can't possibly say. He was not a boy, and he was certainly not an old man. Could I say between twenty-five and fifty? Would that be any use to you?"

Blundell thought it of remarkably little use, but he duly wrote it down. However, he did better than he feared, because Elizabeth Danvers had seen the man depart. She had not been at home when he came, but he was just saying goodbye to her father when she got back, and she had looked at him fairly closely to see if she knew who he was. She would describe him as of middle height—say 5 feet 8 or 9 inches—with longish dark brown hair, tidy, but definitely hanging over his collar. And she would put his age at thirty-five or so, or maybe a bit more—

27

late thirties rather than early thirties, anyway, and she wouldn't be surprised if he turned out to be in his early forties.

"Did he come by car?"

"Yes, he drove up to the house. The gate to the drive is always open nowadays—actually, it has fallen off its hinges."

"Could you say what sort of car?" The rector couldn't, but Elizabeth could. "It was a biggish Vauxhall, an estate car, I think. And it was dark green."

"I suppose you can't recall the number?"

"No," Elizabeth said. "I didn't notice the number, but I can tell you the letters, because they were MEW. I remember them, because they made me think of seagulls."

Blundell was getting quite excited—this was far better than he had hoped. He was exceedingly interested in Mr Platt: what easier way of opening the safe could there be than getting the rector to open it himself? The vestry was far from well lighted, and the rector would, no doubt, have been utterly absorbed in his old registers. It would have been easy enough to take the chalice, and to hide it under one's coat or to slip it in a bag of some sort. Then, if you helped to put back the registers, it would have been easy to stand in front of the safe so that the rector would not notice that the chalice was missing. Was Mr Platt carrying a coat or bag? The rector, alas, had no idea, and when Miss Danvers saw him he was standing by his car, and would have had time to put anything he might have been carrying inside the car. It would have been nice to have more information, but it did not matter much. He had enough to start a police hunt for Mr Platt: he might, of course, be wholly innocent, but he must be found and eliminated from the inquiry —if he was innocent—as soon as possible. Blundell asked permission to use the rectory phone again, and rang Plymouth with the news of Mr Platt, and as full a description as he could give of him. Plymouth was impressed, and undertook to start a hunt for Mr Platt forthwith.

Blundell had intended to begin his round of house-to-house inquiries in Combe as soon as he had taken a statement from the rector, but the emergence of Mr Platt rather changed his thinking. There was no real evidence against Mr Platt, but the circumstantial evidence made it seem quite likely that he had something to do with the theft. The chalice had apparently been in the safe on Sunday, and the rector had not noticed its absence when he opened the safe to get the registers on Wednesday (whether it was still there when he put them back was another matter). After lunch on Thursday afternoon, the chalice had gone. Between Sunday and Thursday the vestry had been entered several times, and such evidence as there was suggested that the door had not been found unlocked. That might not mean very much, but as far as it went it did indicate that the theft was carried out by subterfuge rather than by breaking and entering.

House-to-house inquiries would have to be made, but they could wait a little. Blundell considered whether to recall the transport he had asked for to take the safe for forensic examination, but he decided to leave things here as they were. Expert examination of the safe was a necessary part of the investigation, and if it showed conclusively that the lock had not been tampered with, that at least would be negative information of some value.

While waiting for the photographer and other assistance he had summoned, Blundell turned to finding out as much as he could about the chalice. There were various published descriptions of it, but he himself had never seen it, and he needed a more detailed physical conception of it. But when he began asking questions, the rector said, "You would do better to consult Sir George Dorrance. He is perhaps the greatest living authority on plate of the period, and he is here, in this house. He and Mrs Grainger had arranged to stay the night with us; although they are deeply distressed by what has happened there was no reason to cancel the arrangement. Also, it may be, they did not wish to desert me. Elizabeth, can you find George?"

"I think they are both in the drawing-room. I saw them through the window as we came in."

"Let us go to them, then."

Sir George Dorrance was of the rector's generation, donnishly polite and soft-spoken. The rector formally introduced Blundell, and Elizabeth said practically, "I think we could all do with a cup of tea." She went off to get it, and Blundell asked if he could have a quick description of the chalice.

"I have a small pamphlet concerning it—I wrote it for Canon Danvers some years ago." Sir George had a briefcase with him, and he took the pamphlet from it. "You may keep this," he said. "It will give you all you wish to know."

"But I should still like your views, sir. Can you suggest how a thief would set about disposing of it?"

"I have been thinking of little else, and it would seem a matter of the greatest difficulty. No museum or reputable collector would have anything to do with it—it is much too well-known."

"A disreputable collector, then."

"Well, I suppose there are such, but collectors who can afford to buy such pieces wish to display them. The Combe Dean chalice could never be displayed."

"What, approximately, is it worth?"

"My dear sir, it is literally priceless. It is perhaps the finest piece of sixteenth-century goldsmith's work in existence. If it could be put up for sale openly all the great museums in the world would bid for it. I cannot even suggest what it might fetch—certainly not less than a quarter of a million pounds. But it could be four or five times as much."

"I take it the chalice was insured. What is the insurance value?"

The rector answered unexpectedly. "Sergeant Blundell, I have committed a very grave crime. No, you cannot arrest me for it —it is, perhaps, a sin rather than a crime. But I must be punished, and I shall, of course, see that I punish myself—and Elizabeth, I fear. The chalice was insured—for £5,000. That was the value put on it before the First World War, when £5,000 seemed a great deal of money. The insurance has never been changed.

"You must understand that we are a poor parish—we do not think in terms of huge sums of money. Only last month, at the annual meeting of our Parochial Church Council, some members criticised the insurance premiums we pay—for fire insurance, of course, as well as for the chalice. We know that the chalice is valuable, but we have known it all our lives. And 'valuable' to a moorland farmer means something worth about £50. And for all you read of the permissive society and this secular age, we are God-fearing folk in Combe: until today I should have said that sacrilege in Combe was unthinkable.

"But I can see now that it was criminal to keep the chalice as we did in an unlocked church. I say 'we', but, of course, it is

30

I who am to blame. The chalice was in my custody, and I have betrayed a trust. And yet it was difficult—the chalice, as I told you earlier in the vestry, has been here for 300 years. A few years ago we had a request from the British Museum that we should send our chalice there on permanent loan. Would that we had done so! The matter was discussed by the Parochial Church Council and everyone was against it. So it remained where it was. Well, I have a small sum invested, inherited from my father many years ago, which I have left untouched to provide some safeguard for Elizabeth. That, now, will have to go. And we can sell most of our furniture in the rectory. All this will be nothing compared with the worth of the chalice, but it is all I have, and everything must go to the church to acknowledge my criminal neglect."

"You are talking impious nonsense, Alex," Sir George said. "Everyone has been remiss—the diocesan authorities as much as anyone else. It is not your personal fault. You did not steal the chalice."

"I tolerated the conditions in which it could be stolen. I must make such recompense as I can."

"I shall write to *The Times*. I know the Archbishop of Canterbury slightly—I shall get him to tell the church to refuse the money."

"You will do nothing of the sort, George." The rector spoke sharply. Blundell felt that he was in the presence of a priest, although the rector's spiritual authority was being exercised on himself. He returned to the more practical aspects of the chalice.

"Can you tell me, sir," he asked Sir George, "whether the chalice carried any inscription?"

Sir George was relieved by the change of subject. "No," he said, "that is one of the things that make it so valuable—the workmanship is pure artistry, a coherent whole untroubled by any interference with the design. At the same time, it is rather puzzling. There is no reason to disbelieve the tradition that the chalice was given to Combe Dean church by Sir Francis Drake, though there is no documentary record of the gift. But the period is right, and the tradition is a reasonable explanation of how such a magnificent piece of Spanish craftsmanship came into the possession of a small South Devon parish. I say 'Spanish' because it is almost certainly Spanish work, although the artist is unknown. It is conceivable that it was made by a

Spanish artist working in one of the Spanish dominions in Central America—if so, it is one of the finest works of art ever to come from the New World. The legend that Drake had it made for his friend the rector of Combe Dean out of plate melted down from his booty in the *Golden Hind* is certainly unfounded. Doubtless it came from the booty in the *Golden Hind*, but it came as it was, a piece of exquisite Spanish craftsmanship."

"It could be melted down, I suppose, and sold simply as bullion?"

Sir George shuddered. "It could, of course. But it would be a monstrous act. The chalice weighs about three pounds, and the gold is very pure, so obviously it would have some value as gold. That, however, would be only a minute fraction of its true worth."

"If it could be sold."

"Indeed. One must pray that it has been stolen as a work of art, and not as petty pilfering. Better that it should disappear into some private hoard perhaps for the next century than that it should be destroyed and lost to the world."

"Better still that it should be recovered," Blundell said. "We have only just started to investigate, and while it would be wrong to pretend that you have no cause for anxiety, it would be equally wrong to assume that the chalice is lost for ever."

Elizabeth came in with the tea, and almost at the same moment a police car drove up to the house. Blundell excused himself, and went out to meet the photographer and the constable he had asked for. They were getting hold of a lorry with lifting gear for the safe, the constable explained, but it would take a bit of time to assemble the crew. So he and the photographer had come along in advance of the lorry.

Blundell was pleased to see them. He went back into the house to ask the rector for keys to the vestry and the safe, and he also asked where he would like the parish registers and other contents of the safe put when it was taken away. Elizabeth answered for him. "They'd better come into the rectory," she said. "If you leave them in the vestry, I'll come down and carry them up."

Blundell thought of the heavy, leather-bound registers.

32

"There'll be no need for that," he said. "We'll bring them up for you when we've finished."

The police party went to the vestry, where Blundell and the constable carefully emptied the safe, stacking the contents on the vestry table. "I think we'd better have a list of the contents," he said. "I'll call out the items, and you write them in your notebook. Then we'll get the rector to give us a receipt for them when we take them up to the house."

The photographer had brought a portable floodlamp, which he plugged into the socket of the vestry's single bulb. With this powerful illumination, Blundell again examined the safe. There was a faint ring on the left-hand side of the shelf where the chalice had stood, a slight discoloration of the dark green paint, presumably caused by the weight of the chalice over the years—it must have stood there, Blundell reckoned, for well over a century. He wondered where it had been kept before the Victorian churchwardens had decided to invest in a safe. In the better light he could take in more of the furnishings of the vestry and, against the wall underneath the surplices, he noticed an iron-banded oak chest. "That'll be it, I expect," he thought. "Lord, it really is a miracle that the thing survived so long."

In the safe there was nothing that he had not seen when he examined it earlier with his torch, but in taking out one of the big parish registers he noticed a longish hair caught on a slightly torn edge of the leather binding. The volume was the register of baptisms from June 1815 to December 1837. The hair might or might not be of any significance—it certainly could not be the rector's for it was darkish in colour, and his was short and silvery white. He got a small plastic envelope from his case and put the hair carefully inside it, with a note, witnessed by the constable, of where he had found it.

When the photographer had finished there seemed nothing more to be done in the vestry. Transporting the parish registers, the silver Communion set and a few other oddments that had been in the safe, from the church to the rectory would need two or three journeys. Blundell and the constable each took a load—the photographer was loaded with his own equipment—and walked back to the house. In the drive was yet another police car: this had brought Chief Inspector Evans from Exeter, who had just arrived and was introducing himself to the rector. Blundell set down his load of parish registers in the hall. "I can give you a preliminary report now," he said to the Chief Inspector, "and I expect you'd like to have a look at the vestry, from which the chalice was apparently stolen."

"Let's get down there straight away," the Chief Inspector said.

The photographer, having put his kit in the car, was now available to help with carrying up the contents of the safe. Blundell asked the constable to see to the getting of a receipt from the rector, and he walked back to the vestry with the Chief Inspector.

"This is a bad business, sergeant," the Chief Inspector said. "There'll be a fearful row about it."

"What astonishes me, sir, is that the chalice wasn't stolen ages ago," Blundell observed. "When you see where it was kept I daresay you'll feel the same."

The photographer had replaced the rather dim bulb in the vestry, and the two detectives studied the ill-lit, dusty little room in silence for a bit. The safe, now empty, stood open, and the Chief Inspector looked at it thoughtfully. "No sign of forcible entry," he said.

"No, sir. Have you had my report to Plymouth about the visitor yesterday?"

"No. I left at once, as soon as we got your report about the chalice being missing. Don't think, sergeant, that I came because we haven't got confidence in you—your record is excellent. But this is a hell of a big case, and likely to cause no end of a stink—questions in Parliament and all that sort of thing. So there's got to be somebody to carry the can—I sometimes feel that senior police officers exist simply to be can-carriers."

"I don't know about that, sir, but of course I understand."

"Tell me about yesterday's visitor."

Blundell gave a concise account of everything that had happened since a distracted Elizabeth Danvers had arrived at the police station. The Chief Inspector listened without interrupting, and then said, "Well, sergeant, you seem to have done remarkably well. I agree with you that Mr Platt's visit is, on the face of it, highly suspect, particularly as the ancestor he was inquiring about doesn't seem to exist—not in Combe Dean, anyway. Mr Platt has certainly got to be found. And I'll get in touch with the police in the United States and ask them what is known about him in Boston. But although he's an obvious suspect—indeed, our only suspect so far—we can't assume that he's guilty. You're quite right to carry on with sending the safe for examination: it doesn't look as if it's been tampered with, but when they get the lock stripped they may find some evidence to suggest that it's been interfered with. What else are you thinking of doing locally?"

"If you approve, sir, I think we ought to carry on with house-to-house inquiries in the neighbourhood. There are two things to ask for—whether anyone may have seen a dark green Vauxhall with index letters MEW yesterday—or at any other time, for he may have made a preliminary visit—and whether any other strangers have been seen about the place recently. It's still more or less the holiday season, so we may have to try to trace the movements of quite a lot of people. But we can't really rule out anyone yet."

"You talk about strangers—but we can't wholly rule out the locals."

"No, sir, we can't, and in making house-to-house inquiries of course we must keep our eyes and ears open. But on balance this doesn't strike me as a local effort. There are two main reasons: first, I come from this part of the world, and I'd say that there was still a kind of superstitious feeling which would stop most local people from even thinking of stealing the Combe Dean chalice, and secondly, if a local man wanted to make off with it, why wait till now? It's been an open invitation to thieves for centuries."

"You're probably right, but, as you said, you must carry on with every possible inquiry. It staggers me that the church authorities were willing to leave a thing of such value in an unlocked church."

"They just didn't think about it, sir. I can't excuse them—as we know now it was almost criminal negligence—but I can understand it, at least to some extent. It wasn't a museum-piece in Combe—it was just part of their own church, it always had been part of the church. They just didn't think about guarding it, or getting it properly insured. They're not business men, they're small farmers, and farm-workers. And the rector, Mr Danvers, is much respected and well enough liked, but you couldn't begin to call him a practical man. If anybody runs the parish, it's that daughter of his—it wouldn't surprise me if she has to remind him to call the banns for a wedding."

35

"Well, it all seems pretty crazy, but if it weren't for crazy people there'd be much less opportunity for crime—it happens day in, day out, and nobody ever seems to learn. I'll say good-bye to the rector and then I think I'll go on to Plymouth and find out just what they're doing to get hold of Mr Platt. You carry on as arranged, and give me a ring in the morning. Good luck, Sergeant, and let's hope for developments soon."

The Chief Inspector's hope was not fulfilled. The mysterious Mr Platt became still more mysterious when the police at Boston, Massachusetts reported that there was no such address in Boston as that given on his card. Every police force in Britain was looking out for him, and Interpol was asked to help, but he remained totally elusive. Dark green Vauxhalls were reported from all over the country, but none had registration letters MEW, and all turned out, as far as could be ascertained, to be wholly respectable.

Sergeant Blundell accumulated a large file of statements, but none seemed to have any real bearing on the theft of the chalice. The hair he had found on one of the parish registers went to the forensic laboratory for examination. It was reported to be a human hair, probably male, from the head of someone who enjoyed reasonably good health. There was no trace of dye, and its natural colouring was a darkish shade of brown. It was impossible to make any close estimate of the age of the head from which it came. It was not a child's hair, and it didn't belong to old age. Its owner would probably be someone aged between seventeen and fifty—that was as near as one could get. So far as it went, that fitted the description of Mr Platt—it also fitted most of the brown-haired males in Britain. If Mr Platt were ever found, the hair might be decisive evidence of identity, though since the rector had said that Mr Platt had helped to put back the registers in the safe, it was not evidence that he had taken the chalice. The safe experts reported that the lock, although old, was in good condition. They did not think that it had ever been opened by anything other than a key, although the lock was of a type that a skilled man would have little difficulty in manipulating with a skeleton key. In a negative way this bore out the theory that the rector himself had opened the safe for the thief, but it did not get the police any forrader towards finding the thief. There was one unidentified fingerprint on the shelf in the safe—this might be assumed, Blundell thought, to belong to Mr Platt, but again, it was useless unless Mr Platt could be found. The other fingerprints turned out to have been made by the rector, and one of the churchwardens who doubled as treasurer to the Parochial Church Council and whose duty it was to make an annual check of the contents of the safe.

Blundell himself, with the assistance of two constables, continued with the laborious task of calling from house to house with their questions. There were a number of isolated cottages and outlying farms in the area, and visiting them took a great deal of time. Nothing at all interesting came to light until one evening a constable reported that there seemed to be someone living or hiding in the rocks on Ugborough Moor.

"Have you seen him?" Blundell asked.

"No, Sergeant. I got word of him from a farm where he called to buy eggs. He said he was camping—didn't seem to make any secret of it. I found his camp—very out of the way among the rocks. Neat and tidy, it looked, but there was no one there."

"It's nearly October and a bit late in the year for camping, but it's been reasonably fine, and there's no reason why people shouldn't camp if they want to," Blundell said. "Still, it seems a bit odd, and I think we'd better have a look at him. We can't do much in the dark, so we'll go early tomorrow morning. We'll leave from here at six."

# III

## *Lobsters and Suspicion*

DAVID HAD INCREASED his working capital from £4 to £24.

He had woken early on his first morning at Neolithic Villa, but as he had turned in before it was even dark he enjoyed a long uninterrupted sleep. He was emotionally as well as physically tired—emotional weariness by far the more exhausting—and his sleep restored nerves and confidence. He breakfasted as soon as it was light, and a good pannikin of porridge made him feel better still. It was the third week of September, and the high moorland in the early morning was distinctly chilly. But the porridge warmed him up, and he decided that it was better weather for bicycling than high summer. He was not sure how long he would be able to occupy his camp in the rocks, but he reckoned that it ought to be all right for several weeks. After that? Well, he had to find a job of some sort, and he would see what happened.

As the proverbial crow flies it was barely ten miles from Ugborough Moor to Finmouth, but crows do not have to follow South Devon lanes, and some stretches of the route seemed nearly vertical. True, an uphill trudge when it was too steep to ride offered the compensation of a descent by gravity down the other side of the ridge, but it was not a carefree descent: the winding, narrow road was a succession of blind corners and he had to go carefully to prevent gravity from taking charge and throwing the bicycle out of control. It was not a new bicycle and he was much out of practice as a cyclist. The journey took him the best part of two hours.

He had known Finmouth as a boy, and had often put in there on fishing trips with his father. The entrance could be tricky, for with wind against tide the overfalls on the bar threw a small boat about cruelly, but there was a fair passage if you could find it, and he thought he still could. Approaching the little port by land offered none of these hazards—but it was not without hazards, for he had to brake hard and get off the bicycle to avoid a milk lorry coming out of a farm track completely masked by the high hedges.

The sea was as welcoming as always. David knew enough about the sea to know that the white caps of waves are not made of cotton-wool, and that the picture book loveliness of a seascape can change quickly to an ugly thing, the playful waves becoming battering rams of tremendous power, motivated, apparently, by some malign force determined to beat the heart out of men and boats. He had certainly been afraid at sea: but he knew also that the sea itself is not malign, that it is massively uncaring about human affairs, and that a little boat and a man who keeps his head can usually live through a storm. Perhaps, he thought, as he met the sea that first morning out of Ugborough, it is the unhuman—not inhuman—*un*human— aspect of the sea that gives it such power to bestow peace. The sea asks nothing of man, and offers nothing; though if you care to take from it, it has much to give. The sea cares nothing for what a man is, saint or murderer, failed husband or devoted lover, it is all one to the sea. But a man may challenge the sea and find himself, or something beyond and outside himself which gives meaning to the bewilderment of life.

David felt the peace and cleanliness of the sea as soon as he saw it, and his spirits rose as he rode down towards it. The long bickering with Louise already was beginning to seem far away, a chapter of life closed. He was a little surprised to find that he felt neither remorse nor regret—he had given Louise what she wanted, and now he had nothing left to give that she wanted in any way at all. There could be no going back. The important thing now was to see if Finmouth could provide anything in the way of a job.

He rode down to the quay, propped his bicycle against a stone bollard, and sat on the quayside. Three or four small boats were coming in—lobstermen who must have gone out on an early tide. One boat was singlehanded. He called out to the elderly man at the small wheel aft that he would take her lines, caught the thrown warp deftly and made fast, using a hitch that his grandfather had taught him. For the first time for months he felt that he was actually being useful. "Thanks, mister," said the skipper, as the boat was brought up at the foot of some stone

39

steps. Then, "If you'd like to help some more, I'd be glad of a hand with the baskets." David climbed down the steps and helped to unload the thick lobster baskets. They were heavy to carry up. "Good catch?" he asked.

"So-so," the skipper said. "Catches aren't what they used to be. Too many of those damned skin-divers—thieves, they are. Think nothing of clearing out a man's pots. And the bloody Frenchmen—come right over from Brittany to poach our grounds. Fishery protection? Never see so much as the wake of a Navy vessel. Well, you did me a good turn, mister. Staying in Finmouth?"

"In the neighbourhood, but not actually in Finmouth. I cycled in this morning."

"From the way you made fast, you look as if you know something about a boat. Doing anything for the next few days?"

"Not particularly."

"Can you get up in the morning?"

"Yes, I suppose so. What do you mean?"

"Look, Mister. I'm Jess Grimble. It's my boat, but I've got a mate who works with me. But he's sick—went off to hospital in Plymouth. If you can get up in the morning—tide's right to-morrow around seven—I'd take you out with me. And I'll treat you fair—I'm not asking favours."

"Yes, I can be here by seven. I'm David Grendon."

"Knew a Grendon once—a boatbuilder, over Dartmouth way."

"He was my grandfather."

"Was he now! Small world! Well, he built good craft. Right, Dave—you be here in the morning at seven sharp, and we'll see what your grand-dad may have taught you."

Rather than spend money on food David rode back to the moor for a meal from his own supplies. He was ravenously hungry, and fairly exhausted by some twenty miles of hilly cycling. But he hoped the cycling would become easier as he got more used to it, and if the lobsterman wanted him for a crew, he reckoned he could get to and from Finmouth all right. He turned in early, got up at four, and had a good fill of porridge before setting off shortly before five. His trip began in the dark, and he found it slow going, but he had been careful not to use his lamp much, and the battery was still good. Then it began to get light, he

40

found he was remembering the road from yesterday, and he was able to put on speed a bit.

He got to Finmouth soon after six-thirty. There was a nip in the air, but he was warm from cycling, and he walked up and down the quay to keep himself warm while waiting for Grimble to appear. The boat had been moved from the quay, and was lying to a mooring about half-a-cable off. She looked a good tough fishing-boat. There was no wheelhouse—steering was by a small wheel in the open cockpit aft—but the boat was quarter-decked, and there seemed to be some sort of cuddy forrard. David wondered where the dinghy which they would need to get out to the mooring was kept.

At ten minutes to seven Grimble turned up. He nodded to David. "So you made it," he said. Then he looked at him more closely. "Those clothes are no good. You'll want sea-boots and an oily."

"Well, I haven't got any. I'll be all right."

"Daresay I can find some things to lend you. Come into the shed."

At the back of the quay was a row of old sheds. Grimble went to one of them, unlocked a padlock, and beckoned David inside. There was no light except from the door, and the shed was stacked from floor to roof with the dim shapes of lobster pots, coils of rope, and a clutter of boat-gear. Grimble knew exactly where to go. Moving aside a pile of lobster pots and two oars he reached behind them and brought out a pair of mud-encrusted sea-boots and an ancient oilskin coat. "These'll do," he said. "See if you can get them on."

The boots were on the large side, but David thought that he could wear them, and the coat, which was more or less shapeless, covered him well enough. "What shall I do with my bicycle?" he asked.

"Have to put it in here, with your shoes. Daresay we can just about make room. Now we'll want some fuel. Fill this jerrican from that drum of diesel and take it down. I'll bring the oars."

On the other side of the quay, protected by a stone wall with a narrow entrance, was a boat pool. Not knowing which was Grimble's dinghy, David let him go first. Grimble untied a line from an iron ring in the quayside, and brought an elderly, rather battered rowing-boat to the steps. He walked down with the oars and entered the boat.

The steps were worn and slippery. David was clumsy in the big sea-boots, and carrying the heavy can of fuel he slipped, and all but went in. "Costs money, that does, don't want it in the sea," Grimble said. "Here, give it to me." For all that he must have been at least twice David's age, he took the heavy can with one hand and slung it inboard, apparently without effort. Feeling somewhat shaken, and a bit ashamed of himself, David climbed into the dinghy. There was a fair bit of water over the floor-boards, and he was glad of the sea-boots. Grimble rowed off, with the short, seemingly leisured strokes developed by generations of sea rowing.

When they got to the fishing-boat Grimble heaved the can of fuel on board, and then got in himself. He held the boat for David, then took her painter and made it fast to the mooring. Then he came aft again, took the wooden box-cover off the engine and fiddled with one or two small adjustments. "Tank's aft," he said. "You'll find a funnel in the locker."

David found the funnel, unscrewed the tank cap, and poured in the diesel fuel. The smell took him back: it is a horrible smell, but for him it was associated with boats in which he had been happy. The tank took about three-quarters of the contents of the can. Grimble watched the proceedings, and when David had screwed down the tank cap and replaced the cap on the can, he said, "Put the can in the starboard locker forrard— there's a block of wood to wedge it upright. When you've stowed the can, get ready to cast off, but don't let go till I tell you."

David unhitched the mooring chain and held it with one turn round the samson post when it was ready to run free. Grimble swung the engine, which seemed to be in good condition, for it started at once. "Let go," he said. David threw the chain and its buoy over the side, and went back to the cockpit. It was a good moment for him—it seemed somehow to define the cutting off of his old life.

Grimble had the boat headed a little south of west. "Can you steer?" he asked.

"Yes."

"Well, take over while I light my pipe. I've got two lines of lobster pots. Being singlehanded I worked the near ones yester-day, so today we'll make for the outer pots. They're just a bit seaward of the rocks they call Wadham Rocks. We'll need to go

42

outside the bar to get there, but you can carry on till we're getting towards the bar, and then I'll take over."

"I think I know the passage," David said.

"Do you now! We'll have to see. Carry on, and I'll keep an eye on you."

It was a fair morning, with a wind from the east raising a slight chop, but otherwise calm enough, and visibility was good. The big headland of Bolt Tail was an old friend, and David knew roughly where the passage lay in relation to it. On that morning he didn't think there'd be much trouble with the bar, anyway. Grimble was apparently satisfied with the navigation, for he made no effort to interfere, and sat back, smoking contentedly.

"I told you yesterday I'd treat you fair, didn't I, Dave?"

"You did."

"Well, it's like this. What we make from the catch goes into four shares. I take two, because they're my pots. Fair enough?"

"Yes."

"Then one share goes to the boat. I take that too, because it's my boat, and I've got to pay for the fuel and the gear. The fourth share goes to you. O.K.?"

"Seems O.K. to me."

Having settled the basis of their partnership, Grimble said no more until they were well outside the bar. Then he moved over to the wheel. "You did all right, Dave, but I'll take her now, because we're coming up to the pots, and I know where the buoys are. Go forward and get ready to haul."

It was hard work, but David knew what he was doing, and with Grimble's lifetime of experience they made a good team. Pot after pot came up, and David was impressed by the catch. Then one pot came up too easily, and as David hauled it on board he saw that it was only half a pot. Grimble's whole face seemed to darken with anger. "Look," he said. "Been cut, that has, cut with a knife. One of those damned skin-divers. It's bad enough to pinch the catch, but these chaps think nothing of wrecking a man's gear as well. Trouble is you can never find them at it—they know when we go out, and keep away. Been hellish bad lately—there's a camp of them inshore of here, and they come out when there's nobody around. Asked the police to investigate the camp, but what can they do? Can't identify a lobster even if they find the camp full of them. Me and my mates are thinking of beating up the place, but it's us who'd find ourselves in court. The Frenchmen bring trouble enough, but at least they're proper fishermen. These bloody play-divers are plain swine. If I saw one drowning, I wouldn't stir a hand to save him."

David thought, "You probably would," but he understood Jess Grimble's anger. The pots were the inshore fisherman's capital, the sea area where they were laid as much his as any farmer's fields. Grimble's ground would be recognised as his by every fisherman from Bolt Head to Plymouth—he'd probably inherited the area from his father. There was an ever-present risk of losing gear from storms—deliberately to destroy a pot was indefensible. "Bastards," he said, and Grimble nodded.

There was nothing to be gained by moaning. The useless pot was tossed into the sea, and the two of them went back to work. When they had finished and were heading for home David took the wheel again, and Grimble brought from his pocket a packet of sandwiches wrapped in a bit of old oilskin. "Makes a man hungry, that does," he said. "Got nothing yourself, Dave?"

"No," David said, and cursed himself for not having thought about food.

"Have one of these, then." The sandwich was cold bacon in what tasted like home-made bread. David thought he had never eaten anything better, and wished he had several more. He was not offered another—there were not enough for both of them.

Grimble took over the wheel as they approached the harbour. "Van's in," he said. "We'll get rid of them straight away."

David went forrard and took the bow line. He was more accustomed to the boots now, and as they closed the steps where he had met Grimble yesterday he jumped for them, and ran up to make fast the line. He and Grimble carried up the baskets of lobsters, but this time they did not stack them on the quayside. There was a van at the end of the quay, and they took the baskets to the van. "Chap buys direct for the hotels in Plymouth," Grimble explained. The man with the van weighed the baskets, while Grimble took an equal number of empties from the van. Then the man counted out a wad of notes that seemed to David satisfactorily thick. Grimble pocketed the money.

"Seeing as you did well, Dave," he said. "I'll buy you a pint of beer."

He led the way into a pub appropriately called The Fisherman's Arms and when the beer had been drawn, he said, "Made £32, that lot did. Now, remember what I said about shares?"

"Yes. That makes my share £8."

"Not quite so fast, Dave. The fourth share'd be £8 all right, but you wouldn't hire sea-boots and an oily for nothing, would you now?"

"I suppose not."

"Well, what's it worth? Shall we say a quid for the boots and a quid for the coat?"

"It seems a lot, but I haven't much choice. All right, I'll take £6." He held out his hand.

"Wait a bit, now, Dave. What about the bicycle? Would you expect a good safe lock-up for a bicycle for nothing?"

David began to get angry. "In the circumstances I damned well would," he said. "I'd also expect to be lent the boots and the coat. But I agreed to pay for them, so you can knock £2 off my money. But I'm not renting them, Mr Grimble. I'm buying them—they're mine now. Give me my money and I'll go."

Grimble showed not the slightest sign of resentment.

"In too much of a hurry again, Dave. We haven't fixed up about tomorrow yet."

"I'm not sure that I want to go out with you again."

"Now look here, Dave. A man's got to live, hasn't he? Have you done no buying and selling in your life? Do you blame me for trying to drive a bargain?"

"Not exactly. I just thought it was a bit steep."

"Okay then, and you won. You get a good set of sea-clothes for two quid. Now, what about tomorrow?"

"I'll come, if you really want me again."

"I do want you, Dave. You're a good lad in a boat, and I like your spirit ashore. Tide's later tomorrow, and we'll work the nearer pots, so you can have a bit of a lie-in. We'll go out at eight o'clock. If there's time, we'll work Jim Hiscock's pots for him. His wife's poorly, and he'll maybe not be wanting to go out. When we work another man's pots we go fifty-fifty— but for you and me the half-share from his pots is divided into quarters, as before. Three for me, and one for you. Fair enough?"

"Yes, I think so."

"Well, you can have another beer to settle things." Grimble

called for the beer, and handed over David's £6. David didn't really want another beer—he was extremely hungry. But he was developing a certain respect for Grimble, and thought it politic to accept.

"Now there's another thing, Dave," Grimble said, taking a long pull at his beer. "When you were cross with me you called me Mr Grimble. That won't do. You just call me Jess."

"All right, Jess. I'm not cross now."

"And still another thing, Dave. As my crew, it's your job to put the boat back on her mooring, and bring the tender to the pool. Take down the empty baskets when you go and put them in the boat. There's a bit of old tarpaulin in the port locker forrard that covers them up nicely. Do you want to go now? I'm sitting here for a while."

"Yes, I think I'll go. But I'll need the key to the shed."

"So you will, Dave. And you can have this one. It's my mate's, and he gave it back to me before he went off to hospital. See how I trust you!"

"You can trust me all right, Jess. I won't pinch anything."

"So long, then. Eight o'clock in the morning, sharp."

When he had taken the fishing-boat to her mooring and brought in the dinghy, David recovered his bicycle from the shed, left the dinghy's oars and his own sea-clothes there, and rode off. On the road out of Finmouth he passed a café. He felt too hungry to ride back to the moor, and decided to invest some of his earnings in a meal. After a double portion of bacon, eggs and chips, and three portions of bread and butter he felt better.

Work with Grimble quickly fell into a sort of routine. The long bicycle ride twice a day was tiresome, but it was practicable, and Neolithic Villa was rent free. The boat-work David thoroughly enjoyed—it was good physically, and valuable to him emotionally, for he could feel that it was of some direct value to the world in helping to provide food. Tending the lobster pots seemed to be the main job at the moment, but they did some line-fishing as well, though according to Grimble it was not nearly so profitable. They caught a fair number of mackerel, and could have caught more, but there did not seem much of a market for them. Fresh mackerel, however, are good eating, and Grimble fished mostly for himself and his neighbours. He told David to take what he wanted, and this certainly helped his housekeeping. His earnings varied a good deal, but after four days—and spending a bit on meals in Finmouth and in restocking his larder—he added a net £20 to his capital. How long his job, or his manner of living, could continue he did not know, and for the present he did not much care.

When Grimble settled up with him on the fourth day he announced that he was not going out next morning. "You've worked well, Dave," he said, "and you can have a day off." (It would, David reflected, be unpaid.) Grimble explained that he wanted to go to Plymouth to visit his mate in hospital. His daughter, who was married to a farmer over towards Salcombe, had a car, and she would drive in and take him to Plymouth. Grimble took care to point out that the day off was only for one day. On the following day they would go out as usual, and he fixed a time of departure, adding (again as usual) "and that means sharp, my boy".

David was not sorry to have the day free. He felt fit, but he was still not in training for so much physical work, and he looked forward to a rest. Lying in his sleeping-bag on the night before his day off he contemplated happily how to spend it. It was time he got some laundry done, and he would find a launderette in Totnes. He had noticed what looked like quite a decent bookshop when he was shopping for supplies, and he could do with something more to read. And—feeling flush—he might stand himself lunch in Totnes. With such pleasing thoughts he fell asleep.

The day did not turn out as he had planned. It was barely six-thirty when he was woken up by someone banging on his tent. He opened the flap and found himself looking up at two large men, one a policeman in uniform, the other in plain clothes. The plain-clothes man was apparently also a policeman. for he said, "We are police officers. Are you Mr Wilbur Platt?"

"No. I'm David Grendon." David was half-lying, half-kneeling at the flap of his low tent. It was inconvenient, and a bit embarrassing, to have to talk up to his questioner. "Do you mind if I get up?" he asked.

"I shall be glad if you will, sir. There are a number of questions that I must ask you."

David was sleeping in his shirt and underpants, and it did not take long to put on trousers, pullover and shoes. Feeling tousled and unwashed, he stood up. "What on earth is it all about?" he said.

The plain-clothes man did not answer his question. Instead, he introduced himself. "I am Detective Sergeant Blundell, of the Devon Constabulary. Here is my warrant card." David waved the thing away—he did not doubt the man's credentials. He wanted to know why he was being questioned. The detective went on. "I am investigating a serious crime which took place in this neighbourhood, and I am anxious to interview a man called Wilbur Platt. You say that it is not your name. Is it a name that you have ever used?"

"No, never even heard of it. What's the crime?"

Blundell was silent for a moment. Then he said, "I'm sorry, sir, but I have only your statement that you have never called yourself Wilbur Platt. You are living here in strange and somewhat secretive conditions. This is not a suitable place for what may have to be a long interview. I'm afraid I must ask you to come with me to the police station at Ivybridge."

David was so astounded that he could hardly speak. "Am I under arrest?" he asked.

"No," Blundell said, "you are not under arrest, though you will understand that you could, if necessary, be arrested. It will be much better if you come to the police station voluntarily. If you are innocent, you have nothing to fear, and the sooner your position is cleared up, the better for everybody."

"Shall I be what you call 'helping the police'?"

"You could put it like that." Blundell was not happy. Like all good policemen he was a good practical psychologist, and his instinct told him that this young man was unlikely to turn out to be a crook. He had given not a flicker of recognition at the mention of the name Wilbur Platt. But instinct can be wrong. They had made no progress whatever towards tracing Mr Platt, and it was urgent that he should be found. This young man might not have anything to do with him, but on the other hand it was possible that he might. There was nothing criminal in late-season camping on Dartmoor, but it was slightly eccentric, and eccentricity would be a useful cloak for what seemed a highly-sophisticated crime. The young man would have to give a detailed account of himself.

"Can I have a wash and shave before you take me off?"

48

David asked. Blundell surveyed the austere equipment of the camp.

"Does that mean waiting while you heat some water?" he inquired.

"Not necessarily. It means that I must be allowed to fetch water from the brook, but I shan't run away. Normally I'd light the Primus and use hot water, but I'm not fussy. I've shaved in cold water before."

"You can bring your things and shave at the police station—there's hot water and a proper basin there. I'd rather we got off straight away. This officer will stay here and guard the camp, so you needn't take anything more than you need for washing."

David said nothing. He was not particularly angry at this extraordinary police interference in his affairs, but he was extremely puzzled. When he had seen the uniformed policeman his first thought was that Louise must have reported him as missing—though it would have been wholly out of character, and he did not believe that she cared for him personally enough to bother. And it couldn't be anything to do with Louise, because they hadn't asked if he was David Grendon, and Louise could scarcely have given him any other name. They had talked only of somebody called Platt: who the hell was this Wilbur Platt, and why did they think it was anything to do with him? Anyway, the detective chap was right—the sooner it was cleared up, the better. If they wanted him to go to the police station, he didn't seem to have much choice. They might even give him some breakfast.

He collected a towel and his washing kit and walked with Blundell to the car parked on the track that ran up from the farm.

He did get breakfast. If David was puzzled by the police, Blundell was both puzzled and becoming a little concerned about David. It was no light thing to yank a man into what amounted to police custody on bare suspicion. In the circumstances, Blundell believed that he was justified, but if his suspicions turned out to be wholly unfounded, the young man might have a case for legitimate complaint. However, having gone so far, there was no going back now—and if his long shot did hit the target it would be considered a very good shot indeed. But there must be as little cause for possible complaint as possible. An offer of breakfast would be evidence at least of

49

police readiness to act decently. So the offer was made—and accepted.

A wash and shave in considerably more comfort than Neolithic Villa could provide, and sausages, baked beans, and a cup of tea, had the effect that Blundell hoped, and David showed no particular unwillingness to be questioned.

"You say your name is David Grendon. Have you any way of confirming that identity?" Blundell asked.

"Well, I've got a cheque-book with my name on it—oh, and I've got a driving licence."

David produced both. Blundell studied them, and went on, "Where is your car?"

"I haven't got a car now. The one I had was in London."

"Is this address on the driving licence where you live?"

That was an awkward one. David considered for a moment, and then said, "Well, I suppose it's still my house. But I don't live there any longer. You see, I've left my wife. When things are settled up, I daresay she'll get the house, but it's mine at the moment."

"What is your present address?"

"Oh God, does it matter? In my tent, where I'm living. I call it Neolithic Villa, because it was inhabited before, you know. Stone Age men lived in that cairn."

Blundell felt more and more strongly that his long shot had missed the target altogether. But he went on, "Why did you come to Ugborough Moor?"

"Because my home used to be in Exeter, and my grandfather built boats on the Dart. I knew the district, and when I left Louise I wanted to find peace. Does that sound silly?"

"No, I don't think so." Blundell was a compassionate policeman, and he was beginning to feel rather ashamed of himself. But it was an odd story.

"Is there anyone locally who can identify you?"

David thought of Jess Grimble, but he didn't want Grimble to think that he was involved with the police, and in any case Grimble had either gone, or was on his way, to Plymouth. And Grimble could scarcely be said to know him. "I'm afraid not," he said. "I haven't lived here since my father died." A thought struck him, "Wait a bit, though. Yes—there's your own Chief Constable. My father was a solicitor in Exeter, and for some years he was Clerk to the Justices. The Chief Constable was

50

rather a friend of his. They used to play golf together, and he quite often came to our house. He hasn't seen me for some time, but I expect he'd still recognise me. Would that do? But it would mean going to Exeter, I suppose."

Blundell took a decision. He put back in his pocket the pen with which he had been writing down David's replies, and closed his notebook.

"I'm sorry, Mr Grendon, I've made a mistake," he said. "I'm going to trust you." He recounted the story of the theft of the Combe Dean chalice, and explained the police eagerness to trace Mr Platt, as possibly the last man who had seen it. He did not elaborate—he did not need to, for the implication was plain. As David had been neither buying newspapers nor listening to the radio the story was new to him. "Is that the famous Combe Dean chalice, the one that Sir Francis Drake gave to the church?"

"Yes."

"I've heard of it, of course. In fact, I've even seen it, for it was in an exhibition at Exeter Cathedral when I was at school. I can understand why you want to find Mr Platt, I'm sorry that I can't help you."

"There's one thing you can do, Mr Grendon. It's irregular, and you could probably get me into trouble if you wanted to. But it would clear up the last doubt in my mind about you."

"I don't want to get you into trouble. What is it?"

"Two people saw Mr Platt when he called at Combe Dean, the rector and his daughter. Would you come with me to the rectory and let me ask them if they've ever seen you before? I could arrange a formal identification parade, but it would be quicker if you'd agree to run over to Combe Dean. You don't have to, but it would help me."

"Of course I'll go with you. I don't mind a bit."

"Thank you. Well, I'd better telephone to make sure that they're in."

Blundell telephoned the rectory, and Elizabeth Danvers answered. He did not explain why he wanted to see her and her father—he said simply that there were one or two further points that he'd like to ask them about, and would they be at home if he came straight away? Yes, said Elizabeth, they would both be at home.

David hoped that he did not show the nervousness he felt.

People do make mistakes—by some horrible chance he might even resemble the mysterious Mr Platt. What would happen then? If either the rector or his daughter claimed to recognise him presumably he'd be arrested, and the manner of this apparently quite pleasant detective would change. As he hadn't stolen the chalice, in time he should be able to establish his innocence, but it would take time. He would have to give up his job with Grimble, Louise might have to be fetched to say that he was her husband, it would all be damnable. Oh well, he'd just have to go through with it.

The drive to Combe Dean seemed to take no time at all. For all his nervousness, David couldn't help feeling the sheer beauty of the old rectory, and he was impressed by the saint-like appearance of the rector. Blundell didn't waste time. "Mr Grendon has been camping on Ugborough Moor," he said, "and it is just possible that he may have seen a man resembling Mr Platt. I thought it would be helpful if you could give him a first-hand description of the man who called here."

David appreciated Blundell's delicacy, but he wanted to get things over. "He doesn't mean that at all," he said. "He thinks it a bit odd for anyone to be living out on Dartmoor at this time of year, and he's a bit suspicious that I might *be* your mysterious Mr Platt. He wants you to say if I look at all like him."

"No," said Elizabeth, "you're certainly not the man I saw. He was older, he had dark brown hair whereas yours is fair, and he wasn't as tall as you are."

"I was with Mr Platt for quite a long time. I'm not good at describing people, but I can recognise them," the rector said. "This couldn't be Mr Platt. He looks quite different, and his voice is quite different."

"Thank you," David said.

Blundell had been somewhat taken aback by David's direct approach. "Mr Grendon is quite right," he said. "I wanted to spare both you and him from the embarrassment of a confrontation like this, but the purpose of my call was to ask if you had ever seen him before. The proceeding was quite informal. And it was carried out with Mr Grendon's consent," he added hastily.

"Of course," David said.

"Poor Mr Grendon—how horrid it must have been for you!" Elizabeth said. "I think it would be a good idea if we all had coffee. It won't take a minute to make."

"I feel that I owe Mr Grendon an apology," Blundell said rather unhappily.

"I don't see why—you were only doing your job," David said. "And you did give me some breakfast. I hope you're going to drive me back to my camp."

The most disturbed of all of them was the rector. "What is really dreadful," he said, "is to observe the ripples that flow from one evil act. It is my fault. If I had been less remiss in my guardianship of the chalice this young man would not have had his holiday interrupted. I am deeply sorry. It is I who owe apologies to him."

David said nothing. Blundell said, "Come, sir, you must try to stop looking at things like that. It is true that the chalice might have been better guarded, but as you said yourself, it has been safe enough for 300 years. The evil action was the thief's, not yours."

Elizabeth had just returned with the coffee when the telephone rang. She answered it, looked puzzled for a moment, and then put her hand over the mouthpiece and gasped, "It's Sir George Durrance—he says he's going to offer a reward of £10,000 for the safe return of the chalice."

"It is preposterous—it is nothing to do with him," the rector said. "I must speak to him."

He took the phone from his daughter and proceeded to hold a one-sided conversation, in which expostulations from him were apparently met by dignified firmness at the other end. Finally he put down the phone. "It is no use," he said. "He says he has already given news of his offer to *The Times*." He turned to Blundell. "Is it permissible?" he asked. "Can he do this?"

"It is not uncommon for rewards to be offered when something of great value is stolen," Blundell replied. "I cannot say officially what may be the attitude of the police authorities—a possible objection to such rewards is that they may make the apprehension of a criminal more difficult. In this case the offer of a reward may, perhaps, help, since it would be next to impossible to sell the chalice openly, and £10,000 is substantially more than could be obtained by melting it down. It seems to me a generous offer."

"George is undoubtedly a rich man," the rector said, "but it is I not he who should be offering rewards. May God forgive me for what I have done."

"Daddy, if you go on like this, you will make yourself ill," Elizabeth said. "It's really very exciting. Perhaps the chalice will come back, now. Drink your coffee—and then write a letter to Sir George. I daresay that will make you feel better."

After the diplomatic coffee, Blundell took David back to the police station to collect his washing things. He felt reasonably sure that David's account of himself was true, but he had not yet quite finished with him. There was the unidentified fingerprint on the safe. Blundell had arranged for the knife and fork that David had used for breakfast, and the cup he drank his tea from, to be examined for fingerprints. There were several good ones. Excusing himself from David he compared those prints with the photograph of the print from the safe. They were totally dissimilar. That settled it, then. He drove David back to Ugborough, collected the constable who had been left to guard the camp, and, after further apologies, returned to his routine work.

# IV

# Lily

Jess Grimble had not been inquisitive about David: he employed him, paid him each day, and left it at that. Coming back from working the lobster pots after his trip from Plymouth he asked for the first time about his plans. They had fallen into a comfortable routine, David at the wheel, Jess sitting back on the cockpit thwart eating his bacon sandwiches. David now brought his dinner, too—a couple of hard-boiled eggs, and a good hunk of bread and cheese.

"Look, Dave, my boy," Grimble said, "I've been thinking. You're a good hand in a boat, and you earn your share. How long are you down at Finmouth for?"

David had been living from day to day, getting up early, working hard, cycling twenty miles a day, and falling asleep healthily tired each evening. "I don't know," he answered truthfully.

"Well, my mate's going to be all right. He's coming out of hospital, and he'll soon be coming out with me again."

"I'm glad about that. But I'm sorry too. I've enjoyed working with you, Jess, but I suppose you won't be wanting me any more."

"Not so fast, young Dave, you're always jumping to conclusions. Who said anything about not wanting you?"

"Well, there's plenty of work for two in your boat, but I don't see that there's work for three."

"Ah, but I've got another boat. That's what I've been thinking about, and that's why I asked you."

"I've nothing to take me away from Finmouth. I did have a job in London, but the firm was taken over and I was made redundant. If I can go on working here, I'd like to."

Grimble was silent for a bit. He finished his sandwiches, put away the tattered pieces of oilskin wrapping, and lighted his pipe. "There's still a living to be made at inshore fishing, but there's not many youngsters nowadays willing to do it—work too hard and times too awkward for them. I'm getting on, and my mate's getting on a bit. I've got daughters, good girls, but all married and living away. I've got no son, not even a brother's son. What would you say if I set you up with a boat?"

"I'd be glad to have a go. But I haven't much money for gear and things."

"Jumping ahead again, Dave. I'm not going to give you anything, but I could stake you some gear, and you can pay for it out of your share of the catch. But you'd have to work harder than now. You see my other boat hasn't got an engine."

"Fishermen went out long before boats had engines. I can row and I can sail—my grand-dad taught me to sail."

"Aye, I don't doubt that. And your grand-dad built my boat. She's old, but she's still good. She's lying over at Salcombe where I've been trying to sell her, but nobody wants her because she's heavy, and she has no engine. I thought if we brought her back maybe you could use her."

"That's generous of you, Jess. I could try, anyway. I could go out sometimes and give you a day off. But I could do that in this boat." David was puzzled.

"There's more to it than that. You know my distant pots—the ones we work beyond the Wadham rocks. There used to be several of us fished there—now there's only me. They call my pots Grimble's Ground, not after me, though, after my dad, and maybe my grand-dad. Beyond, there's good fishing on what we call Tiddler's Ground, only there isn't a Tiddler any longer, hasn't been these twenty years. If we worked another boat we could lay out some more pots—nobody'd mind my taking over Tiddler's Ground. What d'you say to that?"

"I'd say it was a good idea."

"Now see here, Dave, it's better for a man to have his own boat. I want to sell my old *Lily*—but you haven't got the money to buy her. So you buy her with work, see? If you take over *Lily* there'll be the same four shares, only you'll take two shares because you're skipper. One share goes to me, because it'll be my gear, and one share goes to the boat. Only the boat's share will go to me too, until there's been enough to pay for her. See? That's how we all worked for our boats when I was a youngster. Fair do's?"

"Fair enough. And I still think it's generous of you, Jess."

56

"Right. I'll ring Bet—that's my Salcombe daughter—this evening, and get her to come over. Then we'll bring *Lily* back here, and get to work on her. She's in good shape, because I tidied her up before trying to sell her. I'm glad now I couldn't sell her—better to keep her in the family."

*Lily* was lying at a small yard on one of the inlets of Salcombe Harbour. They had to watch the tide, because the inlet dried out, though *Lily* didn't mind, for she took the ground quite happily. They also needed the tide to get out of Salcombe Harbour; without an engine *Lily* would simply have been swept back by the flood, so they needed to go out on the ebb. David fell in love with her at first sight. She was built somewhat on the lines of a Brixham lugger, with powerful shoulders and a sweet run aft. It was a moving thought that his grandfather's hands had shaped her. She was rather bigger than Grimble's motor fishing-boat, decked, with a fish-hold amidships and a fo'c'sle with two berths forrard. She was not rigged as a lugger, but as a gaff-sloop. This, David thought, might enable her to make a little progress to windward, but probably not much. With the wind anywhere abaft the beam her big gaff mainsail would have a powerful drive. David thought that he would get a longshaft outboard for her: it would not provide much speed, but it would keep her going when the wind failed. She was big for one man to handle, but boats of her type were designed to be sailed by a man and a boy; David reckoned that he could just about manage her. She was steered by a tiller, a lovely piece of solid oak, shaped with a subtle curve. He remembered seeing tillers just like it in his grandfather's shed—the curve was probably a Grendon tradition.

An outboard would certainly have helped to get her from the inlet into Salcombe Harbour, but the fact that she had none did not worry Grimble. What she did have was a powerful stern sweep. Grimble, standing in the cockpit, worked the sweep, and got her out without difficulty. A small pram dinghy went with *Lily*: it could have been carried on board, stowed over the fish-hold aft of the mast, but as the trip to Finmouth was not far they decided to tow it.

Clear of the inlet they let *Lily*'s sails draw, and a happy little chuckle of water began to come from her forefoot as she gathered way. They were lucky in the wind, a brisk north-

57

easterly, which, with the ebb, took them towards Bolt Head at a fine pace and, once they had cleared the head, gave them a good reach into Bigbury Bay and Finmouth. Apart from taking her out of the inlet with the big sweep, Grimble let David work the boat, and sat quietly smoking his pipe. With that wind the sail to Finmouth was merely a matter of leaving things to *Lily*, but he set himself a private ambition—he would bring her up under sail at the new mooring he and Grimble had laid for her.

He was considerably scared of the other moored boats as they came up, but he kept *Lily* going and tried not to show his doubts of his own ability to bring her up at the right moment. She was a heavy boat, and he reckoned that she would carry her way for some distance. He could only hope that he might judge things about right. He took her a little past the mooring, then, saying a prayer, he put the tiller hard over. *Lily* swung through the wind, stopped, came on the wind and began to move slowly towards the buoy. Letting go the sheets he ran forward and just managed to grab the buoy's line with the boat-hook as she went by. He hauled the buoy on board, got up some cable, and put a couple of turns round the samson post. *Lily* was safe.

"Your grand-dad taught you all right," Grimble said. David did not omit a prayer of thankfulness, but he wondered whether he would ever again be able to bring up *Lily* so elegantly. For this passage, at any rate, all was well.

He got the sails off her and stowed them in the little fo'c'sle through a hatch in the forepeak. Then he hauled up the dinghy, and rowed himself and Grimble to the quay.

*Lily* was registered as a fishing-boat, and Grimble, insisting that everything must be done "proper", proposed to transfer the registration to David. What address did David have? This posed the same problem that had cropped up during Sergeant Blundell's questioning. David didn't think that a tent on Dartmoor was a good address for registering a fishing-boat—and Grimble didn't know that he was living in a tent. "Where are you staying now?" Grimble asked, when he didn't answer. "Any old address will do."

"I'm staying up on Ugborough Moor," David said. "And I don't think it will do; because I'm likely to move out soon." He did not add that all he had to move was a tent.

"You're right out at Ugborough? How do you get to Finmouth?" Grimble was surprised.

"On my bicycle."

"You're a good timekeeper, I'll say that. But you'd do better to come in a bit nearer."

"Yes, I think I will. Look, I've still got my father's old house in Exeter, though it's let to tenants. But anything sent there would find me—it's still my house. Would that do for the registration?"

"Aye, it'll do fine." On his way home David sent a postcard to his tenants asking them to hold any mail that might come for him until he sent a new address. He did not want *Lily*'s registration certificate to go to Louise.

*Lily* made a profound difference to David's life—she gave him something to live for. She also gave him a lot more work. Grimble's mate came out of hospital, but he was not fit to go out fishing straight away, so David carried on as crew of the motor fishing-boat. But instead of cycling back to camp when the day's catch had been landed, he stayed to work on *Lily*. There was much to be done—gear to be rove, a host of small jobs to be carried out on the boat. *Lily*, as Grimble said, was in good shape, but her brightwork was dingy, and she needed paint. David had contrived to keep himself without drawing on what was left of his money; having proved that he could do so, he felt that he could fairly invest a little in *Lily*. He beached her and gave her a thorough coat of anti-fouling, bought paint and varnish and worked on her until her topsides were spotless, and all her brightwork glowed. He got an outboard engine for her, and it performed better than he had hoped, giving her up to about four knots and, more important, providing manoeuvrability, and the power to go out or come home if the wind was foul. Under his agreement with Grimble he did not need to start paying for *Lily* until he began working her, but as he paid no rent and cooked most of his own food he could live cheaply, and he handed over half his earnings from the catch each working day. Grimble wrote down each payment in an old school exercise-book.

David felt that he was using too much time on twice-daily bicycle rides, and decided that he would have to get lodgings in Finmouth—there would be no difficulty about this when the

59

holiday season was over. But he wanted to delay moving for as long as he could, to put his money into *Lily*. He would have to move, he thought, when he started working on his own, but until then he would try to carry on as he was.

Coming home late one afternoon he saw a car on the track below his camp, and outside the camp he met a smallish man in a rather grubby mackintosh. Another policeman? But he did not look like a policeman.

"Good day, sir," said the man. "Can you tell me where I can find a messuage by the name of Neolithic Villa?"

"I don't know about a messuage," David said, "but I call this place Neolithic Villa."

"Ha! Then perhaps you can tell me where I can find a Mr David Grendon."

"That's me." David was extremely puzzled.

The little man seemed to puff himself up. "It is irregular, it is *most* irregular," he said. "Have you no proper address?"

"What's improper about it?" David said, beginning to feel rather annoyed.

"I represent Bray, Bray, Bickersnatch and Bray, solicitors of Lincoln's Inn. I have been instructed to find you to serve notice of Mrs Louise Grendon's intention to institute divorce proceedings against you. I may add that we shall ask for costs, and this ridiculous journey will cost you a pretty penny. I am not accustomed to wasting my time in exploring blasted heaths."

"Come off it," David said. "How on earth did you hear of Neolithic Villa?"

"We were instructed to communicate with a lady in Scotland —a relative of yours, I believe. She furnished what purported to be your address."

David laughed out loud. He remembered writing a cheerful letter to his cousin, in which he had called his camp Neolithic Villa. "You must have had some job to find it," he said.

"I had a great deal of trouble. In the end I went to the police station in Ivybridge, and was directed—most vaguely directed, I may say—to this moor."

"Well, now you've got here, you can serve your notice and go away. Would you like a lobster?"

"A what?"

"I said, 'Would you like a lobster?' It is a very good lobster, cooked only this morning. You can have it to take home, if you like." David, as he sometimes did, had brought back one of Grimble's lobsters, cooked, doubtless by a barter arrangement, at the pub that Grimble used.

The pompous little man began to thaw slightly. "My wife and I are indeed partial to lobster mayonnaise," he said. "But we seldom buy any—they are very expensive."

"Have this one, then."

"How much do you want for it?"

"I don't want anything for it. I'm offering to give it to you."

"You are generous, sir. Yes, I will accept the lobster, though I must warn you that it will make no difference to your costs."

"Oh, shut up! You're welcome to the lobster—something to make up for your journey. What do you want me to do?"

"Mrs Grendon has instructed us to institute proceedings for divorce. I am required to serve notice of those proceedings. May I ask if you are represented?"

"No. Louise can have a divorce if she wants one. What else does she want?"

"If I may say so, you would be wiser to be represented by a solicitor. There will be questions about the division of the matrimonial home."

"There will be nothing of the sort. Louise can have the lot. Have you got a piece of paper?"

"Yes, but—"

"Give me a piece of paper, and something to write with."

From his mackintosh pocket the little man produced a loose-leaf notebook. From another pocket he produced a ballpoint pen. David held out his hand to take them, then he had a better idea. "Look, you're a lawyer," he said. "Write out a statement that I, David Justin Grendon—that's my full name—give my house at Highgate and whatever she wants that's in it to my wife Louise. Then I'll sign it."

"My dear sir, you cannot transfer a property just like that! And—although it is not my task to advise you—I really must counsel you to consider your own interests. I understand that there are no children of the marriage. In the circumstances the Court will probably order the matrimonial home to be divided— it can be sold, if necessary, with half the proceeds going to your wife. The remaining half, of course, will accrue to you. I have been to the Highgate house to take instructions from Mrs Louise

61

Grendon. It is a valuable property. You really must obtain professional advice."

"I don't want advice. I don't want the house. Louise can have it, or sell it, or do whatever she likes. Look, it's getting late, and if you're going back to London you should be on your way. I don't see how you can reasonably get back tonight. If I'm paying, I'll stand you a night in a hotel in Exeter. I'll take the lobster to your car for you."

The little man walked to the car with him. "These papers are for you," he said.

David thrust them into his trouser pocket. "I don't want the bloody things, but you've done your job of serving them on me. What about my Deed of Gift or whatever of the house to Louise?"

"I have explained that you cannot transfer a property like that. I will take note of your intentions, though I disapprove of them, and if you wish I can get a legal document drawn up, and sent to you for you to execute."

"All right, do that."

"But where shall I send it? Is this—this *place*, really your address? Does the postman deliver letters here?"

"No, of course he doesn't. Send your document to my cousin in Scotland, and I'll get her to send it on somewhere."

"Very good. You are a foolish young man, *most* foolish. But a generous one." Shaking his head, the little man drove away.

David was thankful to see him go. Walking back to his camp he wondered whether his visitor had been Mr Bray or Mr Bray or Mr Bickersnatch. In fact his name was Evans, and he was not a solicitor, but—to his own eyes, at any rate—a superior clerk.

David went to sleep thinking about *Lily*.

The weather broke, and it began to rain. The morning after the visit from the representative of Messrs Bray, Bray, Bickersnatch and Bray David got up to a sodden moor. He could not get his Primus going properly, and breakfasted on biscuits and cheese and a mug of cold water. He had a wet ride to Finmouth, and a wet day in the fishing-boat with Grimble. He didn't much mind the weather at sea, though it was depressing, and his chief feeling was of relief that he had got most of *Lily*'s paintwork done. But he had a miserable ride home, and returned to find a small river actually flowing through his cairn. His tent, pitched on ground a few inches higher, was waterproof and seemed just habitable, but the rest of the camp was in a sad mess. There seemed nothing to do but to go to bed. He was tired, anyway, and inside the tent at least he was more or less dry. But he was also cold. Instead of taking off any clothes, he put on an extra pullover.

His tent, being designed for bivouacs at high altitude, offered lying room only. He could just kneel in it, but he couldn't sit with any comfort. It was too early to go to sleep, so he adopted the one non-sleeping position the tent allowed for—lying on his stomach, with his head and shoulders raised on his elbows. He lay with his head to the entrance, so that he could look out, and he watched night come to the already rain-dark moor. It was a dismal prospect, but, as with all the moor's moods, it still had a certain beauty. There was next to nothing to see, but in a way that nothingness had a quality of its own, a sense of space beyond the enveloping rain, of moorland rising to merge with the low clouds, but remaining itself, still granite-hard and strong. David was meditating on the forbidding aspects of Dartmoor, wondering why they still had a sort of appeal even at their most forbidding, when he thought he saw a light. It couldn't possibly be a star—the sky was completely overcast. It disappeared—it must have been some trick of his imagination. Then it returned—it was not imagination, it was a torch, and it was coming towards him.

The police again? Another legal emissary from Louise? Damn the rest of the world, couldn't it leave him alone, even on a night like this? Then there was a woman's voice saying "Is anybody there?"

David switched on his own torch, and crawled out of the tent. A cascade of rainwater collected on the tent flap went down the back of his neck. "Who is it?" he asked.

"Is that Mr Grendon? I'm Elizabeth Danvers—you came to the rectory with a policeman. I was visiting Mrs Dance at the farm, and she said you were still living up here. You must be flooded out. I've come to rescue you. I've got my car on the track—we can put you up at the rectory, there's masses of room."

David didn't feel that he needed rescuing. If it hadn't been for the water down his neck he would probably have thanked

Miss Danvers, and said that he was happy to stay where he was. But he was wet, and damnably uncomfortable. "That's extraordinarily kind of you. All right, I'll come. Give me a moment to collect my rucksack."

The sack, containing his clothes and all his personal belongings, was at the far end of the tent in company with his stove, his stores, and all his possessions except his bicycle. He dug it out, laced the flap of the tent in the hope of keeping the inside at least relatively dry, and said, "I'm ready now." He added, "The way down is worse in this weather than the way up, it's rough and very slippery. I know it pretty well, so I'd better go first." He slung the rucksack on his shoulders, and went ahead. Miss Danvers followed him down.

The car was a couple of hundred yards along the track. On the track they were able to walk side by side. "I don't know how on earth you found the place," David said.

"Well, I know the moor fairly well. In the dark, I wasn't quite sure where to turn off to get to the cairn—that's why I left the car. It was a bit further on than I thought."

"I think it was just marvellous of you." He intended no particular compliment—it was just what he did think.

In the car he realised how cold he was. "I think this really will have to be the end," he said.

"The end of what?" Elizabeth asked.

"The end of living in Neolithic Villa—sorry, you wouldn't know that. It's what I call my camp."

"It's a good name. There must have been a considerable Stone Age population in this part of Dartmoor."

He was pleased that she understood. "They were tougher than I am. They didn't have to be rescued by Good Samaritans on a cold night."

"They were different. They'd never lived in any other sort of house—and quite likely they had a few goats and a pig or two to get up a good warm fug. I'm awfully glad I found you. My father will be delighted. He feels awfully guilty about you. And so, in a way, do I."

"Why on earth should you feel guilty?"

"Because the police upset your holiday. It must have been horrid to be questioned and brought along like that to be looked at. And all because of us."

"It was nothing to do with you."

64

"But it was—it was all because of the chalice. Daddy is dreadfully unhappy about it."

"He can't help being unhappy—it's a miserable business. Has nothing still been heard about it?"

"Nothing. We did so hope that the reward might bring some news, but it hasn't. We're beginning to be afraid that it may already have been melted down."

The gracious old rectory lost all its shabbiness at night. Only two of the front windows were lighted, but this added, somehow, to the sense of friendly welcome, making David feel that a night in bed in a house really was a delightful change in his circumstances.

Elizabeth took him upstairs to a big bedroom with a huge four-poster bed. "Everything in the house is old," she explained, "because we've never been able to afford any new furniture. I expect you'd like a hot bath. Bathrooms in this house, I'm afraid, were a bit of an afterthought, but you'll find a bathroom at the end of the corridor. And we do have hot water. You have a bath, and I'll go and tell Daddy that you've come to stay. When you come down you'll find us in the room to the right of the stairs."

David had a feeling of being left in a dream world. The whole performance seemed all-but unbelievable. He did not then know Elizabeth Danvers, or he would have understood more of the ruthless sense of responsibility for other people with which she had been brought up. All he knew then was that this girl, acting, apparently on some sudden whim, had thought nothing of walking over the rainswept moor in the dark to find and rescue him. She was certainly an odd girl—not pretty in any ordinary sense, but with a nice figure, and features that were alert and curiously attractive. Well, if she was mad, it was a comfortable sort of madness. And he certainly did need a bath.

The temptation was to lie and luxuriate in the bath. Rupert Brooke's line about "the benison of hot water" came into his head—never, he thought, had a writer hit on a more exact piece of observation. The temptation had to be resisted—he was in someone else's house, a guest as yet unknown to his host, although he had acquired a hostess. He had no idea whether they'd had supper, or were waiting to have it—he'd have to go

65

and be polite. He wished he could do more in the way of clean clothes. His rucksack held a pair of jeans marginally less muddy than those he had been wearing when Elizabeth found him, and a clean, though rather crumpled, shirt. At least he had a comb. He did what he could, and went down.

The room seemed to be a combination of living-room and study. There was an enormous fireplace, and a cheerful fire of big logs. The rector was standing in front of the fire as David came in. He held out both hands to greet him. "How good of you to accept our hospitality," he said. "I am thankful that Elizabeth found you, and that we can at least provide an alternative to a night on the moor in this weather. Elizabeth and I drink little, but one of my parishioners generously gives me a case of sherry at Christmas. I think this is an occasion for benefiting from his generosity. May I offer you a glass of sherry? It is a good wine—my parishioner is a retired wine-merchant."

David didn't know what to say. He muttered "It really is extraordinarily good of you ..." but the words seemed so in-adequate as to be almost meaningless. The rector went to a beautiful old corner-cupboard, and got out a bottle of sherry, a small silver tray, and three wineglasses. "Elizabeth will be back in a minute," he said. "Meanwhile, my wronged young friend, I can but repeat the apology I tried to make the other day. And I can at least offer a toast to your health." He poured out sherry for David and himself, and raised his glass.

Elizabeth came in, and her father poured a glass of sherry for her. "We have had no occasion lately for rejoicing, but I felt that we must do what we can for this young man," he said.

Elizabeth laughed. "Why not?" she said. She added, "Daddy gets a dozen bottles of sherry at Christmas. It's getting on towards next Christmas now, and I think we've still got ten of last Christmas's bottles unopened. And eight or nine from the year before. So you're not exactly straining the wine cellar."

"It's nice sherry," David said, awkwardly.

"Yes, isn't it? And it's got quite a history. There aren't many rich people in the parish, but the big house at Combe Episcopi belongs to a family that's had interests in the wine trade at Jerez since the seventeenth century. Each generation is supposed to bring home a beautiful Spanish bride—at least, that's the legend. They're Roman Catholics, but they've always been good to the neighbourhood. The old man—he's retired now, and his son runs the business in Spain—paid for the roof of our church to be mended, and every Christmas he gives Daddy a dozen bottles of sherry."

"Are you a Devon man, Mr Grendon?" The rector asked.

"Yes. I was born in Exeter. But I've been working in London since I came down from Cambridge. My father was a solicitor in Exeter, and my grandfather built boats on the Dart."

"I may have met your father, I think. Didn't he do legal work occasionally for the Diocese? Ah, I thought so. He came here once in connection with a faculty for levelling some of the old, indecipherable headstones in the churchyard, so that we could tidy up the place. But it was many years ago."

"He died nearly ten years ago. My mother is dead, too. I'm the last of our particular Grendons. I've got a cousin living in Scotland, but she is on my mother's side."

They chatted for a few more minutes, and then Elizabeth said, "Do you mind having supper in the kitchen, Mr Grendon? We don't use the dining-room much unless we have guests. It's a big room—all the rooms in the house are big—and it costs too much to keep it warm. So we have our own meals in the kitchen. If I'd known you were coming I'd have put a fire in the dining-room—but, of course, I didn't know in time."

"I'm lucky to be having supper at all. I couldn't get my Primus going in all that rain, and without your rescue work my supper would have been a bit of cheese and a few biscuits."

"Well, you'll still have cheese—I've made a macaroni cheese. But we've some nice home-made bread to go with it. We still use our old baking oven. I baked this morning, so the bread's quite fresh."

David thought the kitchen, with its stone-flagged floor, and a huge kitchen table that looked as if it had been made from ship's timbers, was a most attractive place. Now that he was warm and dry he was also exceedingly hungry. He had two helpings of macaroni cheese, and ate nearly half a loaf of Elizabeth's bread. It was the best meal he had had since he came to Devon, and he enjoyed it enormously.

When they'd finished eating Elizabeth got up to make some coffee, and the rector said, "I don't think I'll wait for coffee, Elizabeth. You know I promised an article to the *Journal of Near Eastern Archaeology*: with all our troubles I just haven't been able to get down to it. So I'd like to try to work on it now, if you will excuse me, Mr Grendon."

"Don't sit up all night, Daddy. You'll get frightfully tired."

"It depends how it goes. . . . We need every penny I can earn, now. But I'll be sensible, of course. Goodnight, Mr Grendon. Please feel that our house is your home."

Elizabeth put the kettle on, and ground some coffee beans in a cast-iron coffee mill that looked, and probably was, at least half a century old. "Poor Daddy, he's desperately, desperately unhappy about the chalice," she said. "I am, too, of course. But I can't see that it was his fault, in the way he feels it is. The churchwarden, the Parochial Church Council, the rural dean, even the bishop all knew where it was kept—it always has been kept in the church. I daresay it was very silly—it's easy to see that now. But Daddy's only done what every rector of Combe Dean has done for centuries. Yet he feels that he is personally to blame for the theft. . . . But you've done him good, Mr Grendon. He's not even thought of Near Eastern Archaeology since the theft. It's good for him to be able to think of it again."

"What branch of archaeology is he concerned with?"

"The Hittite Kingdom in what is now a part of Turkey. They flourished at the time of Agamemnon and the siege of Troy—there is even supposed to have been correspondence between Agamemnon and a Hittite king. Daddy's a priest first, but he's a scholar, too. He's quite famous, in a way. He deciphered some inscriptions in what was then an unknown language, belonging to a sub-kingdom of the Hittites. But he has never been able to afford to do the archaeological work he'd like to do in Turkey. I wonder sometimes whether he wouldn't have been happier if he'd been a don instead of a parson. But no, it wouldn't have worked. He *had* to be a parson—and he's a very good parson, Mr Grendon. At least, he's a very good parish priest. But having this other great interest in his life, he's never bothered about preferment. He's just stayed at Combe Dean. Otherwise, I think, he might have been a bishop. But until this dreadful thing happened he was really quite content. . . . What did you read at Cambridge, Mr Grendon?"

"Maths."

"What do you do now?"

"I'm a fisherman."

"A fisherman? Camping on Dartmoor? What do you catch?"

"I work on a fishing-boat out of Finmouth."

"Are you working now? How do you get there? Where do you keep your car?"

"I haven't got a car. I go on a bicycle. It's rather a complicated story . . ." Over coffee in that friendly kitchen he found himself talking of how things had gone wrong, of how he'd sickened of the paper-money chase, and gone away to find—something or other, himself, perhaps. Then he began telling Elizabeth about *Lily*, and of what he hoped to be able to do with her.

The coffee was long cold, but David went on talking. Elizabeth was a good listener. He told her of his visitor from Bray, Bray, Bickersnatch and Bray, and of his intention to shed everything he'd worked for in London by handing it over to Louise. At last he looked at his watch. Heavens! He'd been talking for nearly two hours! He felt confused and ashamed. "I'm awfully, awfully sorry," he said. "I must have bored you frightfully. And I've kept you away from whatever else you were going to do this evening. Please forgive me."

"You haven't bored me, but I think you must be nearly as mad as Daddy," Elizabeth said.

David tumbled out of his dream world, and began to see a host of practical problems about his truancy from his camp.

"How far is it from here to my bit of moor?" he asked.

"About four miles."

"Well, I shall have to leave early, long before you are up, to get my bicycle. I've got to be in Finmouth by eight—Jess Grimble, the man I work for, will be waiting for me. He's a strict timekeeper, and I haven't let him down yet. So I'll leave about five and walk back to my camp."

"You'll do nothing of the sort. I can drive you into Finmouth. It isn't far."

"But I still won't have my bicycle. I've got to get back, you see."

"I thought you said you were going to pack up your Neolithic Villa. It's absurd to go on living there in weather like this."

"Yes, I am going to pack up. I'm going to get lodgings in Finmouth. But I've got to have my bicycle for transport until I do."

69

Elizabeth said nothing for a moment. Then she said, "Why not come here? It's a lot nearer Finmouth than you are now. And it would help us. We've never had much money, and now we're going to be really desperately hard up. Daddy wants to give half his stipend to the church to go towards the chalice, and he wants to sell most of our furniture. We've nothing really valuable, but a few things that are worth a bit—that corner cupboard where he got the sherry is said to be worth a few hundreds—I've already decided that we must try for some summer visitors next year—it would give me some practice if you came now. Do come. I promise that we'll do everything we can to make you comfortable."

"Don't be silly—the way you've looked after me tonight has been out of this world. But you can't invite me to stay on in your home—you hardly know me."

"I know you just as well as any landlady you ask for lodgings in Finmouth is likely to know you. Better perhaps—after all, we were introduced by a policeman."

"All right—it's a marvellous offer. But there's one condition— if I'm in the least a nuisance, coming and going at odd hours, or eating too much, you must promise to give me notice. When can I move in?"

"Tomorrow, if you like. Let me drive you into Finmouth in the morning. Then I'll go up to the moor to collect your things. And I can pick you up in Finmouth in the evening."

"Look, Miss Danvers, you're supposed to be a landlady, not a free taxi-service. No, I'll leave about five in the morning to collect my bicycle. I'll strike camp when I get back, and come on here."

"You needn't call me Miss Danvers—I'm Elizabeth."

"I can't call my landlady Elizabeth!"

"I don't see why not. I'm going to call you David, anyway. It's still raining, and it will almost certainly go on raining in the morning. It takes barely fifteen minutes to run into Finmouth in the car. You'll fish much better if you have some breakfast. Besides, you can show me your boat."

David gave way. The prospect of walking four miles to the moor through pouring rain in the dark was not enticing. He was already under a huge obligation to this girl, and he felt ashamed to drag her over to Finmouth—but she was quite right, it was much the most sensible thing to do. So it was agreed: and to

70

be on the safe side, Elizabeth suggested a start at twenty minutes to eight. "Breakfast will be ready in the kitchen here at seven," she said.

David enjoyed a glorious night between sheets. He had never needed an alarm clock: from his schooldays he had disciplined himself to wake at whatever time he needed to get up, and that morning he woke at six. He allowed himself a few minutes of sheer comfort, then got up, shaved in the luxury of the bathroom, and made his bed. He was in the kitchen by a quarter to seven. Elizabeth was already there, and there was a lovely smell of freshly made coffee.

"Can you eat bacon and eggs?" she asked.

"I can, but as a rule I don't. At Neolithic Villa my standard breakfast is a mug of porridge."

"Well, you can have bacon and eggs this morning."

They were at the quayside by five minutes to eight, and David was privately pleased to have maintained his record of getting there before Grimble. Elizabeth had been wrong about the rain —at least, partly wrong. It had rained through the night, but with daylight the sky had cleared somewhat, and there was a trace of watery sun. David pointed out Grimble's motor fishing-boat, and his own beloved *Lily*, lying about a cable from her. With her honest, clean lines and new paint she was lovely to look at. David thought suddenly how pleased his grandfather would have been.

On the dot of eight Grimble appeared. "Morning, Dave," he said. Then he noticed Elizabeth, saw that she was apparently with David, and took off the ancient peaked cap that he always wore to go to sea. "Morning, Miss," he added.

David introduced her. "This is Miss Danvers," he said. "Her father is Canon Danvers, the rector of Combe Dean. They've invited me to come down from the moor and stay at the rectory for a bit. It's very good of them, and it will be much handier for getting to Finmouth."

"I should think so," Grimble said. "Well, Dave, you'd better go and get the dinghy, and I'll get the things out of the shed. Is Miss Danvers coming out with us?"

"I'd love to, but I've got to get back, I'm afraid," Elizabeth said. "David, what time do you want me to pick you up?"

71

Grimble answered for him. "I reckon we should be in by two. Say half an hour for tidying up—Dave'll be free around two-thirty. Unless he wants to work on *Lily*."

"I've done most of what I can do for the moment. Two-thirty will be fine for me, if it suits you, Elizabeth."

"Yes, I can manage that all right."

"Good. Then if you can run me up to the moor I'll collect the rest of my kit."

# V

# The Wreck of the Madras

THEY WERE WORKING Grimble's Ground. As often happens after rain, visibility was exceptionally good, and the headland of Stokes Point stood out as sharply as if it had been cut from cardboard.

"Like your girl-friend," Grimble observed as they made their way towards the bar.

"She's not exactly my girl-friend," David said. "She and her father have been very good to me."

"Had some trouble at Combe Dean. Bad business about that chalice."

"Yes, a very bad business. And that's partly why I'm there. The old man is very cut up, and Elizabeth thought it might take his mind off things a bit to have someone else in the house."

"He's well spoken of, the rector. Can't think what people are coming to, robbing a church like that. Worse even than those thieving skin-divers."

In the clear air the coast inland from the rocks was as distinct as David had ever seen it. "They seem to have what looks like a permanent camp there," he said. "Huts and things."

"Aye. Chap started building the place as a holiday camp, but it never got finished. Don't know if it ever will be, though there's talk of getting on with it next year. This diving lot's been down there most of the summer. They're supposed to be working on an old wreck a mile or so this side of the point. Folk say there's treasure still on board, but I don't know about that. What treasure they get is from thieving our lobsters—couple of them have been going round Plymouth offering lobsters for half what we ask. Easy, if you don't have to find your own pots, and don't need to lay out any money for gear. The thieving bastards just use ours, and smash it up, often as not, as you've seen."

"What's the wreck?"

"Old East Indiaman—long before my time, and my dad's,

73

and my grand-dad's, and *his* dad's. Homeward bound she was, coming up Channel, when the wind went foul on her and she was driven inshore. Got caught in the bay this side of the point. She tried to anchor, but her cable broke. Then she tried to beat out, but she didn't have enough room. Nearly made it, though—good ships, those were. But she couldn't clear the point, and struck a ledge that runs out there. They got her off by throwing out cargo and the guns she carried, and they got sail on her again hoping to make Plymouth. But she didn't get far. Too badly holed, she was, and she went down three or four cables beyond the ledge. Least, that's how the story goes. One of her masts came ashore, and they say it's built into a barn over towards Revelstoke. They didn't have time to get any boats away. Half a dozen or so of her people got ashore, clinging to bits of wreckage, but the rest were all lost. This diving lot reckons to have found her, but what else is left to find after all these years I couldn't say. They keep themselves to themselves, and don't ask us for anything. Don't even hire a boat—they've got their own rubber dinghies. They just pinch our fish and our gear."

On the way home Grimble said, "My mate reckons he'll be fit to start coming out again next week. If you like, we'll go out in *Lily* tomorrow, and I'll give you a hand laying some gear on old Tiddler's ground. Then you'll be fit to start on your own."

That afternoon saw David duly installed at Combe Dean rectory. Elizabeth drove him to the track below his camp, and took his kit in the car, while he followed on his bicycle. He insisted on paying a week's rent in advance, and also on paying for petrol for Elizabeth's two trips into Finmouth.

At supper that evening David asked if anything much was known of the wreck of an East Indiaman off Stoke Point.

"Yes," the rector said, "quite a lot is known, although there are aspects of the affair which remain somewhat mysterious. It was one of the worst shipwrecks in this part of the channel. It happened in 1805—the year of Trafalgar. The vessel was the *Madras*, one of the finest ships in the East India Company's fleet. She was nearly new—she was coming home from her maiden voyage out to India. Because she was such a fine ship a number of high-ranking people in India chose her for the passage home—almost all of them were lost. She was embayed

74

near Stoke Point, ran on some rocks and went down. Because there was such heavy loss of life, and because so many of those lost were important people, the shipwreck filled columns of the contemporary papers, and several pamphlets were written about it. The master, and all the officers, went down with the ship. There were various suggestions of negligence—none of them historically substantiated. She was supposed to be carrying a great deal of treasure from India, and I daresay she was, though nothing ever seems to have been recovered. One particularly wild story was that she was not sunk by hitting a rock, but was blown up by a gang on board in league with French pirates. They are said to have killed the master and the officers, and to have made off with the treasure in the ship's boats, leaving the rest of the crew and the passengers to drown. There is no evidence of this. There were a few survivors, and their published accounts have nothing to say on the subject—it was probably just sensational journalism of its time. But the evidence is not very satisfactory. There were no survivors from the crew, and those who managed to get ashore were servants of some of the passengers—Indians who had scarcely a word of English, and a Danish botanist, who was more concerned by the loss of his plants than anything else. They were apparently asleep when the ship foundered, and woke to find themselves struggling in the sea amid the wreckage. They were saved by being carried ashore on floating timbers. They were all half-drowned, and were really in no position to know what may have happened on board. There are several puzzling features. The weather was bad, but it was not exceptionally bad for a well-found ship, and why was she so close inshore instead of being in mid-Channel? It also seems extraordinary that apparently so little effort was made to escape from the wreck. It remains one of the mysteries of the sea.

"You may wonder how I come to know about a shipwreck that occurred more than a century and a half ago. I am not a marine historian, but I have been much concerned with other aspects of history, and I am naturally interested in all history. My friend George Dorrance is a Fine Art historian, and he has been much involved in the study and preservation of objects brought to light by new techniques of marine archaeology—he is president of a scientific body devoted to such matters. A few months ago it was reported that a diving syndicate had found the wreck of the *Madras* and were hoping to recover treasure from her. George and his colleagues are very much concerned— they feel that wrecks should be subject to the same protection as important archaeological sites on land, and that there may be irreparable loss to knowledge of the past if treasure-hunters make free with whatever they can find from ships. There is now an element of Government concern in the matter, but legislative protection is thin, and a wreck has to be designated as being of particular interest before it acquires any protection at all. While Government departments are making up their minds a historic wreck may be gutted for private profit.

"One would have thought that the *Madras* was an obvious case for protection, and when it was reported that she had been found George asked me to obtain as much local knowledge of the circumstances of the shipwreck as I could. I have not had time for detailed research, but there is a good collection of pamphlets and old newspapers in the Plymouth libraries, and I was able to give him much of the information he wanted. Unfortunately nothing has since happened, and the *Madras* has not yet been designated as a wreck of sufficient importance to merit Government action. Apparently, it is largely a question of money—the Government is reluctant to acquire responsibility for wrecks that may qualify for grants for salvage or research."

"Judging by the way they damage our fishing-gear when they pilfer our fish, these divers would not seem a particularly scrupulous lot. The inshore fishermen of Finmouth have had a great deal of trouble from them," David said.

"You do not surprise me. The syndicate, I understand, is a wholly commercial gamble, and its members are doubtless uninhibited about methods of contributing to their costs."

"Does anybody own a wrecked ship?" Elizabeth asked.

"In theory, certainly. The original owners of a ship and her cargo do not forfeit any of their rights if she founders; though they may not, of course, be left in a position to exercise them. Normally, however, a vessel is insured, and if a claim is made and met, whatever can be salvaged belongs to the underwriters —they have, as it were, bought the wreck. But time and circumstance shroud legal rights. The *Madras* belonged to the East India Company, whose rights were transferred to the Crown in 1858. The *Madras* herself was insured by a syndicate at Lloyd's, which duly met a claim for total loss—whatever remains of the

76

hull, therefore, will belong to the legal heirs of those 1805 underwriters. Whether they could now be traced I do not know; it would be a task of immense complexity. The cargo, and what may be more important after all these years, the personal belongings of the passengers, may or may not have been insured. Research could, perhaps, cast some light on this, but it would be of academic value only. The cargo, which seems to have consisted mainly of jute, pepper, and other spices, has long since perished. There may well have been bullion and jewels on board, some being shipped on the East India Company's account, some belonging to the passengers. If any of this could be salvaged it would still be valuable—that, no doubt, is what the treasure-seekers are after. It might be possible in certain cases—if a monogrammed gold snuffbox, say, were recovered— for the heirs of the original owner to establish legal ownership, but it would be difficult, and might require long and costly litigation. Legally, any object brought ashore from a shipwreck ought to be handed to an officer called the Receiver of Wreck, who is responsible for trying to establish ownership. If ownership can be traced, the finder will be entitled to a proportion of the value as salvage. If after a year no owner can be found, the object may be sold, and the proceeds go to the salvor, less certain dues to the Receiver and the Crown. Salvage can thus be very valuable. But legal salvage is one thing, treasure-hunting quite another. A conscientious salvor may declare his finds—if they are particularly valuable it will pay him to do so, to acquire ownership in order that they may be sold openly. But gold coins and jewels are as likely to be pocketed; it would be hard to prove that they came from a particular wreck, even if the question was ever raised."

"It doesn't seem a very satisfactory situation," David said.

"It is not a satisfactory situation. British Governments always seem so obsessed with present problems that they have no time for the care of the past. How many archaeological sites in Britain have disappeared under the plough, or modern bulldozer? We know far more about ancient Crete than we do of ancient Britain. It is fortunate that individual scholars do care, and are able, sometimes, to arouse public opinion to protect a site of outstanding value. But it is the ordinary things of the past, the cooking pots and pins and buttons, that tell us most about our forbears. And these are as likely to be preserved on the seabed as on land—more likely, because there are no ploughs or new housing estates underneath the sea. But it would require an army of inspectors to protect every located wreck for scientific study, and a great expenditure of money. Or, perhaps, a public conscience in such matters; and that, alas, is rarely evident. The pursuit of knowledge has always been at war with Mammon, and Mammon is inclined to triumph. It is a matter both for humility and pride that scholarship has been able to achieve even the little that it has."

The next week passed rapidly for David. It was a great day when he took out *Lily* on her first fishing voyage under his command. He worked over Tiddler's Ground, and since the area had not been fished for a generation his hauls were exceptionally good. He was still a member of Jess Grimble's partnership, and his catch was marketed with Grimble's to the organisation which supplied hotels direct. He began to keep accounts again, and the accountant in him wondered whether they were really making as much as they could by selling as they did—it might pay the inshore fishermen of Finmouth to set up a distribution system of their own, to supply hotels and restaurants under contract instead of selling to a supplying organisation. He decided that he didn't yet know enough about the business, but the thought stayed in his head.

His good catches made up for the fact that he was working singlehanded. Tiddler's Ground was the most distant of the fishing grounds recognised as belonging to the Finmouth men, and it was mainly for that reason that it had been neglected. Deepsea fishermen go much farther after fish now that they work powerful modern vessels, but the powered fishing-boat has tended to reduce the area covered by the inshore men. It costs no more to take a sailing-boat twenty miles than ten, but with fuel costs an important element in the modern fishermen's economy they go no farther than they feel they have to. Of course, there are other social factors involved. When David's grandfather had built *Lily*, a crew expected to be out all night as often as not, and to put up with dreadfully long hours. Men nowadays are reluctant to do so; and the younger wives expect their menfolk to come home regularly.

Working *Lily* under sail as much as he could, David reckoned that he increased his profit substantially. He was impressed by the evidence that sail could still be economic for a working boat, but he realised that there was a price to pay for this. He had to be out longer, and there was always work to be done on sails or rigging when he got back. For himself, he was prepared to accept the price, but he understood why so many nowadays were not.

The arrangement for staying at the rectory worked well. Elizabeth, he thought, was glad to have him there, and for reasons other than his rent. The theft of the chalice had hit her father savagely: he looked now in his late seventies instead of the late sixties, and as the days went by without any news his grief increased visibly. David couldn't help much, but his mere presence helped a little—at meals he could sometimes get the rector to talk about his ancient Hittites, and this was at least a temporary therapy. Elizabeth said to him, "Meals were absolute hell until you came—I could scarcely get Daddy to eat anything. They're still hell, but a little better—more like purgatory, perhaps."

He invited her to spend a day on *Lily*. She was delighted at the chance of getting away from the rectory, but doubtful of her ability as a sailor. "I haven't done much sailing," she said. "But I can swim."

David laughed. "It's a useful accomplishment, but not all that relevant to sailing. If we have to take to swimming I shall consider that my own seamanship has failed. I hope it won't come to that."

It didn't. He took her out to Tiddler's Ground, and she helped him work the pots, making him feel that he really missed a lot by not having a crew. She might know little about sailing, but she picked up things quickly, and mercifully she was not at all seasick.

"Isn't this somewhere near where the *Madras* went down?" she asked.

"I think it was a bit farther out. We can go and have a look if you like—we've got time. The wind's in the south-west, and it will probably hold to take us back."

David didn't know precisely where the *Madras* had foundered, but the rock ledge on which she struck was marked on the chart, and he could estimate roughly where she must have sunk. The ledge was safely covered now, and *Lily*, not needing the depth of a big East Indiaman, could sail over it. At first they

79

could see nothing to indicate a wreck, but after going a mile or so towards the point David spotted a buoy. "That's probably where she is—it'll be a marker buoy put there by the salvage divers, I expect." They sailed over to the buoy and looked into the water round it, but could see nothing. "You couldn't expect to see anything of her," David said. "She'll be lying on the bottom, half buried in sand after all these years—I think it's mostly a sandy bottom round here."

The market-van was waiting for them when they got back. Elizabeth helped to unload *Lily*, and waited on the quay while David put her on her mooring and rowed back in the pram. "I *have* enjoyed today," she said. "Thank you ever so much."

"Well, you gave me transport into Finmouth, and you certainly earned your passage. This is yours." He counted out nine pound notes, and gave them to her.

"What on earth is this for?"

"It's your share of the catch."

"But why should I have a share? I can't possibly take it."

"I'm afraid you'll have to. It's the law of the Medes and Persians round here—two shares for the skipper, one share for the boat, and one share for the crew."

"Well, I've never been paid for enjoying myself before. I hardly ever have any money of my own, and it's a lovely surprise."

They took a lobster home with them for supper.

Thinking about the economics of his job, David concluded that he was wasting working-time, and sometimes petrol for his outboard, by coming in from the fishing grounds each day. *Lily* had a capacious fish-hold, and if he anchored out for the night he could be on the grounds at first light and bring back two days' haul in time to catch the market-van.

*Lily*'s somewhat rudimentary fo'c'sle needed a little work, but it was weathertight, and could be made into a comfortable little cabin. He had spent money so far only on things that mattered for a working boat, but now he gave the inside of the fo'c'sle a coat of white paint, and contrived a folding table to fit between the two bench-bunks. Elizabeth took him into Plymouth one morning, and at a do-it-yourself shop he bought some odd lengths of foam rubber to make a mattress. He had his sleeping-bag and camp kit, and the Primus for a galley stove. He bought two hurricane lamps, and considered that his cabin was now adequately furnished. There was, however, one other piece of equipment that he wanted—a more serviceable dinghy for working single-handed. *Lily*'s pram was a tough little boat, but she was built, like her mistress, out of grown planks—no plywood or plastic about her. This made her heavy, and although she could be carried on board, she was an awkward weight for one man to handle. She could be towed, of course, but a tow is often inclined to be a nuisance, particularly when line-fishing. David wanted an inflatable rubber dinghy, but he hadn't enough cash to buy one. He was making money with *Lily*, but after paying his rent and providing for inescapable necessities he was paying over everything he could save to Grimble, to go towards *Lily*'s purchase price. His private aim was still important to him —to keep himself without drawing on his remaining capital. But he had given himself a dispensation in order to buy *Lily*'s outboard engine, and after much debating with himself he decided that the dispensation could be extended to cover a rubber dinghy —apart from anything else, it would be of real value as a life-raft should *Lily* meet disaster, an important consideration for a man working at sea alone.

So he bought a rubber dinghy. It fitted neatly aft of the mast, which meant that he did not have to re-inflate the dinghy every time he wanted to use it. The dinghy had rope hand-holds, and he devised an excellent system for getting it out of the water. *Lily*'s main halliard had a purchase, and by putting a sling through the hand-holds and attaching it to the halliard, he could get it on board without strain. Equipped with his rubber dinghy, he reckoned that *Lily* was now capable of extended cruising: he could get ashore when he wanted to, and could come and go as he pleased.

Elizabeth had come to look forward to David's return each evening, and was sad about his plans to spend more time at sea. Although she knew everyone in the parish, she had no close friends—the rector's daughter in a country parish tends to be regarded as a universal social welfare worker, the friend of all, but the intimate friend of none. Upkeep of the beautiful but rambling and inconvenient old rectory—built for a retinue of servants—was a strain both on her father's modest income and her own time. She had no social life outside the parish, and visitors to the rectory from the world beyond Combe Dean were

81

few. Those who did come were elderly academic friends of her father, or visiting clergy. David's presence was undoubtedly a help to her father in his misery, but it was also nice for her. She did her best to share his enthusiasm for turning *Lily* into a cruising home, but she rather wished he wouldn't. However, she understood the demands of his job, and helped as much as she could.

David, too, felt that he was missing something when instead of putting over *Lily*'s helm and turning for home he sounded his way cautiously inshore and let go her big fisherman's anchor. The anchorage he had selected was off a small cove or dip in the cliffs, where there was a hundred yards or so of sandy beach. It was not far from the unfinished holiday camp occupied by the diving syndicate. There was a biggish motor cruiser at anchor in the cove, and some dinghies drawn up on the beach nearby. David put them down as probably belonging to the divers. The anchorage was sheltered from the west and north, and the run of the cliffs offered some shelter from the east. It was exposed to the south, but in anything but a southerly gale he reckoned that it would be safe enough.

He had been on *Lily* all day, and when he had anchored and snugged down her sails he felt like a walk ashore. This was where the rubber dinghy came in. He launched it without difficulty and rowed ashore. The tide was making, so he would not have to move it far when he wanted to get back. He hauled it just above the line of wrack that marked the normal range of tide, dug the small CQR anchor that he had bought for the dinghy into the sand, and walked up the beach.

It was good to stretch his legs. There was a path leading up the cliff, and he followed this. It took him up to the cliff road. The holiday camp was about a quarter of a mile to the east. About the same distance westwards there was an isolated building that looked as if it might be a pub.

It was. It stood at a corner where a lane from inland met the cliff road, and a large car-park indicated a thriving summer trade. In this autumn evening, the car-park was almost empty—almost, but not quite, for there was one car there and the pub seemed to be open. David had not so far allowed himself any money to spend in pubs. This evening, feeling lonely at not having Elizabeth to talk to, he told himself that self-discipline could become rather ridiculous: he had set out to keep himself, not to go through life wearing a hair shirt. He could afford to buy himself a drink, and he damned well would. He went in.

There were three other people in the bar, two youngish men and a girl in her early twenties. The girl was sitting on a stool at the end of the bar, with the men standing on each side of her. She was holding an open newspaper, and they were all looking at it. The barman gave him a polite "Good evening", and David ordered a Scotch. "Come far?" the barman asked as he pushed the drink across the counter.

"Not very far, I've walked up from the cove," David said. "I've come off a boat."

One of the men with the girl looked up. "I think I saw you come in. Gaff sloop with a long bowsprit—that your boat?" he asked.

"Yes, she's mine. Only she's not a sloop, she's a cutter. But you wouldn't know that—I came in under only one head sail. She can carry a big staysail, too, but I didn't have it up."

"Nice looking boat."

"She's sixty years old, but she's all right."

The man ordered a round of drinks and glanced at David. "Have one?" he asked.

"That's very nice of you. Thanks very much," David said.

He moved over towards their end of the bar, and the girl showed him the newspaper. "That's us," she said. She pointed to a column headed "Divers Strike It Rich", and handed David the paper. It was a Plymouth evening newspaper, and the story reported the recovery of thirty-eight gold coins and several pieces of jewellery from the wreck of the *Madras*. "Phil Layton —that's our leader—went into Plymouth to see about them, and I suppose that's how the paper picked up the story," the girl said. "Phil said they'd have to be reported to the Customs or something, though I don't quite know why. He found them on the wreck. I was with him."

"You have to report things, Sheila, in order to establish salvage rights," said the man who had stood David a drink. "And it's not the ordinary Customs—it's an official called the Receiver of Wreck. The point is that whatever goes down with a ship technically still belongs to somebody, though with a wreck that's been at the bottom getting on for a couple of centuries it isn't very likely that an owner will be found. Even if he is, you can claim salvage—if he isn't, then the things become yours. That's Phil's job—he doesn't want to keep the things, he wants to sell them. And you get a much better price for jewellery and such like if you can sell it legally at an auction."

"Well, it seems a lot of red tape to me. Phil said I could have one of the brooches."

"And I'm sure you will, my pet. Only you may have to wait for a bit."

"How do you work?" David asked. "Are you all in the diving team?"

"Phil Layton is a professional," the man said. "The rest of us are members of various sub-aqua clubs and come down a week or two at a time for the diving. We pay for our keep, and help with the work. It gives us a cheap holiday, and it provides Phil Layton with crews—it's a good scheme."

"Bill actually helped to find the wreck," the girl said.

"Yes, I was down earlier in the summer when Phil was looking for it. We knew roughly where to look, of course; even so, it's some job to find a wreck that's been on the bottom all those years. In the end we got her mainly by luck. Phil had his harpoon-gun, and saw a big lobster which he thought he'd get. The lobster went into what looked like a crack in some rocks. Phil fired at it as it disappeared—and the harpoon went deep into wood. We didn't bother any more with the lobster, but traced the outline of the wreck. It was the old *Madras* all right."

"And I was there when Phil got up the chest," the girl went on. "I was on *Sea Venturer*—that's Phil's cruiser—and I'd been down with Phil to have a look at things. Phil had been tunnelling into the wreck, and he came on this old wooden chest. It wasn't very big, and I helped him to drag it out. Then I went back up and told the others on the cruiser. We sent down a grapple and a sling, Phil hooked it round the chest, and very, very carefully we got it up. There's a crane on the cruiser, but we had to work it ever so gently in case the wood split, or anything. But it didn't. And when we got the chest on board I thought it was in wonderfully good condition."

"Did you open it on the spot?"

"We wanted to, but Phil said we'd better get it ashore first. He's got special tools and things in a workshop in the camp—he was frightened of damaging anything that might be inside the chest. So we took it ashore, and Phil got to work on it. He wouldn't let any of us stay with him—'It's almost certain to be nothing but a disappointment, and I'd rather take it alone', was what he said. But it wasn't. He called us in a bit later, and there was the chest, open. Inside was a sort of mouldy grey mud that Phil said had been clothes, but underneath the first layers of mud there was something sparkling. He cleared away the mud and there was some lovely old jewellery—bracelets with rubies, and some big emerald ear-rings. And all those gold coins. The jewels and the gold shone like new as soon as they were cleaned up. It was wonderfully exciting."

David bought drinks in his turn. No one else came into the pub, and he spent a pleasant hour chatting to the amateur divers. Then they said they must be getting back to their camp. "We've got a car, and we'll drop you at the top of the cliff path," one of the men said. David accepted the offer.

"Staying here long?" the girl asked as he got out.

"No, I've only put in for the night, and I shall have to be off in the morning. But I may come back—I like your pub."

"Yes, it's not a bad place. We may be seeing you, then. Careful on that path as you go down—it's steep, and horribly slippery in places."

David waved as the car drove off, and then took to the path. It was dark, and he cursed himself for not having brought a torch—but he hadn't set out for more than a short walk along the cliffs. There was a little moon, and some reflected light from the sea; and he was good on hillsides. He managed the descent without breaking anything, found his dinghy, and a few minutes later was safely back on *Lily*. He lit his hurricane lamps, got the Primus going, and cooked himself a meal of fried mackerel. He washed up before turning in, and then lay on his bunk for a bit, enjoying the soft lamplight in *Lily's* newly painted cabin, and the little talkative noises that she made as she rode gently to her anchor. Then he put out the light, and was soon asleep. As he dropped off something was nagging at his mind, but he couldn't determine what.

# VI

## *An Evening Out*

DAVID MADE AN early start, and was back in Finmouth in good time to catch the market-van, with a most satisfactory two days' haul. He got back to the rectory quite early in the afternoon, with a pleasant feeling of an evening and night ahead of him before he needed to go to sea again.

Elizabeth was delighted to see him back so early. "I've brought you some fish for supper," he said.

"There'll be just the two of us. Daddy's gone to a synod in Exeter, and he's staying to dinner with one of the canons. He won't be back till late."

After his extravagance of last night David felt that there was a case for some further relaxation of his private rules. "If your father's not going to be in, why don't you come out and have a meal in Plymouth? The fish was caught today—it will be perfectly good tomorrow. I'd love to take you out to dinner— please let me."

Elizabeth hardly ever had a meal that she had not cooked herself, and she jumped at the invitation. "I'd love it, too," she said. "The only thing is, it will be horribly expensive. Are you sure you can afford it—I mean, the money not going towards buying *Lily*?"

"Well, I had a couple of good days, and the *Lily* account isn't going badly. Do let's go. And let's make an early start, and have time for a civilised drink before dinner. I'll go and get into my one decent suit and be ready to start when you are."

Elizabeth was privately a good deal bothered about what to wear herself. She lived in pullovers which she knitted for herself, and the rest of her wardrobe was sadly thin. But she had one black dress which she had inherited from her mother—it was not hopelessly unfashionable because it had never been particularly fashionable. This would have to do. David, who used to irritate Louise by seldom noticing the new clothes which she was always buying, couldn't have said whether the inherited black dress was fashionable or not. He thought simply that Elizabeth looked stunning.

David's knowledge of Plymouth was a decade or so out of date. He could still find his way by sea to the boat harbour at Sutton Pool, but he knew nothing of the tower blocks of hotels which have sprung up round the Hoe. Elizabeth, who occasionally went into Plymouth to shop, was equally ignorant of Plymouth restaurants, but had heard that the roof-top restaurant of one of the new hotels was good. So they went there. It was a magnificent site—a penthouse high above the Hoe, with a tremendous view of the Sound and, in the far distance, the Eddystone light just beginning to wink.

They sat for drinks at an immense window, with the green Hoe and then the vast seascape reaching away beneath them. David felt completely happy—and then the nagging thought which had come into the edge of his mind last night returned.

David had earned his living as an accountant, which does not call for particularly high-grade maths. By nature, however, he was a mathematical philosopher, he had been a Wrangler at Cambridge, and he had a good logical mind.

"Cast your mind back, Elizabeth, to when that policeman of yours was trying to run me in."

"He wasn't trying to run you in," Elizabeth said indignantly. "He was looking for Mr Platt, who he thinks—and I think—stole the chalice. He didn't know who you were: he just had to eliminate you from the inquiry."

"All right, all right. I don't hold it against him—actually, I thought he was a rather nice policeman. The man he was looking for was called Platt. Yes? Well, go on a bit to the night you rescued me from my camp. Do you remember at supper telling me more of the story of Mr Platt? What was the name of the ancestor he was looking for in your parish registers?"

"Layton—James or John Layton he wasn't sure which."

"So that's it. Well, I've just come across a Mr Layton." He told her of his encounter with the divers.

"It can't have anything to do with Mr Platt. Layton was the name of his mother's father, or grandfather perhaps. It wasn't his name."

'And he didn't exist—at any rate in the Combe Dean registers. But Mr Platt doesn't exist either, so they're all square so far. How good are you at inventing names? Obviously ones like Smith or Jones wouldn't quite do. Mr Platt had to have two names—the fake Platt, which he'd thought up at leisure, and got a fake visiting card for, and a name for his ancestor. Now a *mother's* ancestor couldn't be any give away—it couldn't be his name, because that would be his father's. *Why not use his own name?* It would be realistic and sound good. I can imagine doing it myself if I suddenly had to find a name for one of my mother's relations that I didn't want traced to me. It would be better, in a way, than a random name, because in the nature of things it *couldn't* be my own real name."

"It sounds very involved. But I see what you mean. Only there must be hundreds of Laytons around, and there is nothing whatever to relate your Mr Layton to our Mr Platt."

"No. But there is a little more to it. Suppose there are 100,000 Laytons in England. And suppose one of them is also Mr Platt. The crude odds against picking the right Mr Layton at random are 99,999 to 1. Once you know anything about them, the odds alter—some Mr Laytons will be over eighty, others may have one leg, or be blind, or otherwise ruled out. Geography is not a very strong ruling-in factor, but it *is* a factor. If you are looking for a Layton-Platt and you find a Layton within a dozen miles or so of where Mr Layton-Platt was last seen, it's mildly interesting, to say the least. There's something else as well."

"What's that?"

"The chest that the girl said was brought up from the wreck. She saw it come up—remarked on its good condition. It had to be taken ashore to be opened with special tools, or that's what Mr Layton said. Your father told us that the *Madras* went down in 1805. Do you think that a wooden chest that's been on the seabed since 1805 would come up in good condition? I think it would have disintegrated long ago."

"David, what on earth are you driving at?"

"I've been wondering what I would do if I wanted to make money out of very valuable stolen goods—big jewels, or your chalice. There's a crook's market, of course—fences who are ready to buy stolen things. But they don't give very good prices —they can't, because they're taking a lot of risk themselves. Salvage from an old wreck would be a marvellous way of acquiring a legal title to sell things. No one knows what went down in the *Madras*—no one can say for certain what comes up. Major pieces of jewellery can usually be identified by insurance records, but the stones themselves can be re-set, or even re-cut. If you found an old chest on a wreck and got it up, wouldn't you be so excited that you'd want to open it straight away? The girl said she and the others did want to open it, but Mr Layton wouldn't let them. If what she told me is accurate—and I can't see that she had any reason to lie about it—no one, apart from Mr Layton, actually saw the chest opened. He has witnesses to prove what came *out* of it—there's no evidence of when any of it went in."

"You've certainly got a powerful imagination! But how could the chalice come into it?"

"Doesn't it strike you as odd that no one has tried to claim the £10,000 reward? I grant you, it could have been melted down before the reward was offered—in which case the thief must be kicking himself. But would anyone go to all the trouble of getting fake visiting cards printed and concocting a story about his mother's ancestors to steal the chalice just to melt it down? The sneak thief and the sophisticated thief have different sorts of mind. I don't believe this was a sneak thief's job, nor do you, nor do the police.

"I think I told you—or if I didn't tell you, I certainly told your policeman—that I've seen your chalice. I remember it very well—it was in an exhibition of church plate in Exeter, and we had a lecture on it when I was at school. There is no inscription on the chalice—that's one of the things that casts a little doubt on the Francis Drake story, though I remember the lecturer telling us that it's hard to see how else anything so valuable could have got to Combe Dean. Its beauty is in its shape and workmanship. It's been measured and recorded, of course, but if witnesses saw it coming out of the wreck of the *Madras*, who could prove that it wasn't another chalice, an unknown replica, or one of an unknown pair? Museums or rich private collectors would bid eagerly for it—if they could!"

Elizabeth gazed out of the encircling window at lights springing up along the Hoe, against the huge backcloth of now nearly-dark sea. "Do you think there is even a chance that the chalice still exists?" she asked wistfully.

"I should think it almost certain," David said. "Whether it can be recovered is another matter. But I should rate the chances of that as reasonably good, too."

"Oh David . . . it would transform Daddy's life. He's saying now that he feels he ought to resign the living. And I don't know where we'd go, or what he'd do. . . . Do you really think there's anything in your Layton-Platt theory?"

"I don't know. I've never been a proper philosopher, though perhaps I could have been. I think I could have stayed at Cambridge, but my parents were both dead, and I felt awfully restless. I liked climbing, and I wanted to get out into the world. But I had a good education in mathematical logic. Suppose you want to account for something . . . you devise a theory that seems to fit the known facts, and you stick to this until you have proved it to be wrong, or some other fact turns up which doesn't fit. That's what I feel now. My theory seems to fit the facts, but there must be a lot of other facts that we don't know. I'd like to try to find out those other facts, but I'm not a policeman. I've thought of something, though, that I *could* do."

"What's that?"

"Well, the chief constable at Exeter used to be a friend of my father's, and I think he'd remember me. I could go to see him, tell him what I feel about the diving operation, and leave it to him."

Elizabeth considered this. Then she said, "You know, David, I don't think you ought to do that. He'll be a very busy man— a bit like a bishop, I'd imagine. If you go direct to the bishop about something that needs doing in the parish it's fine if he has time to be interested. But if he *doesn't* do anything about it, then you're stuck—having gone to the bishop you can't very well go to anybody else. I think you should go to Sergeant Blundell. He'd probably have to do the investigating in any case, and he'll be much more enthusiastic about it if the idea comes to him directly instead of being passed down by the high-ups. He's an intelligent man, and a nice man, and I'm sure he'd listen to you."

"I don't mind doing that, but you'd better come with me. He may still be a bit suspicious of me for all I know. If you are with me at least he'll realise that I haven't tried to run away. . . . And now we really ought to have our dinner—the chap with the menus seems to be getting a bit restless."

On the way home they arranged a plan of campaign. David didn't want to lose a day's work, but by going out early in the morning, around six, he could be in by about noon. During the morning Elizabeth would telephone Sergeant Blundell and try to make an appointment with him. She would meet David at noon, and they'd fit in with whatever time Blundell suggested.

When David brought in *Lily* Elizabeth was waiting on the quay. "I'm sorry, David," she said, 'but I'm afraid there's a bit of a rush. Sergeant Blundell was very friendly, but he says the only time he can see us today is at the police station at twelve-thirty. I'll help you unload *Lily*. We should just about make it."

"He'll have to put up with my fishing clothes," David said.

"You again," said Blundell, but he said it pleasantly.

"You did me a good turn by arresting me," David said. "It's really because of that that I'm staying at the rectory."

"I didn't arrest you. And I knew about your going to the rectory."

"How on earth—"

Blundell smiled. "You may think that village people take no notice of you, but in a village everyone knows practically everything about everyone else. Sometimes I think it's a kind of instinct. People keep themselves to themselves, but you can't put on a new pair of shoes without somebody's knowing about it. I heard about your striking camp and going to the rectory the day after you got there. You mustn't misunderstand me, Mr Grendon, but I had to check up as far as I could on the things you told me. Everything you said seems to have been quite accurate."

David was slightly taken aback. "Since it was all true it could hardly have been anything else," he said. "But I don't hold it against you—rather, it makes me a bit happier about coming to see you now. It makes me hope that you may take seriously some ideas I've formed about the chalice."

"Of course I'll take them seriously. Tell me about them."

David recounted the theories he had discussed with Elizabeth the night before. Blundell listened without interrupting, making an occasional note on a pad.

"Finmouth fishermen don't exactly love those divers, do they?" he remarked when David had finished.

"We've no cause to love them. They take our fish and, what is far worse, they wreck our gear. I've seen almost new lobster pots cut to pieces with a knife. We can't prove that the divers do it, but I can't see how else it could happen."

Blundell was a South Devon man, and he understood the fishermen's feelings. "It's a rotten business," he said. "One of your mates brought in just such a slashed pot. I wish we could do something about it, but without a constant sea patrol there isn't much we can do. I mentioned your relations with the divers only because it's the sort of question my superiors will ask me. I'm not really suggesting that you thought up your ideas to try to make trouble for them."

"No, it's not that at all." This was a point of view that hadn't occurred to David, but he was naturally an honest person, and he accepted Blundell's observation as quite reasonable. "I suppose it could look like that, though."

"I don't suppose it does," Blundell said. "I like your point about the Layton name. I ought to have thought of it, but I didn't. Of course, there's no evidence one way or the other, but it's one of those funny little coincidences that need to be looked into. I also like your point about the condition of the chest after all those years at the bottom of the sea. But you didn't see the chest yourself?"

"No. I only heard about it from the girl. But her account of how it had to be taken ashore to be opened suggests that at least it wasn't falling to pieces."

"Yes, that's a good point, too. But again there's no sort of evidence. But that's our job. I think I'd like to have a look at that chest. Another thing, Mr Grendon—did any of the people you met say anything about Huntingdon? Did they come from Huntingdon, perhaps?"

"I haven't the least idea. Why Huntingdon?"

"The car-registration MEW that Miss Danvers noticed is a Huntingdonshire registration."

"It made me think of sea-birds. I remember it very clearly," Elizabeth said.

"I only met three of them in the pub," David said. "They were all amateur divers, and I got the impression that they weren't local, but they didn't say where they came from. I gathered that there was a pretty constant flow of people from various sub-aqua clubs coming for a sort of working holiday. The lot I met had a car, but I'm afraid I didn't notice the registration number."

"It was just a thought. If there was an MEW vehicle in the camp it would be evidence to support your theories. If there isn't—or wasn't at the time of Mr Platt's visit to the rectory— it doesn't necessarily rule out the theories, of course. I take it that Miss Danvers hasn't seen Mr Layton?"

"No, neither of us has."

"I wonder if it could be arranged. I could ask Mr Layton to call here—as I asked you—but I'd rather the police kept in the background at present. If Miss Danvers could see Mr Layton, she could tell us whether or not he bore any resemblance to the man she met as Mr Platt. That would be an important step towards deciding if there really is a case for investigation."

"I told the people I met that I liked their pub, and that I might come back. I could try to find out if Mr Layton ever goes there, and if he does there's no reason why I shouldn't take Miss Danvers with me one evening when he's likely to be there. Or we might think up some reason for calling at the camp—I could say I'd lost an anchor, and wondered if the divers could help me to recover it."

"I must say I hope you don't take to crime, Mr Grendon. You have a horribly subtle mind."

"I'm a mathematician, really. It's just a question of trying to solve a problem."

"The pub would be the better plan, I think, because it's more casual. Could you manage to get back there fairly soon?"

"Yes, I could go by road this evening, if you like."

"That would be admirable. And if you do manage to see Mr Layton, let me know as soon as possible. I'll give you my home telephone number, so that you can get hold of me if it's out of office hours. And there are one or two discreet inquiries that I can make in the meantime. Well, Mr Grendon, obviously I don't know whether there is anything in your ideas or not, but I'm exceedingly grateful to you both for coming to see me. I don't need to tell you to be very careful in anything you do or say."

"We want to get back the chalice," Elizabeth said.

Blundell was considerably impressed by David's visit. His theorising was pretty wild, and yet in an odd way it held together. It was not so much any one thing as a combination of little things which added up to a sort of circumstantial evidence.

93

The story of the chest—if true, and it was no more than hearsay based on a girl's pub chatter—was a queer one. And they had all been so busy looking for a man called Platt that nobody had thought of looking for anyone called Layton. Yet Layton was a name at least as important in the story as Platt. If the disappearing Mr Platt was really Mr Layton, his choice of a name for one of his mother's ancestors was a good one—it was the last name anyone would think of as applying to him. Blundell had one piece of evidence which could settle the matter one way or the other—the so far unidentified fingerprint on the safe. But if by any chance Mr Layton was the mysterious Mr Platt, an official visit from the police before they knew anything more about him would probably put paid to all hopes of recovering the chalice: he could scarcely be expected to tell them where it was on a preliminary visit, and while inquiries were being made he would have plenty of opportunity to dispose of it. Without the chalice, or some really hard evidence that he had something to do with it, the fingerprint alone was not enough to proceed on. If it was Mr Layton-Platt's fingerprint it would be highly suspicious, but there was no evidence to say when it was made. Mr Layton-Platt could say that he had wanted to speak to the rector about something or other and had followed him into the vestry one Sunday morning after a service. The safe would be open for putting away the ordinary Communion plate, and he must just have put his hand on it. A thin story, but with the help of a clever counsel one that it would be next to impossible to disprove. The rector might say that he had no recollection of the incident —but it would not need much cross-examination to suggest that his memory was scarcely to be relied upon. Of course, there was the additional possibility that the rector and Miss Danvers might recognise Mr Layton as the man they knew as Platt— but the kind of ingenuity they were dealing with suggested that Mr Platt would not be easily identified with anyone.

And if that Mr Grendon's ideas had anything in them, the chalice was only part of an ingenious use of an old wreck to dispose of stolen jewellery. If—if—if—Blundell decided to go to Plymouth to discuss things with his inspector.

"What do we know of this chap Grendon?" the inspector asked after listening to Blundell's story.

"Nothing much, really. You'll remember that I put in a report about interviewing him in the early days of our search for the man Platt—he was camping out on a lonely part of Ugborough Moor, and we were interviewing all strangers in the vicinity. Grendon gave a reasonable account of himself, and made no objection when I asked if I could take him to Combe Dean to see if either Canon Danvers or his daughter could identify him. They both said he was nothing like the man they knew as Platt, and I was able to check his fingerprints against the unidentified print on the safe—it was certainly not him. All that seemed to let him out completely. I did ask the Exeter people about his story of having lived in Exeter, and it seems to be quite true. There was a Samuel Grendon, who was a well-known Exeter solicitor, and there isn't any doubt that he was a friend of the Chief Constable. Of course, I haven't seen young Grendon's birth certificate, but there doesn't seem any need to. As far as I know he's exactly what he says he is."

"And now he's turned up living at Combe Dean rectory. Queer, that."

"I don't think it's particularly queer. He told me that he'd left his wife and come to Devon to try to make a living as a fisherman. He worked at first for old Jess Grimble at Finmouth, and he's now working Grimble's old *Lily* on his own, or in some sort of partnership with Grimble. I had a word with the Finmouth people before I came over here. Young Grendon's been around just as he says he has, and the other fishermen seem to think well of him, as a good boat-hand and a willing worker. As for living at the rectory—he hadn't anywhere else to go. The local story is that Miss Danvers rescued him from his camp one pouring wet night, and that he's staying on as a paying guest. It's just the sort of thing the Danvers girl would do—she has a name for helping people in the parish. And I daresay they need the money. That rectory is a huge rambling old place—it must cost a mint of money to keep up, and I've never heard that Canon Danvers was a rich man."

"Okay then, if you're satisfied about him. What do you yourself make of his story?"

"It's hard to say. I just feel there could be something in it. It's a question whether you feel it's worth going into seriously. It can't be done locally."

"Well, we're at a dead end otherwise. The high-ups are

getting restive about complete lack of progress in the Combe Dean chalice case. At least this is a line of some sort to work on. And some of these treasure-hunters aren't all that scrupulous. If there's anything in the Grendon story, I take it the jewels said to have been found in the chest were presumably stolen."

"That would be the idea, yes."

"I'll start by getting the cutting from the evening paper. What would be the date? Day before yesterday? Shouldn't be any difficulty about that. Matter of fact, I think I remember reading the story—I thought, 'How bloody lucky some people are!' Funny if it turned out they weren't so lucky after all. And I know the Receiver of Wreck. I can have a word with him, and get a proper description of what is supposed to have come from the chest."

"Damn the expense," David said as he and Elizabeth left the police station. "Let's have some lunch at a hotel."

"We can't. What about Daddy?"

"Ring him up and explain. I expect you left everything ready for lunch, anyway."

"Well, yes, I did. But David, I'm costing you a fearful lot of money. And you have to go to that pub again this evening."

"That's what I want to talk about. We must have a plan of campaign. Ring your father and tell him we're stuck here for lunch."

Feeling guiltily that she was living in an extravagant world of meals out, Elizabeth found a telephone box and explained matters to her father. When she rejoined David, he was beginning to have second thoughts. "The question is," he said, "whether I'm fit to be seen with you in these clothes."

Elizabeth laughed. "What's the matter with them? They'll think you're a yachtsman. You look rather nice."

The summer visitors having departed, those hotels which were still open were left to their permanent residents, most of whom ate early. David and Elizabeth had a dining-room almost to themselves. "What do you think your policeman made of us?" David asked.

"I'm sure he took us seriously. Oh, David, I wonder if you could possibly be right?"

"Well, we've got to go on until we're proved wrong. I'm thinking about tonight. Could you come with me?"

"But we've no idea whether Mr Layton will be there."

"It's worth a gamble. There's nothing to do in that camp in the evenings, and I should think most of the people there go to the pub. The Layton man wasn't there the time I went because he'd gone to Plymouth to deal with the Customs or whatever about his finds. If he's around, he'll quite likely visit the pub. And if we're lucky you'll see him at once, and that will save a lot of time. There's another thing. If we go to the pub together, it's quite natural. If I go by myself and start asking about Mr Layton it will mean going back there again with you, and if anyone is at all suspicious they'll begin to wonder why I'm interested. It would be far better if we could just be there casually when he came in."

"I see what you mean. I've never thought about being a detective before—it's awfully exciting. Of course I'll come with you."

"Can you remember what you were wearing on the day Mr Platt came to the rectory?"

"A skirt and jumper, I suppose—what I'm wearing now, although it may have been a yellow jumper instead of this one. There was nothing special about the day, and I certainly wasn't dressed up for anything."

"Put on a long skirt, or something quite different for tonight. And do your hair a bit differently if you can. We don't want to run any chance of his recognising you. If by any chance I have to introduce you I shall call you Anne—and it mustn't be Anne Danvers. What about Anne Cameron?"

"All right. It doesn't sound a bit like me, but I'll try to remember my name. Is there any reason why I shouldn't call you David?"

"None at all—I don't come into the picture at that point. Mr Platt may have done some homework about your father and you before his visit, but he'll have kept well away from Combe Dean afterwards. We'd better give ourselves a bit of background for this evening, though. If we meet any of the people I met before, they know I have a boat. I didn't say I was a fisherman, and I'd rather they didn't know that. Relations between Finmouth fishermen and the divers are not good, and they'll think I'm just out to spy. They've seen *Lily* because they

97

saw me anchoring in the cove. But although *Lily* is a fishing-boat she's the sort of boat that any cruising yachtsman might have. I didn't say I was a yachtsman, but I didn't say I wasn't. If they like to think I am, so much the better. I came by boat the day before yesterday, now I'm come back by land.... What have I done? I put in at Finmouth to see my friend, Anne Cameron. You live—no, better, you're *staying* with some people there. I think you live in London. You're a fashion designer . . ."

"But I don't know anything about fashion."

"All right, you're not a fashion designer. What would you like to be? A schoolmistress? No, that wouldn't do, it's term-time now. A shorthand-typist in a City office, taking a late holiday."

"I *do* know shorthand—I do nearly all Daddy's letters for him. Do we have to say what office?"

"No. You said you could swim—skin-diving could be one of your hobbies."

"It could be, but it isn't. And these people are experts—they belong to clubs, and know all about it. I'd make some awful mistake."

"Just be decorative, then. You can do that very well."

"Thank you!" They both laughed. Elizabeth was shocked to find that she was actually enjoying herself. It seemed all wrong that the misery of the chalice should produce anything nice.

But it did. She was not used to being taken out to pubs, and the prospect was exciting. She was again bothered about her wardrobe. She possessed only one long skirt, a nondescript affair which she had bought at a sale to go with her father to the annual guest-dinner of the Combe Dean Women's Institute. She wondered if a real London typist would be seen dead in it. However, she did have a rather pretty Turkish blouse which her father had brought back some years before when he had been invited to Turkey to lecture on the Hittites, and this, she felt, might make up to some extent for the rather dowdy skirt. She brushed her hair back, holding it in place with a band, and put on a pair of ornate Victorian ear-rings that had belonged to her grandmother. Studying herself in a mirror, she concluded that the total effect was really rather dashing. At least it was quite unlike her normal appearance.

David had met the divers early in the evening. That was little to go on, but it suggested that they went to the pub before rather than after their evening meal. He thought, therefore, that they had better get there soon after opening time, but to be prepared, if necessary, for a longish stay there. He remembered seeing some sandwiches behind the bar: they would help to fill in time.

They were both so keyed up that they started earlier than they needed to, and got to the pub a few minutes before it opened. So they drove along the coast road to the cove where David had anchored *Lily*. The cruiser was still there. David would have liked to explore a little, but Elizabeth's long skirt inhibited scrambling down the steep cliff path. He studied the anchorage from the cliff-top. On the cruiser he could see the crane that the girl had talked about—a squat thing rather like the hoists on the back of break-down lorries. The dinghies were drawn up on the beach, as before. Whatever the divers were doing, they were still there.

The car-park by the pub was deserted when they got there, and they were the first customers in the bar. The barman remembered David. "Brought your boat back?" he asked.

"No," David said. "I put in at Finmouth to see Miss Cameron—she's staying with some people there. She came down from London by car, so she has her car with her. We just came out to have a look at your pub. I rather hoped to meet some of those divers again."

"They'll be in—a bunch of them usually come along. It's a bit early yet."

David ordered whisky for himself and sherry for Elizabeth. When the man brought the drinks David asked if he would join them. He accepted a half-pint of bitter, pulled it, and said "Cheers".

"Does the boss of the outfit come in at all?" David asked. "I read about him in the paper—name of Layton, isn't it?"

"Aye, he's often in with the others. Not the last couple of nights, though—I heard he's been away. But his boat was out this morning, and it doesn't generally go out unless he's with it. So it looks like he's back."

99

They chatted for about twenty minutes, and the bar remained empty. David was wondering how to spin out the evening without drinking too much, when there was the noise of a car outside and a few minutes later three people came in. One was the girl called Sheila whom he had met before. With her were two men, both strangers.

"Evening, Miss, evening Mr Layton," the barman said.

The girl noticed David. "Hullo," she said. "Back again? Your friend sail with you?"

"No, landsman tonight," David said. "Anne's staying at Finmouth, and we drove over. Can I get you a drink? What will your friends have?"

The girl said she'd like a gin and orange. One of the men asked for beer, the other, who it turned out was Mr Layton, said he'd join Sheila in the gin, but not with the orange juice. Could he have a pink gin? David ordered the round, and the girl introduced him. "We met on the night you were in Plymouth dealing with the treasure," she said. "David, isn't it?"

"Yes, David Grendon. This is Anne Cameron."

"Phil Layton, and Robert Ogilvy," the girl said.

"I read about you in the paper," David said. "It must have been a great occasion. But I bet it took months of work."

"You a diver?" the man called Layton asked.

"No, I try to stay on top of the water." They all laughed.

"Well, I wish they wouldn't put these things in the papers. I had to go to London yesterday, and I came back to find twenty-three begging letters waiting for me. It's all very well, but people don't understand. Yes, we've had a bit of luck, but diving is a damnably expensive business. It can take two or three years' work to find a wreck, and what you recover when you've found one is anybody's guess. Then you have to wait while the officials go through all their rigmarole. If you break even over the years, you're lucky."

"But it's frightfully exciting," Sheila said.

"All right for you, poppet—you're having a holiday." He put his arm round her shoulders. "Don't get me wrong—I couldn't do without you. And yes, it's better than working in an office. But it's also a job with plenty of headaches—like any other."

David was trying hard to assess what Elizabeth was thinking. She sat on her high stool at the bar, looking into her glass of

100

sherry. She had taken no part in the conversation. Mr Layton began to order another round of drinks and asked her what she would like. She replied in a queer voice, not much more than a whisper. "I'm awfully sorry, but really we ought to be on our way. We've got a date. David, don't you think we should be getting on?"

David glanced at his watch. "Lord, we certainly should," he said. Then to the others, "Will you excuse us?"

"Of course," they muttered politely.

"Going back to Finmouth?" Layton asked.

"No—we've got a dinner date in Plymouth," David said. "We can just about make it, if we hurry."

"Nice to have met you again," Sheila said. "Give yourself more time when you drop in next."

"I will. Good night."

Elizabeth looked white and worried as they went out to the car. David offered to drive, but Elizabeth said she had to drive because—to keep down the premium—the Mini was insured only for her own driving. On the way out of the car-park she trod hard on the brake—"Look!" she said. Then, "But it isn't. You see, it can't be!"

She was about to turn to go back towards Combe when David said, "We told them we were going to Plymouth. We'd better go in the Plymouth direction for a bit, anyway."

They took the cliff road which at least led towards Plymouth, though if they decided to go right into Plymouth they would have to turn inland after a few miles to cross the Yealm at Yealmpton. It was dark, and although the Mini's headlamps were quite good Elizabeth drove slowly. David said nothing, waiting for her to talk. In daylight, the stretch of road they were now on would have been breathtakingly beautiful—it ran close to the cliff-edge, the cliffs falling steeply, in places almost sheer, to the rocks and the sea below. They had gone perhaps two miles when they saw the lights of a car coming out of a side turning on their right, about a quarter of a mile ahead. It turned towards them, and Elizabeth dipped her headlamps. The other car did not dip: it gathered speed and raced towards them, hugging the crown of the road. As it came up it moved over towards their side of the road.

David began to gasp "He must be mad" but there wasn't time to get all the words out. Elizabeth could do nothing but swerve to the nearside—towards the cliff-edge. The other car roared past them and the Mini left the road. The other driver made no attempt to stop.

A few yards farther on they would have gone over a sheer cliff and crashed into the sea. Where they did leave the road there was a narrow, boulder-strewn ledge between the verge and the actual cliff-top. The nearside front wheel of the Mini hit a big boulder, mercifully deeply embedded, on the very rim of the cliff. This stopped the car, and also slewed it round and toppled it over on David's side.

In her eagerness to get away from the pub Elizabeth had forgotten about her seat-belt. The first shock of impact with the boulder had flung her forward, but as the car had also slewed she was hurled not directly on to the steering-wheel but between the wheel and the door. Perhaps the door was not quite properly shut, anyway, the crash burst it open, and she was flung out of it and over the edge of the cliff. The door, torn off its hinges, went with her over the edge.

David had clipped on his seat-belt automatically as they drove away from the pub. The belt saved him from being flung into the windscreen, and as the car toppled over he was left huddled on his side. He was cut and bruised, but nothing was broken, and his first thought was to call out to Elizabeth. She did not answer, because she was no longer in the car. The crash had put out the lights, and David, tangled in the wreckage, was in total darkness.

He knew that there was a torch on the shelf under the dashboard: could he possibly find it? Even in the chaos of the crash his mind worked in its accustomed habit of logical analysis. Everything in the car must have been thrown forward in the sudden deceleration of the crash; therefore the torch must be somewhere at the fore end of the shelf. It might, of course, be smashed, but it was rubber-covered, and should stand a reasonable chance of survival. The immediate need was to free himself to get at it. The safety belt which tied him to the car unclipped without difficulty, but he could not get it off his shoulders because one of the straps seemed caught in some twisted bit of metal. His hands were free, however, and he had his pocket knife. This was in a trousers' pocket and it required some contortion to get at it, but he managed it. The strap was tough and hard to cut, but David was a practical seaman and kept his knife sharp. As soon as he could cut himself free he began feeling for the torch, working gingerly, because there were many sharp edges of torn metal.

He found the torch, jammed against an AA book that had also been on the shelf. The book had also helped to protect it, and the torch worked. He saw a gaping hole where the door on Elizabeth's side had been, called out to her again, and again got no answer. Desperately worried, he scrambled over the wreckage of the seats and climbed out through the door-hole, stopping himself just in time from going over the cliff-top by grabbing at the rock which held the wreckage of the car. The torch showed a horrible situation. The boulder which had stopped the car was on a small promontory extending only a few yards from the edge of the cliff. Between the wreckage of the car and the sheer face of the cliff was a ledge of no more than a few inches. Below was blackness, which he could investigate only a little way in the thin beam of the torch.

It was the long skirt that saved her. Elizabeth had been flung clear over the cliff-top, but at the point where she had gone over it was not quite sheer. About fifteen feet from the top a gnarled and wizened tree had managed to root itself and, somehow, to survive. In order to survive it had to be tough, and its thin, twisted branches were in fact exceedingly strong. One of them had pierced and caught a fold of Elizabeth's long skirt and, whatever its inadequacies of fashion, its fabric had a good Women's Institute quality of strength. David's torch found her apparently hanging upside down from the tree, although she was actually lying along the branch, her head and shoulders pressed against the cliff-face. She had been dazed into semi-consciousness and had not heard him call, but the beam of the torch revived her, and when he called again she was able to call back, "I'm all right—at least I think I am."

"Whatever you do don't move," David said. "Do you have a tow-rope in the car?"

"Yes. In the boot."

"I'm going to get it. I shall have to use the torch, so you'll be in the dark again. Get your arms round the tree and just hang on. I'll be as quick as I can."

Most of the damage was to the front of the car, and the boot was still openable. David was terrified that it might be locked, but whatever the sins of the countryside there is seldom any need to lock the boot of the rectory car in a remote moorland parish. David found the tow-rope and went back to the cliff-top.

The rope was not as long as he would have liked, but it would have to do. Near the big boulder that had stopped the car was a smaller rock that seemed firm, and which would not take up too much rope for a coil to be passed round it. He anchored the tow-rope to this, tested it as far as he could by leaning back against the rope, and then let himself over the edge. He needed all his skill as a rock climber to get down to Elizabeth: in daylight it would have been easy enough, but in darkness it was a terrifying climb. He tied his handkerchief round the torch so that he could hold it in his teeth: it was hard to keep the thing steady, but at least it left his hands free. He made for the tree on the far side of the branch that held Elizabeth. When he got level with the tree things became slightly easier, for it had spreading roots, and he was able to find a firm foothold against a root. He worked his way round the tree until he was a little above Elizabeth and could get his left arm round her shoulders.

"Anything hurt?" he asked.

Elizabeth managed a small laugh. "Lots of things," she said. "But I think it's mostly scratches."

"I can hold you quite safely like this. Do you think you could hold the torch?"

"Yes, I think so."

He gave her the torch, and said, "Don't try to move round. Shine it on the cliff-face and we'll get just about enough reflected light to see where we are."

He rested for a few moments while Elizabeth manoeuvred the torch. Then he got his knee into the crook of a branch and put both arms round Elizabeth. "I'm going to put the rope under your armpits," he said, "and then I'll lift you off the branch. Don't try to do anything for yourself yet—just be as limp and relaxed as you can manage, and go on holding the torch."

There was just enough rope to go round her. He made it secure, and said, "You're held by the rope now, and you can't fall any farther. The next thing is to free your dress from the tree. When I've done that I'm going back upstairs, and I can pull you up from the top. If you can manage to hold yourself out a bit from the cliff-face as you go up, it will be a help. If anything hurts badly, give a shout and I'll come down again. I'll take the torch now—I shall need it at the top, and you'll want your hands free for coming up. I shan't need it to climb back, because I've got the rope, so I'll put it in my pocket."

Elizabeth felt a sudden, desperate loneliness when David left her to begin his climb, but the rope round her shoulders was a comfort. She moved into a sitting—or rather, squatting—position, holding the branch with her legs and the tree-trunk with her hands. She wriggled her feet and bent her knees—no, nothing was broken.

David found going up easier than coming down. With the rope to guide him he had no need to worry about where he was going, and the rough cliff-face offered some reasonably good toeholds. He was back at the top in a few minutes, and shone down the torch at Elizabeth.

"All right?" he asked.

"Fine, thanks."

"Ready to come up?"

"Yes."

"Well, don't move until I tell you. I must check the rope before we start."

With the torch he examined the coil of rope round the boulder. It did not seem to have frayed materially, and when he pulled up Elizabeth the strain would be taken by him. He had to find a secure hauling position for himself, but that was not too difficult, for the cliff-edge was hard and firm. He balanced himself and called down to Elizabeth. "Ready now?"

"Okay."

"Right. Starting to haul. I'll go very gently."

Elizabeth felt the rope tug at her shoulders. She grasped it with her hands as well, and as she was pulled clear from the tree she found the cliff-face with her feet. David pulled her up very slowly, and from time to time she took some of her own weight on her toes. She had lost her shoes, which helped her to find toeholds: in the irrational way in which the trivial suddenly intrudes on the important she said to herself, "That's the end of these tights. And they really were my best pair."

When she was about three feet from the top David rested for a bit. Then, "Last lap," he said. "As soon as you can get a grip on the edge with your arms, tell me, and I'll lift you over."

One more heave with the rope did it. Elizabeth reached over the cliff-edge, digging her fingers into the coarse, strong grass. Putting a turn of the rope round his left wrist, David knelt down, got his arms round her, and pulled her over the top. As soon as she was safe, he was swept by utter exhaustion. For several minutes they lay on the cliff-top, clinging to each other.

# VII

## *The Cliff Road*

E LIZABETH RECOVERED FIRST. She sat up, and said, "Thank you for saving my life. What do we do now?"

David had slipped into near-unconsciousness, compounded of shock, relief, and sheer physical exhaustion from his climb and the effort of hauling Elizabeth to safety. He dragged himself back to wakefulness by an effort almost as great as that of pulling Elizabeth up the cliff.

"Well, I suppose the first thing is to try to work out what happened."

"Oh, David! And I've always thought of you as such a practical person. Yes, there's a frightful lot to talk about, but we can't stay here all night. I'm sure you've got hurts that ought to be looked at, and I'm scratched and torn all over. And my clothes are in a fearful state—I must look a dreadful sight."

"You couldn't look a dreadful sight, and anyway, it's quite dark. And what we do must depend to some extent on what we think happened." David went on pulling himself together. "But I see what you mean. I think we'd better find a telephone and ring somewhere for a taxi. And we ought to do something about the car."

"Have you any idea of the time? My watch has gone—the strap wasn't very good. I'm sad about it, because it belonged to my mother."

David's watch was still on his wrist, and still going, although the glass was cracked. It was just after ten o'clock.

"It feels like hours after midnight, but it isn't really very late. Do you know what I think would be the best thing to do? Let's telephone Sergeant Blundell at the home number he gave us. I've got the bit of paper with the number on it in my bag— if we can find the bag. It was in the car, between the front seats."

"Then it's probably still somewhere in the car. I don't

remember coming across it when I was hunting for the torch, but I wasn't thinking about it, so that doesn't mean much. I'll go and have a look."

"No, David. You've had a worse time than I had. You stay here, and I'll go. Can you lay hands on the torch?"

"Yes, it's still in my pocket."

He gave her the torch, and Elizabeth got up. "Ouch!" she said. "No—I'm all right. Only I haven't any shoes, and my tights don't seem to have any feet left. I just stood on a sharp stone."

"Be very careful. We're horribly near the cliff-edge. You'd better let me go."

"No, you've done more than your share already. I'll be all right when I can see where I'm going."

A few minutes later she called back, "I've got it, David! And I've got the car-keys, too. We passed an AA phone box not so very far back. Now I've got the key, we can use that."

She returned to where David was still sitting on the ground, and sat down beside him. Hunting in her bag with the torch she found the bit of paper with Sergeant Blundell's telephone number. "All we've got to do now is to get to the phone box," she said.

David got up. "You can't walk there without any shoes," he said. "I'm better now, and I can get there all right. I think I remember seeing the box—I don't think it can be more than a mile back, perhaps not quite as much."

Elizabeth hated his going off, but she had to accept that he would get to the telephone far more quickly than she could without shoes. She gave him the piece of paper, and as she shone the torch for him to take it was horrified to see that his sleeve was badly torn, and covered with blood. "Oh, David, you must be badly hurt," she said. "Take off your coat and let me see if I can do anything."

"I don't think it's much," he said. "I remember cutting my arm on something as I climbed out of the car." He took off his jacket, and Elizabeth gently rolled back his shirt sleeve. There was a nasty gash on his forearm, but it didn't seem particularly deep. His handkerchief was still tied round the torch. Elizabeth untied it and bound up the cut as well as she could. "Feels better already," David said. "It can't be all that serious, or it would have bled much worse."

"It's bled quite enough," she said. "I hope the bandage will help to stop it, but we must get it treated properly as soon as we can. Try not to move the arm too much when you walk. I know—I'll tear off a strip from my skirt, and make a sling."

"Please don't! What about your skirt?"

"It's torn to ribbons already—one more tear doesn't matter. And I'm in charge of you for the moment, so you'll have to do what I say."

David took this meekly: he was too tired to argue with her, and it was rather comforting to be taken care of. Elizabeth got a good piece of material from her skirt, and improvised an effective sling. She tucked his arm in it, and said, "That should help a bit. And if you can try to keep the forearm raised a little it will control the bleeding. You must take the torch."

"I don't need a torch for walking along the road. You keep it, you might want it for something. I'll start off now. Promise me you'll keep away from the edge."

Elizabeth laughed. "You're the one who needs looking after —I'm supposed to be the nurse. But all right, I promise."

Detective Sergeant Blundell was getting ready to go to bed when the phone rang. He half-expected the call—a man he suspected of setting fire to hayricks had been arrested that afternoon for another offence at Totnes, and Blundell thought it likely that he would be charged with the rick-fires as well. But the call was not from Totnes police station. A voice he did not at once recognise asked, "May I speak to Detective Sergeant Blundell?"

"Who is it?" Blundell asked a little guardedly.

"David Grendon. I want to speak to Detective Sergeant Blundell, please. We need some help."

"Blundell speaking. What's the trouble?"

"It's too long to go into over the telephone. We went to that pub we talked about, and there's been an accident. At least, I don't think it was an accident. We were pushed over a cliff."

Blundell was now keenly interested. "Where are you speaking from?"

"A phone box on the cliff road, about two miles on from the pub."

"Are you hurt?"

"A bit. Miss Danvers is, too. But chiefly we want to talk to you. Only we haven't got a car any longer because ours is smashed up, so we can't come in to see you."

"Do you mean you're stranded on the cliff road?"

"Yes—well, we are for the moment. I could telephone for a taxi, of course, only Elizabeth—that's Miss Danvers—said we ought to tell you about it first."

"I'll come out at once. Do you need an ambulance?"

"No, I don't think so. We'll need a breakdown lorry for the car, I suppose, but that can wait. It's off the road, and not a danger to anybody else."

"We can see about that when I get there. Where, exactly, are you?"

"Keep to the cliff road, and drive on past the pub. About two miles on you'll see an AA box on the right-hand side of the road. We're about a mile on from the box, on the cliff side. We've got a torch, but you'll probably see us in your headlights."

"Right. I'll be with you just as soon as I can."

Mrs Blundell was in the kitchen, making the cocoa that they usually had as a nightcap. She had heard the phone ring, and was already putting her husband's cocoa in a vacuum flask. Blundell explained what was happening, and she kissed him. "I just hate it when policemen are called 'pigs'," she said.

David had driven himself half-running to get to the telephone, but anxious as he was to get back to Elizabeth he could not make the same speed going back. He was near exhaustion, and his legs kept flagging. He had the best part of a mile to go, and he had barely time to tell Elizabeth that the sergeant had undertaken to come to their rescue before the lights of Blundell's car appeared. He took one look at them in the illumination of his headlamps, and said "I'm going to take the pair of you straight to hospital. Get in the car, and you can tell me all about it later."

"No, no," Elizabeth pleaded. "I can't possibly go to hospital. There's no one at home to look after Daddy. Besides, it could be terribly bad for him. Mummy was killed in a car accident, and if he's told that I'm in hospital after an accident I really think it might kill him. He's desperately worried and unhappy

110

as it is. I'm sure that David ought to go to hospital, but please take me home. I'll be perfectly all right."

"I'm not going to hospital either," David said slowly. "I've been thinking all the way back from the telephone. And if I'm anything like right, Miss Danvers may be in considerable danger. She's not going back to the rectory alone."

Blundell was uncertain what to do. His instinct was that both the girl and the young man needed hospital treatment, and after any other road accident he would have called an ambulance as a matter of course. But perhaps this wasn't quite an ordinary road accident; perhaps there was something in what this strange young man had said. He gave in to the extent of saying, "Well, you'd better try to tell me just what happened. Did you manage to see Mr Layton in the pub?"

"Yes, and it was a very queer experience," Elizabeth said. "He looked quite different, and he talked quite differently, from the man I met as Mr Platt, but I'm almost sure it was the same man. What is much more important is that I'm *quite* sure he recognised me."

"But Mr Platt—if this man is Platt—only saw you for a moment at the rectory. You had on different clothes and you'd done your hair another way tonight," David said. "I don't see how he could have recognised you."

"I don't know how he did either, but I know that he did. That's why I tried not to say anything and when I had to spoke in that sort of whisper. That's why I wanted to get away. He recognised me more than I could recognise him. The man I saw as Mr Platt had glasses, and talked with a slight American accent. Mr Layton didn't have glasses, or any particular accent. Mr Platt was wearing a sort of business suit; Mr Layton was in sailing clothes. Mr Platt took off his hat politely when he met me, and his hair was brushed back. Mr Layton had rather untidy hair falling over his forehead. In most ways I *didn't* recognise him. But he *did* recognise me."

"I suppose he could have recognised your car—you drove up in your car when he was saying goodbye to your father. We got there first tonight, and your car was in the park when he came," David said.

"I hadn't thought of that—yes, that may be it. I only know that he recognised me, and all the time he was talking to you he kept having little side-looks at me."

111

"I didn't know what you've just told Sergeant Blundell," David said, "because we haven't had a chance to talk. I did know something had upset you, of course. What you say fits in with my own thinking. I'm certain that car deliberately tried to push us over the cliff. I can't think of anyone who might want to kill me. So whoever it is must want to get at you. That's why I said that I thought you might be in danger—having failed once, he may have another go. If Mr Layton is really Mr Platt, you are very dangerous to him. It makes sense."

"There's another thing," Elizabeth said, "but it doesn't make sense. Do you remember how startled I was when we were driving away from the car-park? That was because I saw an estate car that looked exactly like the one Mr Platt had when he came to the rectory. But it couldn't have been his car, because it had a quite different number. I'm certain the letters on Mr Platt's car were MEW. Tonight's car was JLP, so it couldn't have been the same. But it was a queer coincidence."

"You haven't told me about the accident yet," Blundell said patiently.

David explained how they'd said they had a date in Plymouth and started off, how the other car had come out of a side road in front of them, come at them very fast, and driven on without stopping, although the driver must have heard the crash as the Mini hit the rock. Blundell examined the wreckage of the Mini with his torch, and shone it over the edge of the cliff to the tree that had caught Elizabeth. There were streamers of torn fabric from her skirt clearly visible among the branches.

"Do you mean to say you got up from there in the dark without help?" he asked.

"David got me up," Elizabeth said.

"We had the tow-rope," David added.

"You did miraculously," Blundell said. "I should scarcely have believed it possible. You had a very, very narrow escape. Did any other car pass while you were here?"

"I don't remember one. There doesn't seem to be much traffic on this road."

"There wouldn't be at this time of year. It's really a scenic road. In summer hundreds of people come out for the view, but there's not much call to use it now unless you're going to the pub. You can get to Yealmpton and Plymouth, but it's a long way round—the best route runs inland."

"We said we were going to Plymouth, so we thought we'd better start off in that direction. That's why we were on the road."

"Yes. I understand that. Let's have a look at the road itself."

Blundell switched on the headlights of his car and studied the road surface where the Mini had gone over the edge. He knelt down and looked at the road closely, using his torch as well. "There are certainly tyre-marks here," he said, "and if they were made by the car coming towards you it was right over on your side of the road, and you had no room at all. The marks look recent, but of course we can't prove when they were made. I think it might be worth getting a photographer out to photograph the marks—they might be useful evidence if we ever find the car that fits them. There's one thing I must ask you, though. You'd both come straight from the pub—how much had you been drinking?"

"Elizabeth was driving. She had one small sherry, and she made it last—I don't think she quite finished it. We left in rather a rush. I think I had three small whiskies. I'm sure we didn't imagine anything. And there's evidence that we were sober—we couldn't have done that climb if we'd had too much to drink."

"I don't doubt you," Blundell said, "but I had to ask. I'm quite sure drink doesn't come into it."

After some further discussion Blundell decided what to do. He agreed to take them back to the rectory on condition that they saw a police doctor. He got through to headquarters on his radio and asked for a photographer with flashlight equipment to be sent at once to the cliff road—he wanted photographs of the tyre-marks before there was rain or other traffic to blur them. He would wait, he said, for the photographer before setting off for Combe Dean. Meanwhile, could the doctor be asked to stand by to go out to Combe Dean? He would call up again just before he started, so that the doctor wouldn't get there first.

He was worried about David and Elizabeth, who were both beginning to shiver—with shock, or reaction, or cold, or a combination of all three. He wanted to get them back home, but he didn't want to leave the place until the photographer arrived. If there was anything in this extraordinary story it was an ugly business—for all he knew someone else might have

113

thought of tyre-marks, and come back to disfigure them. The best he could do for the moment was to put David and Elizabeth in the back of his car and give them a rug.

Having settled them as well as he could he studied the map with his torch. Yes, it was quite possible: a car leaving the pub after the Mini could have cut inland at the crossroads and taken a lane to meet the cliff road at the point where they had seen the other car come out. If it were driven fast, it could easily have got there ahead of the Mini—the inland distance was in fact considerably shorter, because the cliff road wound along the coast. But how on earth could any of this be proved? And what would it prove, anyway? That some drunk had driven dangerously? There was nothing but the purest speculation to link the curious accident on the cliff road with events earlier in the evening.

Nothing? Well, there was Elizabeth Danvers's strange story. But what did that amount to? She couldn't swear that the man she met as Mr Layton was the man she had met before as Mr Platt—indeed, she had thought he looked quite different. Under cross-examination any hope of her evidence establishing identity would fall to pieces. Yet she felt that *he* had recognised *her*. She could easily be wrong, of course, but her evidence could not be discounted altogether. It is quite possible to have a feeling that somebody recognises you—it is a common human feeling, and it is often right. *If* the man Layton were really the man Platt, and *if* he was engaged in camouflaging stolen jewels as finds from old wrecks, he had a lot to protect. The rector and his daughter were the only people who had even seen Mr Platt—the emergence of the daughter on Mr Layton's doorstep could be regarded as very dangerous indeed. From then on the story of the queer accident on the cliff road held together. But it was all *if—if—if* . . . "Are we ever going to get a grain of fact in this blasted case?" Blundell sighed to himself.

His speculations at least filled in the time while waiting for the photographer. David and Elizabeth were quiet in the back of the car. David had more or less passed out, and Elizabeth was so worried about him, and about whether she was doing right by insisting on going home instead of to hospital, that she didn't want to talk. The arrival of the police photographer roused them, but Blundell told them to stay in the car—there was no point in their getting out. Instructions to the photo-

114

grapher were soon given, Blundell radioed headquarters that he was about to leave for Combe Dean, and set off thankfully.

Elizabeth was even more thankful to get home. Her father had long since gone to bed, but he slept badly nowadays and she thought that she had better give him some explanation of what had happened. Fortunately she looked at herself in a mirror before going into his room—she was dressed in rags, covered in dust and had a long scratch down one cheek. She washed and changed hurriedly and went to comfort her father.

The doctor arrived while she was with him. He helped David to undress and examined him thoroughly. The cut on his forearm was not particularly serious, but he had a much deeper cut in his left thigh from which he had lost a good deal of blood. His other injuries were bruises, painful, but not serious.

Elizabeth reappeared while the doctor was examining David, got water for his wounds to be cleaned up, and helped the doctor to get him to bed. Then it was her turn to be examined. She was much bruised and scratched, but had got off considerably more lightly than David. The doctor made her go to bed, and then returned downstairs for a word with Blundell.

"The man has been severely shocked and has a nasty wound in his thigh, as well as a badly cut arm. Normally, I'd send him into hospital for a day or two, but he's young and seems fit and he'll probably be all right. The girl is less badly hurt, though she, too, has been severely shocked. Her main need is simply rest, but she ought to get her own doctor to come round in the morning."

"If you don't mind," Blundell said, "I'd much rather not involve her own doctor at the moment. There's something very odd about that accident, and it may be connected with another case we're investigating. No, there's nothing suspicious about the couple themselves, but the girl could be an important witness in this other case, and it's just possible that the accident was engineered to get rid of her. The less known about it beyond ourselves, the better. They'll have to have been in an accident, of course—you can't keep anything that happens to the rector's daughter secret in a small village. But I want it to be as vague as possible, and particularly I don't want it to be related to the cliff road. I shall have the wreckage of the car moved before daylight—it's a lonely spot at this time of year, and with luck there'll be nobody around to ask awkward questions. Could you look after them if they need any more doctoring?"

"Yes, certainly," the doctor said. "I think I won't come unless they ask for me—if you want to keep the whole thing quiet it would be better that way. But I'll come at once if they telephone. Will you be seeing them again in the morning?"

"Yes, I shall have to."

"Well, give them my telephone number, and I'll look after them as well as I can."

"Thanks a lot, doctor. And I really am grateful to you for everything."

After the doctor had gone Blundell telephoned for a police breakdown lorry to go at once to the cliff road to remove all obvious traces of the wrecked Mini before daylight. There seemed nothing more he could do at the rectory, but he was reluctant to leave. In the end he decided to spend the night on the couch in the rector's study. He hated waking up his wife in the middle of the night, but he knew that she would rather be telephoned than left to worry if he did not come home. That had been a nice remark of hers when he'd been called out— "I hate it when policemen are called pigs." Ought he to leave the Force to try to give her a better life? But she wouldn't want that—she was a marvellous woman to be married to, and he was just damned lucky.

# VIII

## Fisherman's Bait

THE COUCH WAS old, big and comfortable, and Blundell, who was tired, got about four hours sleep. He woke suddenly to a little pattering noise, jumped up, and startled Elizabeth, who had come downstairs to cook breakfast.

"What on earth are you doing here?" she asked.

"And why aren't you in bed?"

"Well, Daddy usually has breakfast quite early. And so do I. I don't think I'll disturb David."

But David, in pyjamas, was at the top of the stairs. "What's going on?" he said. "I heard someone moving about."

Blundell laughed. "You two are incorrigible. You're both supposed to be under doctor's orders and I find you wandering about the house."

"But you haven't explained what you're doing here," David said.

"You thought there might be some further danger to Miss Danvers, so I decided to stay around."

"So you take us seriously! But what happens next?"

"I think we'd all better have some breakfast," Elizabeth said practically. "David, if you're going to be up, you'd better get some clothes on. Sergeant Blundell, if you'll come into the kitchen it will be warmer than it is here, and there'll be some coffee in a minute."

Both men obeyed her. Blundell, who had taken off his shoes when he lay down, put them on again and followed her into the kitchen. David went back to get dressed.

Elizabeth was putting things on a tray. "Daddy only has coffee and some toast, and usually I take it up to him," she said. "David and I have breakfast down here. I'll get Daddy's tray out of the way, and then I'll cook some bacon and eggs for us. It was very good of you to stay here last night, Sergeant Blundell."

117

The coffee was soon made, and Elizabeth poured out a cup for Blundell, then she took the tray up to her father. David came down while she was upstairs. "How are you feeling?" Blundell asked him.

"Not so bad, considering. But I'm worried about Elizabeth. I've been thinking about things."

"And what have you thought?"

"That Elizabeth ought to go away. But I've got a sort of plan. I don't suppose you'd like it, though."

He didn't explain further because Elizabeth came back. Blundell, who wanted a shave and who had thought earlier that he wouldn't stay at the rectory for breakfast, changed his mind and decided to wait to hear what David had to say.

They were all hungry, and Blundell asked no questions while they ate. Then he said, "That was a wonderful breakfast, Miss Danvers. Thank you very much. Can we talk briefly about your plans?"

"I suppose the first thing is to get something done about the car," Elizabeth said. "I'm afraid it's beyond mending, but I can't just leave it lying there. And I'll have to tell the insurance company. I don't know what I'm going to do without a car."

"As far as the wreckage is concerned you needn't do anything. I had it moved during the night."

David looked at him sharply. "That was a very good idea," he said. "So as far as anyone knows this morning, we disappeared over the cliff?"

"I think so, yes."

"They'll find out later, of course. If I'd engineered that accident, I'd want to know what happened—I'd have a look at the rocks below the cliff. They cover at high tide, and the tide will be making now, so there won't be anything to see for a bit. That gives us a little time in hand—I mean, before he knows for certain that we're not dead."

"You think it quite certain that somebody did try to kill you?"

"Yes. And so do you, or you wouldn't have stayed on guard here all night."

Blundell ran his fingers through his hair in a little, worried gesture. "Mr Grendon," he said, "I don't know what to think. I'm a policeman, and I have to act on evidence. There is no

118

*evidence* to relate your Mr Layton to the Mr Platt whom we believe to have been concerned in the theft of the chalice."

"The attempt to push us over the cliff is evidence of something."

"Yes, if it happened. Please—don't misunderstand me! I have to look at things as a lawyer would look at them. There is your statement, confirmed by Miss Danvers, that a car appeared to drive at you last night and forced you off the road. I fully accept that you both believe this happened, and the tyre marks on the road to some extent support you, although we cannot say just when those marks were made. But there is nothing to indicate who the other driver was, and neither of you can give a description of the car."

"It was dark, and we were dazzled by the headlights. I was just conscious that it was a biggish car—all I could think about was getting out of the way," Elizabeth said.

"That's completely understandable, but it means that there is awfully little to go on. I agree that it would have been possible for Mr Layton to leave the pub after you, cut inland, and meet you on the cliff road. But there's nothing to suggest that he did do any of this."

"You could find out if he left immediately after us by asking at the pub," David said.

"Yes. But it wouldn't prove where he went. And once the police start asking that sort of question it alerts everyone. All it would do at the moment is to give a guilty individual—if there *is* a guilty individual—time and opportunity to cover up. I'm in no position even to contemplate making an arrest."

"You arrested me," David said.

"I *didn't* arrest you. I invited you to come to the police station to help with my inquiries. Once you'd given an account of yourself I couldn't have held you. I could do the same to Mr Layton, but on what we know at present I couldn't hold him. I'm taking you sufficiently seriously not to want to start questioning him unless there is some evidence on which I could hold him."

"There is one bit of evidence you could get without his knowing anything about it," David said slowly.

"What is that?"

"Well, I *know* that someone did try to push us over the cliff —maybe I can't prove it, but I still know it. If I were in his

119

position I'd have to find out what happened. If our car went over the cliff—and since you've taken away the wreckage he can assume that it did—there'll be traces of it, and presumably of us, on the rocks at low tide. There's no beach there, there's no easy way of climbing down at that point—the best way would be to go by sea. If you could have someone watching the place he could see if anyone came to search the rocks. If Layton's cruiser came, it would be pretty good evidence that he knows something about it. If he didn't show any interest in the place, it would tend to rule him out. It will be low water around mid-day. If you can't send anyone, I'll go myself—I can easily find somewhere to watch where I can't be seen."

"There's no need for you to go—it would be much better not. I don't want to claim credit for your ideas, but that was one of the things I had in mind when I decided to get the wreckage moved before daylight. If Mr Layton—or anyone else—turns up to search the rocks it will be interesting, but it won't really prove anything in itself. He could say he was looking for oysters."

"He could say so, but it wouldn't be true, because there aren't any oysters on those particular rocks. I'm a fisherman, and I know."

"Well, mussels, then." Blundell laughed. "It doesn't matter, anyway, because what we really want to know is simply whether anyone turns up." He looked at his watch. "If I can use your telephone, I'll get that laid on straightaway."

He went off to telephone. "What have you told your father?" David asked Elizabeth.

"Not very much. I told him that the car had skidded and gone off the road, and that it had taken us hours to get home. I also said that nobody else was involved, that we were a bit shaken but not hurt, and that he was to try not to worry."

"I'm not sure that you're right. I'd like to ask Sergeant Blundell about it when he comes back."

When Blundell returned from his telephoning, David said, "There's one very important thing we haven't mentioned. You see, I really do think that Elizabeth is in danger."

Blundell didn't reply for a moment. Then he said, "So far we've been talking about *evidence*. I told you that a policeman has to act on evidence, and that's true. But it's not the whole truth. A policeman has thoughts and feelings like anybody else, and sometimes he's got to use imagination. I can't say whether you are right or wrong about Mr Layton, but you have made me feel that there's a lot to be explained. If you're right, then Miss Danvers is a vital witness, and it would obviously be in somebody's interest to get her out of the way. Your feeling about this certainly influenced me last night—that's why I stayed around. In the cold light of day—God knows. I'm not happy about Miss Danvers, but on the evidence available I don't know what I can do. I can scarcely put her under police guard all the time. If I can talk as a human being and not as a policeman, I just don't know what to do."

"I can only carry on with my own theory until we get some new fact that proves it wrong," David said. "If I'm right, then Miss Danvers's father is also in some danger, and more, perhaps, than she is, for he was with Mr Platt far longer than she was, and would be a better witness for identification. I don't think they were in any particular danger until last night. I don't know what we did wrong last night, but something happened to warn Mr Layton that we were interested in him not as Mr Layton but as a candidate for being Mr Platt. Until last night he reckoned that he was safe enough. Now he's very much worried. He thought of a way to get rid of Elizabeth— and me, though he can't know how I came into it—on the spur of the moment. He doesn't know yet that he didn't get rid of us. He'll want to make sure, and that's why I expect he'll want to have a look at things at low tide. As soon as he's satisfied that he's dealt with us, I should expect him to have a go at Canon Danvers. He's horribly unprotected. I think both he and Elizabeth ought to go away at once."

"I'm not saying you're wrong. And I'd be a good deal happier if they could go away for a bit," Blundell said. "Is there anywhere you could go at short notice, Miss Danvers?"

"Offhand, I can't think of anywhere particular for me, but Daddy could go to Oxford. He's a Visiting Fellow of All Saints, and they're always glad to see him. It only needs a telephone call to fix it up."

"I've got a plan for Elizabeth, if she'll accept it," David said.

"What's that?"

"Well, I thought we might go off in *Lily* for a couple of days. But it's a bit like baiting a trap. After low tide this morning, he'll either think that we're dead and safely carried out to sea, or that we're not dead, but have disappeared. If we bring back *Lily* into the cove, say the day after tomorrow, and we stand about on deck so that we're sure to be seen by somebody, he'll get very agitated indeed. And if we anchor off for the night without going ashore, I'd expect something to happen. If we could have a policeman on board that night, Sergeant Blundell might get enough evidence to do something."

"I'm game," Elizabeth said excitedly. "It's a marvellous idea."

"I don't like it at all," Blundell said. "If you're anything like right you're likely to be in very considerable danger."

"But we'd have a policeman with us!"

Blundell laughed. "It's nice to have such faith in the police, but I'm thinking of a man who may be a very dangerous criminal. He may also be pretty desperate. Anything could happen."

"Look," David said, "there are two possibilities. One—I'm wrong, and in that case nothing will happen. Two—I'm right, or partly right, in which case something is almost bound to happen. And we *want* something to happen, because then the police will be able to act. We may waste a policeman's time for one night—or we may give the police at any rate some of the evidence they need. It seems to me a wholly justifiable risk. In any case, you can't stop me going out in *Lily* with Elizabeth. If it's not the sort of thing the police can help with, we'll go it alone, and report what happens."

Blundell walked up and down the kitchen without saying anything. The human being part of him agreed with Elizabeth, that David had put up a marvellous idea. The more cautious policeman couldn't approve of members of the public using themselves as bait for a trap. But why not? This was something the police *couldn't* do themselves—if it was to be done at all, it had to be the Danvers girl. Should it be done at all? Well, it offered a chance of clearing up things. If nothing happened, if they spent a peaceful night at anchor, it would be a reasonable indication that there was nothing in Grendon's wild ideas, and they could stop wasting time on them. If there were any sort of attack on the boat he could make an arrest. Unless anything very violent occurred it would only be a holding charge, but it would provide an opportunity for the detailed inquiries that he didn't see how to make at present. And if the man Layton—or one of his friends—tried to board Grendon's boat in the middle of the night it would be strong evidence that something very odd was going on.

A thought struck him—he could spend a night on *Lily* without its having anything to do with all these other matters. The Finmouth fishermen had complained about lobster-poaching and damage to their gear—what could be more reasonable than to go out with a Finmouth fisherman for an unobtrusive watch? "All right," he said, "I'll come with you. We'd better make some plans."

There was no point in Sergeant Blundell's going off with David and Elizabeth that morning. David intended to get Elizabeth away as soon as they could fix up her father's departure for Oxford, but he didn't want to lay his trap too soon. As far as Finmouth people were concerned, they were now used to his going off in *Lily* for a day or two at a time, and they'd think nothing of her absence from the port. To keep out of the way he'd go well out to sea, and stay at sea for thirty-six hours or so. Then he'd put in at Plymouth, pick up Sergeant Blundell there, and sail back to the cove from Plymouth. Today was Wednesday: he arranged to pick up Blundell from the Mayflower Steps in Sutton Harbour on Friday morning.

The rector of Combe Dean might be vague and impractical in everyday affairs, but he had a fine scholar's mind. When the events of last night were explained to him he was neither shocked nor frightened—Elizabeth was privately very proud of him, and agreed with David that she had been wrong in editing facts to try to spare him. He saw the point about his and Elizabeth's going away at once. "I can certainly go to Oxford —there are several things I want to do there," he said. "I'll telephone George Dorrance, and he will fix up a room for me at All Saints. Making arrangements here is more of a problem. I'll ring Truslove, my churchwarden, and explain that both Elizabeth and I are called away. Would it be wrong, do you think, to imply that urgent family matters require us to go to Manchester? We have, indeed, next to no family, but we do have a second cousin who is headmaster of a school in Manchester. I needn't explain that to Truslove, of course—I just feel that it might be wiser not to let it be known precisely where we are going. After all, St Paul observed that not all

123

things are expedient—an accurate statement of our movements would not, I feel, be expedient. Let me see, the old Archdeacon of Barnstaple is retired and living at Exeter. I met him at the synod the other day, and he offered to come and take a service for me—the poor old man is really rather bored, I think, and he would probably be glad to have something to do. I'll ring him before I speak to Truslove, and then there'll be no question of leaving the parish in the lurch."

Elizabeth remembered that she had no car. "It's an imposition on you," she said to Blundell, "but do you think you could run us to Finmouth? I can get a taxi from Ivybridge to take Daddy to Totnes for his train, but it might be better for nobody but you to know that David and I have gone to Finmouth."

"It would be better for nobody to know that you haven't gone with your father," Blundell said. "Of course I'll take you to Finmouth, and I'll take Canon Danvers to Totnes, or arrange for a police car to take him. I'd like to leave as soon as you can get ready, because I've an awful lot to do."

After depositing David and Elizabeth at Finmouth, Blundell took the rector to the police station at Ivybridge and asked a constable to drive him to Totnes. He didn't go himself because he decided to return to the cliff road, to see for himself whether anything occurred at low tide. They'd breakfasted so early that it was still only ten o'clock, and he reckoned that he would have time to get to the cliff road and find an observation point well before low water. So he countermanded his earlier instructions for a detective-constable to be sent to keep watch, and set off himself.

He drove about half a mile beyond the place where Elizabeth's car had gone off the road, left his own car in a lay-by where it wouldn't attract notice, and walked back. He found a large rock, screened by some bushes, where he could get a good view of the coast below without being seen either from the road or from the shoreline, and settled down to watch. The tide was already fairly well out, and the jagged rocks below the cliffs were uncovered. He shivered slightly as he studied them—no one in a car plunging on to those rocks from the cliff-top would have stood a chance of survival.

Something glittering caught his eye. He had brought field-glasses, and he focused them on the spot. Yes, there was something there—the remains of a car-door caught between two rocks. He remembered Elizabeth's telling him how she had been thrown out of the car after the door had been torn off—there had been no reason to disbelieve her, but here at least was proof of her story.

No one appeared on the shore below, and there was no boat out to sea. It was certainly low water now, and the tide would soon start to come in again. Blundell was disappointed, and felt somehow let down. Grendon's logical analysis of the situation had been so impressive that he really had hoped for something to bear it out—well, that came of letting oneself be hypnotised by theorising. Obviously there was nothing in it, and he wouldn't waste any more time.

He had been looking seaward and downward. As he turned to go he stopped himself quickly—there was somebody on the cliff-top by the road, just about where the car had crashed, also studying the shore through field-glasses. Confident that he himself could not be seen, Blundell focused his own glasses on the observer. He got a considerable surprise—it was not a man, but a woman, who on earth was she? Whoever she was, she was deeply interested in the rocks below the cliff. She was doing precisely what Blundell himself had been doing a little earlier—studying the remains of the car-door through field-glasses.

Blundell thought, If you are looking for the wreckage of a car, and you see bits of a car where you expect the wreckage to be, you may reasonably think that the rest of the car is somewhere there as well. An observer on the cliff-top could not know that only the door had actually gone over the cliff. There would be signs of the crash on the cliff-top, but the body of the car had been taken away, and there was nothing to indicate that it hadn't gone over the edge. A tide had come and gone—bodies flung out in the crash might have been carried out to sea, other bits of wreckage might have been sunk around the rocks and covered by sand. The watcher on the cliff-top couldn't know how much of the car remained to be seen—the fact that a substantial mass of metal was there among the rocks would certainly suggest that the car and its occupants had gone into the sea.

All Blundell's disappointment left him, and was replaced by that tingling in the tips of the fingers that comes to detectives—

and mathematicians—when an apparently insoluble equation suddenly shows signs of working out. Theory suggested that *if* a deliberate effort had been made last night to kill Elizabeth and David in their car, someone would turn up this morning to have a look. Someone *had* turned up—with field-glasses, too. Did that prove that there really had been an attempt to wreck the Mini last night? Blundell had to admit that it did not. The appearance of the watcher on the cliff-top in itself proved nothing—she might be a birdwatcher, or a late tourist simply having a look at the rocks. As an event in a chain of circumstance, however, it was at least significant.

Then he realised that far from being on the way towards solution, the equation had simply acquired a new unknown quantity. Miss Danvers thought that she had been recognised in the pub by Mr Layton. The mysterious visitor to the rectory had certainly appeared to be a man. If there was anything in David Grendon's theorising, the Mr Layton of the diving camp was—or at least had something to do with—the elusive Mr Platt. If Mr Layton had been responsible for the accident to the Mini, it was Mr Layton who might be expected to be interested in the outcome of the crash. Of course Mr Layton might have sent the woman to have a look at things for him, but if so, and unless Mr Layton was a very skilful maker-up of credible stories, the woman must presumably be implicated with him. And they had no idea who she was, or where she came from.

Still confident that he could not himself be seen, Blundell studied the woman as closely as he could. She would presumably have come by car, and yes, there was a car a little way down the road, although it was half hidden by rocks. Blundell trained his glasses on it. It was biggish, dark green in colour, and possibly an estate car of some sort, though he couldn't be sure of this because he could see only the front. But with his glasses he could make out the letters on the number plate— JLP. Those were the letters that Miss Danvers had seen on the car outside the pub, which she thought resembled Mr Platt's car, but which couldn't be the same because Mr Platt's car had been lettered MEW—and she was convinced of that. That this car resembled the vehicle described by Miss Danvers at least suggested that the woman on the cliff-top was mixed up in the affair in some way, but in what way he was no nearer knowing.

The woman spent another five minutes examining the foreshore, and then walked back to the road. Blundell heard a car door slam, and a moment later the car drove off. He got a glimpse of the whole car as it passed on the road—it was certainly an estate car, though he could not be sure of the make. He was glad that his own car was parked unobtrusively in the lay-by some distance away, and that it had no marks indicating police.

Blundell waited another quarter of an hour. The car did not return, so presumably it had gone on towards Newton Ferrers and Yealmpton, or had cut inland at one of the side roads meeting the cliff road. The tide had definitely turned, and there did not seem anything more to be gained by keeping observation. He left his hide in the rocks, walked back to the road, and returned to his own car. He decided to go on into Plymouth and have another talk with his inspector.

Detective Inspector Cornish was a good policeman. The crimes he dealt with were seldom of a dramatic sort, but he was painstaking and shrewd, and the local community owed him a good deal more than it would ever recognise for helping to keep its society relatively wholesome. The inspector had a considerable respect for, and no jealousy of, the much younger Sergeant Blundell. He accepted without rancour that Blundell had enjoyed a better education than he had, and that the sergeant had qualities of imagination that he himself lacked. In his view, Blundell was likely to go far. Meanwhile, Blundell was an excellent subordinate, and if at times his enthusiasm needed tempering with common sense, that was all part of the process of gaining experience. Blundell, for his part, had a genuine affection for the older man, and recognised the value of his immense practical knowledge of the detection and prevention of crime.

When he got to headquarters, Blundell was told that Inspector Cornish was engaged, and likely to be for some time. However, when the duty officer rang through to the inspector's room to say that Blundell was waiting to see him, the sergeant was asked to come up forthwith.

"The very man I want to see," the inspector said. "I rang you at Ivybridge earlier and was told you'd been out all night.

I hope you're not too tired—I must say you're looking fairly spry."

"Clear conscience, perhaps. But it was an interesting night. I've come to tell you about it."

"Well, it may have to wait a little. These gentlemen would like to talk to you first." The inspector had two men with him, and he introduced them as Commander Furness, of the special Fine Art squad of the Metropolitan Police, and Mr Alexander Gathermore, of Gathermore International, the big firm of auctioneers. The Inspector explained, "After our last talk, John, I sent a report to Exeter, and they got in touch with the specialists at New Scotland Yard who deal with art robberies and big jewel thefts. The commander was very much interested, and he's come down with Mr Gathermore, who is a jewellery expert, to have a look at the finds from the wreck of the *Madras* that are being held for the moment by the Receiver of Wreck here."

"Do they think there could be anything in our theory?" Blundell asked.

Commander Furness replied for him. "It's hard to say, but yes, there could be something in it. There have been four big jewel robberies over the past couple of years, and although we have our ears pretty close to the ground we've not picked up the slightest indication of any attempt to dispose of the stolen goods. That is, until you came along. Mr Gathermore is extremely interested in a big ruby brooch that we saw this morning in the *Madras* collection at the Customs place here. He can't swear to it, but he thinks the stone—a particularly big one—has a considerable resemblance to the Countess of Holmfirth's ruby that was stolen after a ball at Holmfirth Castle just before Christmas last year."

"We know the stone," said Mr Gathermore, "because we sold it to the present earl's grandfather—the fourth earl—in 1898, and of course we have records of everything that passes through our salerooms. This particular stone has in fact been through our hands twice—the previous owner bought it through us. It was all a long time ago, but after the recent Holmfirth Castle robbery we naturally received a list of what was stolen so that we could keep an eye out for it, and I checked back in our records. It is a famous stone, and was brought to England originally by a soldier who served in India with Clive.

128

"When the fourth Earl of Holmfirth bought the stone in 1898 he had it reset, in a heavy gold brooch, a typical late-Victorian setting. The ruby in what I may call the *Madras* collection is in an eighteenth-century setting, which might reasonably be found in a ship wrecked in 1805, but there is something very odd about it. It is remarkably like a piece by the famous French goldsmith Louis Grandjean which, surrounding a small pearl-set locket, was stolen in another jewel robbery a few months ago. Grandjean's work fetches very high prices nowadays, and I am familiar with this locket-setting because I sold it myself to the present owner—I mean, the owner from whom it was stolen, the Hon. Mrs Christopher Sighurst—only eighteen months ago. Of course Grandjean could have made more than one setting to a similar design, although that would have been unusual, but the occurrence of a Grandjean setting with a ruby jewel would be unique—it is a feature of his work that he would never set rubies, which he considered to be unlucky."

"The stone from one brooch could have been reset in another, I suppose," Blundell said.

"Yes. But a stone as well-recorded as the Holmfirth ruby would be identifiable, unless it was recut. I cannot be sure of the stone in the *Madras* collection because I have not been able to remove it from the setting for complete examination, but there are slight indications of a recent cut—a cut that could not have been on a stone that went down with a ship in 1805 because it employs a technique that was not developed until the early years of the present century. It is extremely puzzling."

"If the jewels we have seen today were brought to you for auction, would you accept them?" asked Commander Furness.

"We would require proof of ownership, of course. Apart from the big ruby, the other pieces are not in any way outstanding. They are pleasant enough pieces of about the right date, though a pair of ear-rings look to me rather late—more Victorian than suitable for 1805. But with small, relatively unimportant pieces of jewellery, it is often impossible to be completely sure of a period. And ownership is often far from easy to prove—rings and brooches may have been in a family for generations, and unless they are of exceptional value they may never have been listed properly for probate, or insurance purposes. We do the best we can—the fact that we have been established since the eighteenth century with a business that has long been world-wide, is, perhaps, an indication of the precautions we take.

"The big ruby is in a different category. A stone of that size and quality ought to have a history, and we would require to be satisfied of its provenance before we handled it. The possible Louis Grandjean setting would make me doubly concerned to find out everything I could about it—but that may be partly because Grandjean's work has been a particular study of mine for many years."

"If you were told that the jewels were salvage from a wreck, with proof that they had been through the office of the Receiver of Wreck, would that satisfy you?" Commander Furness said.

Mr Gathermore paused. "It could be considered a reasonable title, I suppose—in certain circumstances, that is," he replied cautiously. "We should need to know, of course, of any insurance interest, or other possible claims."

"Salvage from a ship that went down getting on for two centuries ago would not be likely to produce such claims."

"No, perhaps not. It is an interesting situation."

"Have you met it before?"

"Yes, but always in rather special circumstances. Some years ago, for instance, we acted for a Scandinavian Government in selling a number of finds raised from a wreck in the Baltic— they were articles judged surplus to the requirements of the national museum, and were sold to help to finance further work in marine archaeology. And we have acted from time to time for insurance companies when they have been able to salvage articles of value from wrecks on which they have paid claims for total loss. But those are relatively modern wrecks. We have never, I think, acted for a private individual in selling salvaged valuables, but there is no reason in principle why we shouldn't, and I daresay some other firms have. There has been a considerable increase in salvage from old wrecks over the past few years."

"Would you handle the sale of an article as valuable as the Combe Dean chalice if it were brought to you as salvage from a wreck?" Blundell asked.

"My dear Sir! The Combe Dean chalice is world famous: if by any chance it were brought to us, we should, of course, notify the police immediately."

"Yes, but that would be if you could identify it. While the

130

measurements and the design of the chalice are presumed to be unique, I understand that it bears no marks by which it can positively be identified. If it were found, say, in the wreck of the *Madras*, it would be hard to prove that it was not a hitherto unknown replica. Could it not be offered for sale as a replica of unknown origin? What would be its value as such?"

Mr Gathermore considered. "Given a provenance of finding in a wreck as far back as 1805," he said at last, "I should expect its value to be very great. Experts would no doubt argue about it, but that would enhance publicity. Museums and private collectors from all over the world would bid for it. Yes, it would fetch a very large sum indeed. But we are speaking hypothetically: nothing remotely resembling the chalice has so far been found, and as far as I know there is nothing to suggest that it ever will be."

Blundell said nothing. Mr Gathermore looked at his watch, and murmured about his need to return to London. "There's a fast train to Paddington in just over half an hour," Inspector Cornish said.

"I think I'll stay in Plymouth tonight—there are several other matters that I want to discuss," said Commander Furness. "Inspector, can you fix up a car to take Mr Gathermore to the station?"

The inspector could, and did. After Mr Gathermore's departure the three policemen reassembled in the inspector's room.

"You know much more about all this than either of us do," Inspector Cornish said to the man from New Scotland Yard. "Do you think we're just wasting police time in trying to find a link between the salvage divers and the theft of the Combe Dean chalice?"

"No," Commander Furness said. "If I did, I wouldn't be here. I think you've hit on a novel and most ingenious way of disposing of stolen jewellery. Whether anyone has yet tried to use it is another matter, and whether we can ever prove anything about these particular finds is another matter still. But the method has such potentialities for covering up crime that the investigation must certainly continue."

"I haven't told you yet about last night," Blundell put in. "You may think it has some bearing on what we've been discussing."

He gave an account of events from David's telephone call to his house after the car crash to his own observation of the watcher on the cliff-top that morning. The two senior men listened without interrupting. Then Commander Furness said, "I've studied all the papers in the Combe Dean case very thoroughly indeed, and there's one aspect of Sergeant Blundell's story that I find particularly interesting. Most human activities —not only criminal ones—tend to follow a pattern: individuals act in particular ways because their minds work like that. There's a curious pattern here. If this man Layton is really our suspect Platt, he disguised his own identity in a simple but extremely subtle way—by using his own name in a context that couldn't possibly relate to him, that is, by giving it to one of his alleged maternal ancestors. The one name that one would assume couldn't possibly be his own is Layton. There is a similar pattern about the estate car that seems to feature in the case. The car that Mr Platt used, and for which every police force in the country has been looking, seems somewhat similar to the car that Miss Danvers thought she saw outside the pub last night, but which couldn't be the same vehicle because Miss Danvers has a clear recollection of the unusual registration letters MEW on the Platt car. Of course this could be the simplest form of eye-wash—it needs no more than fitting an MEW registration plate to a car that normally has a completely different index number. After the visit to the rectory, the MEW plate disappears, the original plate comes back, and the Platt car to all intents and purposes has vanished into thin air. The one car that couldn't be Mr Platt's green estate car is another green estate car in everyday use, but with a wholly different registration. His own name, his own car, but in contexts that virtually couldn't be related to him. There *is* a sort of pattern, you know."

"You could say that there's the same sort of pattern about the finds from the wreck: jewels, even the chalice, in a context that *can't* be suspicious," Sergeant Blundell observed.

"You could say so.... But we're running away with ourselves," said Commander Furness. "What evidence have we got?"

"None, at least none that would stand up to cross-examination," Blundell said, "unless you can regard the appearance of a watcher on the cliff this morning as some sort of circumstantial evidence. But it's not even circumstantial evidence against Mr Layton, because the watcher wasn't Mr Layton, but a hitherto unknown woman. There's no woman in the Platt case so far—at least none that we've ever heard about. What do you make of last night's happenings on the cliff-top? Do you think there's anything in Mr Grendon's and Miss Danvers's story that they were deliberately pushed off the road?"

"It's a queer story," the inspector said. "There's no obvious reason for a car to leave the road like that. You're quite satisfied that they weren't drunk?"

"Quite."

"And it's odd that someone should turn up to inspect the foreshore through field-glasses, as if that someone expected to see the remains of a car there," said the Commander. "Don't you think that's enough for a formal visit to make inquiries at the diving camp?"

"We've got an unidentified fingerprint on the safe, and I'd dearly like to compare that with Mr Layton's prints," Blundell said. "But I don't think we've got enough to hold him, and I do think that once we show our hand it's goodbye to the chalice, and to any hope of clearing up any of the other jewel robberies—if he's mixed up with them in any way. Mr Grendon, who's certainly got his wits about him, has a plan for setting a sort of trap. I don't like it much, but I can't very well stop him from going ahead." He outlined David's plan for reappearing in the cove, with Elizabeth on board *Lily*. He explained his commitment to go with them, pointing out that he could be there ostensibly to investigate damage to the lobster fishermen's gear. To his surprise, neither of his seniors poured cold water on the scheme.

"I don't think that's a bad idea at all," Commander Furness said. "Of course, nothing may come of it—but that's a risk we're taking all the time, in any investigation. More seriously, if anything does come of it, it's likely to be nasty. Can that boat take another man?"

"She's a biggish boat. I don't know how many she can sleep, but she could carry a dozen men easily enough."

"Well, I think you should have one man with you, possibly two. And while we're about it, we might be able to kill two birds with one stone. I'd very much like to have a report on that wreck. Inspector Cornish, do you think you could get hold of a police frogman—preferably two, it's always better if they can work in pairs—who could go down and have a look at the wreck? They could be extra manpower for your party, Sergeant Blundell, and while you've got a boat at your disposal they might go down and inspect the wreck."

"We've got a fine police diving school. I'm sure I can find a couple of men—they'd be keen on the job," said the inspector.

"We'd have to be a bit careful," Blundell said. "It wouldn't do for any of the Layton group to see us investigating their wreck."

"It's not their wreck—we've a perfect right to investigate the seabed without a search warrant," Commander Furness replied. "I agree, though, that you don't want to be seen doing it. And although they've got no rights in a wreck of this sort, some of these treasure-hunting groups go to great lengths to keep other people off. There was that case somewhere in the north last year when two rival groups attacked each other, and a man in one boat was badly injured by a crowbar. We don't want to get involved in trouble of that sort. But they can't be diving all the time. You'll be at sea, you're a fishing-boat, and I daresay you can find an opportunity to put our chaps over the side when there's no one else about. Anyway, you can try."

"We can certainly try," Blundell said.

"Have you been able to find out anything about the man Layton?" the inspector asked.

"I put inquiries in motion as soon as I got your report from Exeter," Commander Furness answered. "There hasn't been much time, and there's very little to go on. He's got no criminal record—at least, not under that name. The marine division knows a lot about divers—all this oil work in the North Sea has raised a number of new problems. A man called Philip Layton, who fits the description of your chap, came out of the Navy some years back with good Naval qualifications as a diver. He worked for a time on an oil-rig, and then, apparently, set himself up as a freelance. I can't tell you any more—and unless we can question him, I doubt if we can find out much more."

"He negotiated for quarters in the unfinished holiday camp near Finmouth quite openly," Blundell said. "He seems to run a sort of club for amateurs, who provide the crews he needs for his salvage work in return for a holiday. The place isn't licensed—they use the pub—but they've got a mess hut, and a sort of club room. We've had complaints from the local fishermen about them, and while it's hard to prove anything I think there's no doubt that they do help themselves from the men's lobster pots, or some of them do, and they're not over-careful about the way they treat the gear. I've seen three or four pots that have been deliberately cut. That may be no more than thoughtless high spirits—people who don't come from a fishing community may not realise what a crime it really is. We'd like to put a stop to it, but it's not easy to act. Apart from this, they've caused no trouble in the neighbourhood: they seem to keep themselves pretty much to themselves. If anybody finds out about our police divers, we can always say that we're investigating alleged damage to fishing-gear. Then if nothing comes of the other business, no harm's done, and no one need be any the wiser."

"That's a good point. And if you don't clear up any jewel robberies, at least you may do something to help the fishermen," the Commander said.

# XI

## *On The Tamar*

I T W A S S T I L L quite early when David and Elizabeth were deposited at Finmouth, and hardly anyone was about. Those fishermen who were going out had already left, to get their work done and return on a making tide in the afternoon. David doubted if anyone noticed them as they walked along the quay and down the steps to the small-boat quay, where *Lily*'s rubber dinghy lay. All the same, he was nervous until they could get away, and thankful when they boarded *Lily*. On a falling tide he'd have to be careful about the bar, but he knew the passage well now, and in reasonable weather *Lily* could get out at any state of the tide.

It was a calm morning, with a gentle offshore breeze. He decided to sail out, partly because he did not have a great deal of fuel for the outboard, partly because he did not want to attract attention by the engine-noise. When he had the rubber dinghy stowed and the sails up he wondered why he was feeling so uneasy—it must simply be reaction from last night, he thought, for there was no occasion for anyone in Finmouth to be particularly interested in his movements. It was perfectly normal for him to go out in *Lily*, and although it was not quite normal for anyone to be with him, there was no earthly reason why he shouldn't go out with a girl. He wanted some stores— would it not be sensible to bring *Lily* to the quay and shop in Finmouth? No, he wanted to get away: he had a breaker full of fresh water, and all the food they really needed, though it would be nicer to give Elizabeth something slightly less spartan than rye bread and hard cheese. But with some forty-eight hours in hand before their rendezvous with Sergeant Blundell in Plymouth there were plenty of places they could put in: once clear of the bay and beyond any possible observation from the cliff-top they could go where they liked.

He let *Lily* drift clear of the other moored boats, and then let the sails draw and headed for the passage across the bar. With the light offshore breeze it was a gentle run. *Lily* began her small, familiar chatter as she gathered way, and David felt a profound sense of escape as the land fell behind them.

Elizabeth was frankly enjoying herself. "I've never thought much of mathematical logic before," she said, "but I must say it has a lot to be said for it when it takes people on holiday cruises."

"This isn't exactly a holiday," David said.

"Well, it is for me. And you can think of it as a holiday, too —you're not going fishing on this trip."

"We might need to catch a fish for dinner. And we are going fishing, in a way. Only I've no idea what we're likely to catch— if anything."

"That doesn't come until Friday. We've got today and the whole of tomorrow to go cruising. Oh, David, if you knew how dull my life really is—I could almost bless our accident last night."

David said nothing. He was thinking of equations—$X +$ wreck $+$ (perhaps) chalice $=$ attempted murder $+$ what? And he was thinking, too, of this girl who had so oddly come into his life. That could be expressed as an equation, too—only there were so many unknown terms that it wasn't a very satisfactory one. He thought suddenly of Louise—how she would have hated going off in a boat without a cabin and a private bathroom. This girl didn't seem to care tuppence about *Lily*'s lack of practically every comfort. And he could talk to her in a way he had never been able to talk to Louise. Oh, well—he was presumably still married to Louise, and that was that.

Clear of the point, the wind freshened though it was still northerly. It was a good reaching wind for Plymouth, and although he didn't want to go to Plymouth yet, David decided to make across the mouth of Plymouth Sound to Cawsand Bay. It was only nine or ten miles away, and they should make it comfortably by lunchtime, and he could take Elizabeth ashore for lunch in Cawsand village. There was a good anchorage off the beach, and they could row ashore easily. They could shop in Cawsand—and there seemed not the remotest possibility that anyone interested in their movements would be looking for them in Cawsand.

He explained this to Elizabeth. "Cawsand is a pretty little place," he said. "Have you ever been there?"

"No," she replied, "but I think I've heard of it. Isn't it in Cornwall?"

David laughed. "As a Devon man myself I accept that Cornwall is a foreign country. But as a Devon seaman it isn't quite the same. Cawsand, Looe, Fowey, Falmouth, are all in Cornwall, of course, but they all belong to the sea that belongs to us. I don't feel the same about the North Cornish coast—but that's a horrible coast, anyway. The Channel coast, though—that's all home ground."

"I suppose I must be a Devon landswoman, then. Do you know, I don't think I have ever been across the Tamar."

"You're crossing it now—at least, you're crossing the great Sound that it helps to form."

"I really do feel that I'm going abroad. Do you think the natives will be friendly?"

There are no dangers in the approach to Cawsand. David brought *Lily* into the wind about a cable off the beach, and anchored in a couple of fathoms of beautifully clear water. He was launching the dinghy to row ashore for lunch, when Elizabeth said, "Do we have to go ashore yet?"

"Well, we do if you want a decent meal. I've only hard tack and a few emergency tins on board."

"I'm sure we can manage on what you've got. I'm enjoying *Lily* so much that I don't want to wake up. What have you got?"

"Some ship's biscuits and packets of pumpernickel—that's wholemeal rye bread, the 'black bread' that peasants used to eat. Some people think it repulsive, but it keeps fairly well at sea, and I can eat it. There's some rather hard cheese, but I haven't got any butter. There aren't any vegetables—unless you count baked beans. And there are a few tins of soup."

"Enough for a feast! I'm quite good with Primuses, so I'll start with some soup. I know where things are from the last trip you gave me."

"All right. I'll leave the dinghy in the water, though, because I'll have to go ashore after lunch. I must get some more petrol for the outboard, and the larder has got to be improved. I don't keep fresh food on board—normally I get what I need in

138

Finmouth before I go out. I didn't today because I wanted to get away from the place. But we've got to spend at least a couple of days on board, and there's no call to turn old *Lily* into a prison ship."

Elizabeth didn't answer, because she'd gone forward to the cuddy where David had his galley, sleeping quarters, and everything else that *Lily* could offer in the way of living accommodation. David stayed aft, contemplating the beach, the wooded hillside rising up to Maker Heights, and the sheer beauty of the anchorage. It was hard to believe that only last night there had been a murderous attempt to send him and Elizabeth plunging to death over the cliffs of Bigbury Bay. That there had been such an attempt he was quite certain—and it was because of that that they were in this quiet anchorage now. Elizabeth had a valuable quality of detachment—she could enjoy whatever seemed good at the moment without letting concern for the future spoil it. He wondered whether this was essentially a female characteristic. Louise had it to some extent: but Louise was just improvident—she wanted enjoyment, and didn't care a damn what it cost, or who paid for it. This girl was not improvident—indeed, part of her reason for not wanting to have lunch ashore was to save David's money. But she did seem to have a rather wonderful capacity for making the best of the calm in the eye of a storm. She had enough on her plate, poor kid—anxiety about her father, the constant strain of running that rambling old rectory, and most of the humdrum work of the parish, on nothing like enough money. If she could enjoy these couple of days, good luck to her.

For himself, he had much harsher things to think about. He believed that both Elizabeth and her father were in real danger —and so, apparently, did the police, although perhaps not with his own degree of conviction. Danger didn't seem to worry either the rector or his daughter: they were co-operating sensibly in keeping out of the way, but he doubted if either of them would have thought of going away if he hadn't more or less made them do it. And what came next? They couldn't stay away for ever—but until the mystery of the chalice was cleared up, he was convinced that neither of them could safely go back to Combe Dean. Could the mystery be cleared up? He was pinning his faith to pure theoretical reasoning. Mathematical logic was a powerful form of reason, but its deductive process required reliable facts—nice clean mathematical facts, like the beautiful relationship between the squares on the sides of right-angled triangles. Applied to irrational human actions, the possibilities of error were enormous. Yet there were some facts. X + wreck + chalice (for he was ready to include the chalice as a term of that equation) had already equalled attempted murder. X + reappearance of supposedly murdered victims must equal something—it *must* lead to some further action on X's part. But what action? He could speculate endlessly, but he could not predict. If there was anything in his theory, if X had devised a method of acquiring a legal title to the proceeds of jewel robberies, he had a profitable secret to preserve. If that secret were threatened by the possibility of Elizabeth's, or her father's, recognising X, it would be worth going a long way to remove the danger—to remove Elizabeth and her father. X had tried—perhaps thought he had succeeded—in removing Elizabeth. Given proof that he had failed, what could he be expected to do? Try again? Melt down the chalice and give up? Logic was no help here, because X's reaction would depend on his human make-up, on the qualities of determination and ruthlessness in his personality. On past form he was sufficiently ruthless to have another go, but where human actions were concerned form was an unreliable guide. Logic could calculate on *some* action—it couldn't suggest what. And X's reaction might remain unknown, a purely private decision taken within himself, never manifested in the external world.

Unsatisfactory as all this was, even the assumption of *some* reaction on X's part depended on the theory's being right, or on the right lines. Suppose it were wholly wrong? Suppose the diving-scheme was precisely what it was said to be, treasure-hunting on an old wreck, with nothing to do with stolen jewels, the chalice, or anything else? Then the elaborate scheme for staging Elizabeth's reappearance would achieve nothing, because nobody in the diving outfit would be in the least concerned whether she was around or not. But David, and Elizabeth herself, and her father, and the police, could not know this: they would know that for some reason their scheme had failed, but they could not know why it had failed. Elizabeth and her father would have to go home and take up their lives again with the threat of danger still around them, any noise in the night, the appearance of the most innocent stranger in the village bringing fear. If nothing happened, such fears would lessen in time, but it would be a long time, a hellish time of corrosive anxiety and suspicion. And it would be his, David's, fault: he would have returned Elizabeth's kindness to him by giving her a lifelong worry. He had approached the possible connection of the theft of the chalice with diving-work on the wreck as an interesting mental exercise—was it not really a grossly irresponsible game with other people's lives? Would he ever know? And would he ever be able to forgive himself? Yet *someone* had attempted to kill Elizabeth, immediately after she thought that the man in the pub had recognised her. Those were facts of a sort—they had *not* sprung simply from his own imagination. But it was his imagination that produced the situation in which these other events had happened—or were thought to have happened. Elizabeth might feel that she was on holiday, but he had a hellish two days to get through.

These disquieting reflections were interrupted by Elizabeth's call from the galley. "Lunch is ready now, David. Shall we have it in here, or shall I bring it on deck?"

"I think we'd better eat in the cuddy—it's not all that warm out here when you're sitting still," he said. He went forward, and even in his gloomy mood he had a moment of sheer pleasure at seeing what Elizabeth had done. She had found a piece of old sail and folded it to make a tablecloth for the board that he used as a cabin table. *Lily*'s cutlery, practically all of it, for he had only two spoons and a few odd knives and forks, was neatly laid out, and there were two steaming mugs of soup —he had neither soup-plates nor bowls—on the table. Beside each mug was a piece of pumpernickel. "You've certainly done us proud," he said, determined to put away his own worries as far as he could so as not to spoil her sense of holiday. These might be the last two more or less carefree days she would know for a long time—he must help her make the most of them.

"Some of Drake's fleet anchored here after that famous game of bowls in July 1587, when they were assembling to leave Plymouth to go out to fight the Spanish Armada," he said. "They had an anxious night. Half the fleet was still in harbour being victualled, and when one of Drake's pinnaces brought news of the Armada they had to warp out as quickly as they could. Those that were ready first hung about around here.

Then they had to get out into the Channel, and that wasn't easy, because they had a south-westerly wind. That meant they had to beat out—and those sixteenth-century ships weren't handy at going to windward. But they managed it, and by mid-morning most of them were clear of the Eddystone Rocks—there wasn't an Eddystone Lighthouse then—and on their way to fight."

"We're waiting to go out to fight, in a sort of way," Elizabeth said.

"Yes. And at least we can think of Drake's fleet as an example. They had a lot against them." Her remark made him feel a lot better.

Cawsand, and the neighbouring Kingsand, a little to the north-east, were originally fishing villages. Trade with summer visitors has given them shops and services that fishing villages could not support, and would, perhaps, not need. Having rowed ashore after lunch, David was able to get all he wanted in the way of supplies. He also telephoned the Met station in Plymouth for a weather forecast. This was not optimistic. The northerly wind which had brought them comfortably into Cawsand Bay was expected to increase, and then veer to the east, with the possibility of an easterly gale later on. Back on board *Lily* he considered the position. His earlier intention had been to spend the waiting period, between leaving Finmouth and springing the trap with Elizabeth as bait, well out to sea, safely out of the way of any possible observers. But that was before his decision to leave Finmouth without shopping for supplies. Several things now combined to make him change his plans. The most compelling was the weather forecast. They had a rendezvous to keep in Plymouth the day after tomorrow and if they were caught by a gale at sea they might be delayed in getting back to Plymouth. But there were other reasons, too. He was more tired after last night's excitements and the severe cut in his leg than he had reckoned on, and the prospect of a battering at sea was not enticing: he had no doubt of *Lily*'s ability to stand a gale, but he was responsible for Elizabeth, and he distrusted his own weariness. Next, it was ridiculous to suppose that the diving organisation, even assuming that it was a cloak for more sinister activities, was capable of maintaining a watch over the whole West Country. He felt safe enough in

Cawsand—why not, instead of putting back to sea, run up the River Tamar? They could find a quiet anchorage somewhere in the river, no one would think of looking for them there, and they could get back to Plymouth for their rendezvous without hazard. He had an Ordnance map of Plymouth as well as his charts, and he got out this and studied it. There seemed to be no difficulties. All they had to do was to sail into Plymouth Sound, round Picklecombe Point on the Cornish shore, and then take the passage by Drake's Island into the Hamoaze, which was really the combined mouth of the Tamar and the St Germans' (or Lynher) River, flowing in from the west above Torpoint. Once past Devonport they could go a long way up the Tamar: there was a good channel, and as long as he kept an eye on depth when anchoring there seemed nothing at all to worry about. He put the idea to Elizabeth, and she jumped at it. "It will mean that I really can cross the Tamar now, and it will be much nicer than being at sea if it's likely to get rough," she said.

Considering the chart again, David decided to make the passage under power from the outboard. The wind had certainly increased, and although it was forecast to veer, it had not done so yet, and was still northerly. That meant that he would have to beat up river, and as there were various ferries and a good deal of shipping around Devonport, it would be easier to handle *Lily* under power than to be going about constantly in a confined waterway.

There was nothing to keep them in Cawsand, and with some hours of daylight left it seemed sensible to make for the Tamar forthwith. With the wind in the north, *Lily* more or less took herself out of the anchorage. David didn't bother with the mainsail, but gave *Lily* a jib to control her. Once clear of the shore he started the outboard, dropped the jib, and headed for Picklecombe Point.

The woods on Mount Edgecumbe were mostly bare now, but the westering sun came through the clouds a little as they cleared the point, touching the trees with crimson. *Lily* was heavy for the outboard, but, once moving, it gave her four knots or so, and she plodded on steadily. Elizabeth stood in the bows, the wind ruffling her hair, and sending a strand or two streaming backwards, like a picture David had once seen somewhere of Athene driving a chariot.

They made the passage by Drake's Island and the narrows by Devil's Point without problems. The Cremyll ferry crossed a cable or so ahead of them, and David was glad of the manoeuvrability that the outboard gave. Devonport, with its lines of shipyards, was soon to starboard. They watched a newly painted Royal Navy frigate come out, her clean lines giving her a wonderful sense of purpose. Soon they were past the Torpoint ferry, and the Tamar widened as the St German's river joined it. They went on upstream, the built-up banks of Saltash and St Budeaux falling away as they moved into the world of the open river. A couple of miles above Saltash they rounded Weir Point, and were attracted by a wide pool to port below the little village of Cargreen. "What about this?" David called to Elizabeth. "It's secluded enough, and seems pretty well sheltered. How about stopping here? There's probably a pub ashore in the village."

Elizabeth came aft, and stood in the cockpit beside him. "It's utterly peaceful and lovely," she said. "Is this Cornwall?"

"Yes, this is the Cornish bank. The only doubt in my mind is how much of this pool dries out. It must be about half-tide now, and the tide's making." He throttled back the outboard to leave *Lily* just with steerage way. "Can you get me the lead?" he asked. "It's in that locker beside you."

Elizabeth got the leadline, and David asked her to take the tiller while he swung the lead. "Keep her moving gently as she is," he said. "I'll see what happens to the depths over this part of the pool as we go upstream."

He swung the lead three or four times. "There's plenty of water for us here at the moment," he said, "but I don't know the Tamar, and I don't know what happens here at low tide. I should think we'd be all right, but I think we'll anchor a little farther out. We must watch the tide when we go ashore. The rubber dinghy draws next to nothing, but even that can't float on mud. *Lily* takes the ground quite happily and will come to no harm, but we don't want to be cut off from her. We'll be all right this evening—it was low tide around midday, you remember. I wonder if Sergeant Blundell saw anyone looking for a wrecked Mini on the rocks? Well, we can't know about that yet. I think I'll bring her up about here. Shut off the engine, and I'll let go the anchor."

*Lily* lay docilely to her anchor, and David tidied up. There

144

was not much to do, for having come up-river under power, her sails were already down. It was getting dusk, and he got out *Lily*'s stormproof lantern. "There doesn't seem much shipping about as far upstream as this, and we're well out of the fairway, anyhow, but we'll have a riding light," he explained to Elizabeth. "If you're game, I'd like to go ashore for a drink, and come back for supper on board—the larder's better stocked now. But it'll be dark when we come back, and the riding light will help us to find *Lily*."

"You're turning me into quite a pub-crawler," Elizabeth said, "but it will be nice to go to a pub where we don't have to look out for anybody."

They came back to *Lily* after spending about an hour ashore in a friendly small pub that they found on the waterfront. There was no problem finding *Lily* in the darkness, because her lantern shone out like a lighthouse-beacon for them. David lit the two lamps in the fo'c'sle, and soon had a good stew ready from meat and fresh vegetables that he had bought in Cawsand. They were both tired, and after supper were quite ready for bed, but there was a situation that David had been rather dreading. The only thing to do, he felt, was to discuss it frankly.

"Look," he said to Elizabeth, "I'm afraid we've got to share the fo'c'sle. I could spend the night in the cockpit, I suppose, but it would be wretchedly cold, and it seems damned silly. It wouldn't be honest to pretend that I don't find you disturbing— you're a very attractive woman, and I do. More than half of me wants to make love to you. But I'm not free yet to ask you to marry me, I've had one marriage that turned out very badly, and I'm not at all sure that I'd be much of a husband even if you thought about accepting me. And there's another thing— important to me, anyhow. We're not here because I took you for a cruise on my boat simply to be with you—we're here because I've put you in what I believe to be some real danger, and that danger isn't over yet. One day, perhaps, I can properly tell you that I love you, but it would be all wrong and jangling to get it mixed up with the beastly business that has brought us here. I should hate you to think that I don't want to make love to you. And I want you to understand why I'm not going to."

Elizabeth laughed—just nervous tension, in no sense mockery.

145

"You're a dear person, David," she said. "I've never had a love affair—I've never met anyone to have a love affair with. You say you want to be honest—well so do I. I could horribly easily be in love with you if I let myself. But it would make Daddy dreadfully ashamed—and I'd be ashamed, too. I suppose a lot of people would think this quite ridiculous. But what they call the Permissive Society hasn't got to Combe Dean—and I don't think I want it to, anyway. I keep telling myself that I mustn't do anything, ever, that might stop you going back to your wife."

"There is no chance whatever of my going back to Louise. She doesn't want me, I'm no use to her any longer, and I don't want ever again to have anything to do with the kind of life she represents. You've given me a sort of dream of what a marriage might be—but there's a nightmare to be woken up from first."

Elizabeth kissed him lightly on the forehead. "I suppose that isn't quite fair. But you mustn't forget that I'm a woman."

"I'm not in the least likely to forget it. There's only one sleeping bag, but it's a high-altitude mountaineering bag, and a very good one. You have that—I've got enough blankets to be comfortable. You must sleep to port—there's an unwritten law that skippers always have to berth to starboard. Now I'm going out to study my navigation—"

"At anchor?"

"Well, to contemplate the night if you like, while you do whatever undressing you're inclined to. Goodnight, Elizabeth— and thank you for all sorts of things."

David left the fo'c'sle and went aft to the cockpit. Emotionally, he was much disturbed, but he also felt curiously happy. *Lily's* old brass lantern made a pool of dim light on the foredeck, and the lights of the village twinkled in the distance, but the rest of the world was darkness. There was a faint whisper from tide or current meeting *Lily's* forefoot, but so faint that it simply emphasised the silence. What a clean, beautiful place the world could be—and what hellishness men and women made of it! Well, perhaps not always. David thought of those ships of nearly 400 years ago, whose anchorage they had briefly shared in Cawsand Bay. They had to beat out against a south-westerly wind to meet the great Armada. Their men must have wondered if they'd ever come home: and some of them never came home. But some did—the dreadful shadow of the

Armada lifted for ever. That wasn't chance—they lifted the shadow of invasion from England by their own guts and seamanship. Would the shadow of the stolen chalice ever be lifted from their own lives? Perhaps you had to go through hell to win anything worth while. Perhaps . . .

David's thoughts raced on, until he suddenly realised that he was exceedingly cold. He looked at his watch and discovered that he had been sitting in the cockpit for nearly an hour and a half. Elizabeth would surely be tucked in now. He went back to the fo'c'sle and opened the door quietly. The lamps were still burning: but Elizabeth was fast asleep, one cheek and a tendril of hair just appearing from the down of the sleeping bag. David put out the lights, undressed to his shirt—he had no pyjamas on board—and got into his own blankets. He was overwhelmingly tired, and the gash in his thigh hurt, but he felt utterly at peace. It seemed wholly natural for Elizabeth to be sleeping beside him.

Thursday, the epicentre of their private hurricane, was a happy day for both of them. Neither referred to the conversation of last night, and they were completely at ease in each other's company. They rowed ashore after breakfast, and went for a long walk through winding Cornish lanes to King's Mill and Botus Fleming—where they lunched on bread and cheese at an inn. Elizabeth surprised David by being able to interpret the "Botus" in the village's queer name. "It's an old Cornish word for 'house'," she explained. "Daddy makes rather a study of place names, and he has a lot of books about them. We had a retired clergyman to preach once, he'd been vicar of Botus Fleming. It was such an odd name that I looked it up—it was years ago, but I've always remembered it. I never thought that I'd actually be in Botus Fleming one day!"

The walk back to Cargreen was cold and wet—the weather was definitely worsening, though neither noticed it. David's seaman's instinct felt the weather as soon as they got back to the dinghy. The anchorage was safe enough, but it was a hard row out to *Lily* against a cold easterly wind. Yesterday's forecast was turning out to be accurate—the wind was now strongly in the east, and conditions out at sea would not be pleasant.

147

Well, they were all right for tonight: it was no use worrying about the morning until it came.

Their rendezvous with Sergeant Blundell at the Mayflower Steps in Plymouth's Sutton Harbour was at ten o'clock. David was awake soon after 4 a.m., and had he been alone he would have got up and made some coffee. But he didn't want to wake Elizabeth sooner than need be for what was bound to be a worrying and exhausting day. Elizabeth, however, was also awake. She sensed David's restlessness, and asked, "What's the time? My watch is no good in the dark."

David told her, adding, "It's awfully early, but I don't think I shall manage to get to sleep again. How about you? Would you like some coffee, or can you go back to sleep?"

"I'll settle for coffee. What time do we have to start?"

"Well, we haven't far to go—less than ten miles. We'll have the ebb with us, and the stream. The wind still seems to be in the east, but it won't affect us much in the river. When we get out into the Sound it will be dead against us, but it's not much of a passage. We'll go down on the engine, and we should do the trip in well under two hours. It doesn't matter if we get in early, though, and to be on the safe side I reckon we should start at eight o'clock. There's nothing much to do before we start, except to have some breakfast and stow the dinghy, so we've got hours of time. But I think I'd like a cup of coffee now."

"So would I. Go and study navigation for a few minutes while I get dressed and get the Primus going. I'll make the coffee."

They were both thankful when it was light and time to do something. It was a matter of minutes only to stow the dinghy, but there is never absolutely nothing to do on a boat and David kept himself busy by reeving a new halliard for *Lily*'s staysail. Elizabeth washed up the breakfast things—again a matter of minutes—and then decided to reorganise the stowage in the food locker. "That's all very well," said David when he saw what she was doing, "but unless you come to live on *Lily* I shall never be able to find anything."

"You will, because the new system is just common sense. You've got some bacon stowed at the back, and coffee, and tins

148

of things that will keep, taking up all the room in front. I'm putting perishables in front and the keeping things at the back."

"Well, I'm sure it's a good idea, but I'm not so sure of my own ability to practise common sense when I want something in a hurry."

"Pooh!" Elizabeth said.

They were so anxious to get under way that they started well before eight o'clock, and got to Sutton Harbour with about three-quarters of an hour in hand. "We shouldn't be here long, so I don't suppose it matters if we use a vacant mooring," David said. "I'll put *Lily* on this buoy and hope for the best." He made fast, then launched the dinghy and rowed across to the jetty and the memorial commemorating the departure of the *Mayflower* with the Pilgrim Fathers for a new world. "I don't know whether the *Mayflower* was able to come alongside, or whether the passengers were taken on board by boat from these steps," he said. "Some of them probably used the steps, or some steps that were here then, anyway—there'd be friends waiting to the last minute to say goodbye, people to be taken on board after she'd warped out into the pool. We're in good company—first Drake's fleet, and now the *Mayflower*."

Sergeant Blundell arrived promptly at five minutes to ten. David was relieved to see him—the whole business had begun to seem so unreal that it was somehow reassuring to find that the police still took it seriously. Blundell had two men with him. He introduced them as Constables Fraser and Martinson, explaining, "The high-ups thought that we'd better have a stronger police party on board, and Fraser and Martinson volunteered for the job. But there's more to it than that. They're both expert frogmen from the police diving school, and if we get a chance we want them to have a look at the wreck. Can you manage to take the three of us?"

"As far as *Lily* is concerned, easily," David said. "But I can't offer much in the way of comfort. She's a working boat with only a small fo'c'sle with two berths."

"Don't worry about that. We've brought plenty of pullovers, and—I nearly said 'Worse things happen at sea', then I remembered that we're going to *be* at sea."

They all laughed. "I took on some stores for the trip, and at least I think we've got enough food," David said.

The rubber dinghy was supposed to support six men in an emergency, but Sergeant Blundell and the constables were all on the large side, and David decided to make two trips out to *Lily*. He took Elizabeth and Sergeant Blundell first, and came back for the two constables. On board, he had a brief conference with Sergeant Blundell. "We've only got eleven or twelve miles to go," he said, "but once out of the Sound the wind will be dead against us, and it'll be a beat the whole way. The day looks pretty rotten, and the weather is quite likely to get worse. We can easily take about four hours for the passage, and it may be a bit more. We want to be anchored in the cove with plenty of daylight left for Elizabeth to be seen, so I think we ought to set off at once, if that suits you."

"Suits us fine, that's what we're here for," Blundell said. "The only thing is—I've done a bit of sailing, but I can't guarantee not to be seasick."

"No one ever can," David replied. "Anyone who says 'I'm never seasick' has either never been to sea, or is just a plain liar."

"Well, I've got some quite interesting things to tell you—they'll keep my mind off thinking of being seasick. Both the constables can handle a boat, so when you've got under way you can leave her to them, and I can bring you up to date."

While David and the sergeant were talking Elizabeth had been making coffee. She brought four mugs to the cockpit, and on that cold morning it was particularly welcome. David decided to leave harbour under power, and to set the sails when *Lily* was clear of the entrance. Constable Fraser went forward and cast off, and they were under way.

As soon as they were well into the Sound, David asked Constable Martinson to take the helm while he got up the sails. He had a respect for the outboard but it was always a good moment when he could shut off the engine. *Lily* felt happier under sail, and in anything of a wind she could go much faster, too. The first leg of the passage, from the Sound to clear the Mew Stone was almost due south, and the strong easterly suited *Lily* well enough. Once out to sea they would have to turn east, and the wind would be dead on the nose; clear of the land, it would be also a good deal stronger, probably not far short of a gale. *Lily*, herself, would not mind that, but beating into a gale in a rough sea would not be comfortable. Still, they didn't have far to go, and for about half the passage they would be fairly sheltered by the land. Having laid a course to take them out beyond the Mew Stone, David left *Lily* to the constables and joined Elizabeth and Sergeant Blundell in the fo'c'sle. "Did anyone come to the cliff?" he asked.

"Yes, but it couldn't have been Mr Layton, because it was a woman." He described his watch on the rocks, and how the Mini's door had been clearly visible from the cliff-top. David listened to all this, and then asked, "Did you get a good look at the woman?"

"Yes. I had a good pair of Service binoculars. But she was well wrapped up, wearing a jacket with a hood, so I couldn't see her face very well. She was using binoculars most of the time, too."

"You are quite sure it was a woman?"

"As sure as one can be. She had the figure of a woman, and she was wearing a skirt."

"What sort of age?"

"I got the impression of someone fairly young, but it was no more than an impression: I couldn't even guess her age. She walked briskly when she went back to the car, though that's not much to go by."

David shrugged. "Well, somebody came, so it looks as if someone knew about the Mini. Nobody passed us on the road, so unless the police reported the accident straight away to the morning papers or to the local radio the only people who *could* have known about it were whoever it was tried to push us off the road. I must say it's a bit of a disappointment that it wasn't the Layton man who turned up, but he could have sent somebody."

"The accident wasn't reported. There's something else—it doesn't necessarily bear out your theory, but it does suggest that something happened when you went to the pub that stirred whoever took the chalice into action. The rectory was entered last night."

"Thank God Daddy wasn't there," Elizabeth said. "What happened?"

"In the light of what did happen I could kick myself, but it's easy to be wise after the event. I was impressed—I still am—by your theory. The only people known to have seen Mr Platt

151

are Miss Danvers and the rector. If your accident was not an accident, and the watcher on the cliff-top took in the significance of the wreckage of the car-door on the rocks, Miss Danvers could be presumed to be dead. That left the rector. We know that he wasn't there last night, and the churchwarden knew, and doubtless other people in the village, but there's no reason why anyone else should have known. On the chance that someone might want to attack the rector we put a man in the house last night. I wish now that we'd put a dozen men—if we had, the case might be all over. But we haven't all that many men, it was a long chance, and I don't think I *really* expected anything to happen. But about one o'clock this morning the man in the house—he was upstairs, in the rector's bedroom, with the door open—heard a slight noise apparently coming from the passage leading to the kitchen. He crept to the top of the stairs and saw someone with a torch in the passage. He rushed down to try to grab the intruder, but whoever it was was too quick for him. There's a window in that passage, it was open, and the intruder was out of it in a flash. Our chap gave chase, but it was hopeless. It was pitch dark, there's a thick shrubbery, very much overgrown, along that wall of the house, and the intruder just disappeared. Our chap got on the phone at once and a couple of police cars were at the rectory within about twenty minutes, but it was no good. The significant thing is that our man is fairly sure the intruder was a woman. He can't be quite sure because whoever it was was in a dark sort of boiler suit, with a hood, or close-fitting cap. But he had a strong impression that it was a woman, and even thinks that he caught a slight whiff of scent—though that may be imagination. There were footmarks under the window where the intruder jumped down, apparently made by shoes about size 5. That is more a woman's size of shoe than a man's, but they were shoes of some plimsoll type, which might be worn by either a woman or a man with small feet. So the evidence is not at all conclusive, although the possible reappearance of a woman is certainly interesting."

"The catch on that window has been broken for years," Elizabeth said. 'I suppose I ought to have got it mended, but somehow I never got around to it."

Blundell sighed. "People simply invite thieves into their homes," he said. "Thousands of man-hours of police time would be saved if simple precautions about door-locks and window-latches were taken. But good door-locks and well-fitting windows protect against casual breakers-in: I don't think we can regard the intruder in the rectory last night as a villager having a look round. An old house like your rectory is seldom really very secure—anyone determined to get in could probably do so without much difficulty. You were certainly careless about that passage window, but I doubt if your carelessness had much to do with the entry, although it made it a bit easier for whoever it was to get in."

David was about to say something, when there was a hail from the cockpit. "Well clear of the Mew Stone now, sir, reckon it's about time to change course."

He went aft to have a look at things. He'd been so immersed in Blundell's story that he hadn't noticed the weather. It had markedly deteriorated. *Lily* was still heading more or less due south, and was now standing out into the Channel. She could still carry her full mainsail, but she was pressed hard over, and a vicious short sea was running at her. The Great Mew Stone rock was almost out of sight astern—it was high time to turn east to make their way towards Stoke Point and back into Bigbury Bay. This leg of the passage was not going to be comfortable.

Before putting *Lily* on the wind David decided to put two reefs in the mainsail. He reckoned that she could still carry her normal working jib, but she would be happier now with the reefed main. Martinson stayed at the tiller, and Fraser gave a hand with the reefing. When the sail was settled David took the tiller himself. Fraser took the jib sheets. "Ready about!" David said, then, "Lee-O!" He put the helm over, *Lily* came up into the wind, lost way, but went across sweetly. They hardened the sheets and began their beat towards Stoke Point.

Fortunately, they hadn't far to go—not much more than four miles of very uncomfortable sailing. But it was slow work. *Lily* gradually clawed her way to windward, but cascades of water swept her deck. As her bow slammed into the waves, the fo'c'sle became the most uncomfortable place on board. Blundell and Elizabeth were both seasick. Asking Martinson to take the tiller again, David went forward to persuade them to come into the cockpit. "Put on everything you've got in the way of warm clothes, and come into the open. It's cold and a bit wet, but you'll feel a lot better." Elizabeth went first, and Blundell followed. It was not easy to walk along the steeply heeled deck, and David tied a line to each of them in turn for the trip.

Safely in the cockpit, Elizabeth, now acutely unhappy, huddled on a thwart, and retched as unobtrusively as she could over the side. Blundell was equally unhappy, but did his best to talk in the intervals of being sick.

"We must pass pretty close to the site of the wreck, I suppose. Any chance of one of the divers going down?"

"Not in this weather," David said. "With luck it will moderate during the night, and we'll see what we can do tomorrow—that is, unless we have other things to deal with." His chief concern was to round Stoke Point and get to the anchorage near the diving camp. That was a reasonably sheltered cove, and once he could stop *Lily*'s pounding and get some hot drinks into the invalids, they'd soon begin to feel better. The two constables, with much more experience of small boats, were taking things quietly enough. It was a great help to have such a powerful crew with him.

At last the horrible passage came to an end. Once round Stoke Point *Lily* rode more easily. With about a half a mile to go before making the anchorage, David said, "If anybody sees us as we come in, it's important that only Elizabeth and I should appear to be on board. Can the rest of you go to the fo'c'sle? It's quieter now, and it won't be so bad in there. As soon as I've anchored, we'll have some hot soup."

"I'll get the Primus going, and if you'll tell me where the tins are, I'll make the soup," Fraser said.

"Good work. You'll find everything pretty well to hand." David explained where the food locker was, and added, "There's a choice of celery, Scotch broth, and tomato soup. I'd recommend tomato—it's one of the best things for settling an uneasy tummy. But go ahead and use whichever you like. You'll find mugs in the rack to port."

The three men went below, and Elizabeth got up gallantly to make herself conspicuous. "Oh, David," she said. "I'm so sorry to have let you down like this."

"You haven't let anybody down. Nobody can help being seasick, and it was a rotten trip."

She managed a rather wan smile, and went and stood near

154

the mast, holding on to one of the shrouds. David, accustomed to handling *Lily* singlehanded, took her just inside the cove and ran forward to let go the anchor. He was a bit farther out than he had been before, but he wanted to be sure that nobody who might be interested in *Lily* should be able to hear anything to suggest that there were more than two people on board.

With *Lily* at rest, and the hot soup inside them, they discussed a plan of action. It turned out to be a plan of inaction. David suggested that he and Elizabeth might go ashore, but Blundell was against this. "It's late in the afternoon," he said, "and although there's plenty of light now for people to have seen us come in, it will be dusk before much longer. This is a pretty deserted stretch of coast at this time of year, and if anybody has anything against you or Miss Danvers, it would be easy to have a go at you. And if you just didn't come back, we shouldn't know where to begin looking—besides, you'd have the dinghy ashore."

The wisdom of this seemed obvious. David and Elizabeth went on deck from time to time until it got dark, but Blundell and the constables kept below out of sight. There was not room for five people to lie down in *Lily*'s sparse accommodation, and they spent a wearisome and uncomfortable night. Tiresome as their cramped conditions were, David was bitterly disappointed when dawn came. Nothing at all had happened during the night.

# X

## *At Sea*

SERGEANT BLUNDELL WAS philosophical about
things. "It was worth a try," he said. "I suppose four-fifths of
our work is going up blind alleys—but unless you toil up and
down the blind alleys, you'll never find a through road. Don't
worry, Mr Grendon. You did everything in good faith, and
we'll just have to think of something else."

David was not comforted. He was not greatly upset at being
proved wrong—his theory remained a valid intellectual exercise,
and was wrong only because he hadn't known enough facts.
But it was not an intellectual exercise. He was convinced that
the threat to Elizabeth and her father was real—a conviction
borne out by the break-in at the rectory. He had hoped desperately that the reappearance of Elizabeth after she was supposed to be dead would prompt some action to indicate who
was endangering her. It hadn't, and now they were back where
they started, without the least idea of who was threatening her.
Or rather, they were worse off than when they started. The
theft of the chalice in itself had not seemed to pose any particular threat either to the rector, or his daughter. Life at the
rectory had gone on quite normally, with no sinister happenings. The threats had come because he, David, had interfered—
if he hadn't taken Elizabeth to the pub, nothing would have
happened. But if the accident to the Mini, the break-in at the
rectory, had happened *because* he had taken Elizabeth to the
pub, then he *couldn't* be wholly wrong—*somebody* connected
either with the diving camp or, perhaps, with the pub on the
cliff road, had something to do with the theft of the chalice,
and regarded the arrival of Elizabeth at the pub as a threat to
his or her security. Or her? Who was this woman who had
appeared twice in the case? So far as he knew, the police had
found nothing to indicate a woman as concerned in any way
with the theft. The mysterious Mr Platt might have been a

woman disguised as a man, but it didn't seem likely. Of course, Sergeant Blundell might know more than he had disclosed, but somehow David didn't think so.

He went on deck to have a look round. The cove was much as it was when he had last anchored in it—the diving team's cruiser was moored to a buoy off the beach, and there were various dinghies drawn up on the shore. There was no other sign of life, but there hadn't been before—and people wouldn't hang about in the cove when they had their camp to go to. Work on the wreck, presumably, was still going on, though how often the divers went out to it he didn't know.

Automatically, he took in the weather. The wind had backed a bit during the night, and was now coming more from the north again. The cove was well sheltered from the north so it was quiet enough where they lay, but it might still be blowing quite hard outside. He felt, though, that the wind had moderated. There were still white horses out to sea, but the waves didn't look as vicious as they had been yesterday.

He went below again to find Elizabeth and the policemen discussing breakfast. "Can we go on deck now?" Constable Fraser asked. "I'd rather like to have breakfast in the cockpit after a night cooped up in here."

David looked at the sergeant. "There's nobody about on the beach," he said, "but of course we can be seen plainly enough from the cliffs. Having gone so far, I feel we'd better carry the thing through. We've failed to achieve anything up to now, but we don't know how absolutely we've failed. We might want to try the plan again. If you can bear it, I think it would be better for everyone but Elizabeth and me to stay out of sight until we can't be seen from the shore."

Sergeant Blundell agreed. "Just as well not to give anything away," he said. "If the diving people don't show up, what are the chances of getting down to the wreck this morning?"

"Reasonably good, I should think," David replied. "It's not a nice day, but it's better than yesterday, and the wind's gone back to the north, which means that we'll get a bit of shelter from the land even when we go outside. I'm not a diver, so I don't know what conditions you can work in. But I'm confident that I can keep *Lily* in position to pick up anybody who can go down."

"Surface conditions don't make much difference once you're

157

fifteen feet or so below," Constable Martinson said. "And once you're on the seabed there can be a howling storm on top, and you'd never notice it. If you're using a diving suit and air line, you need a fairly calm surface for handling the gear, but for free-swimming skin diving all that really matters is for the boat to be able to stand by. I'd certainly like to go down, and I don't see why we shouldn't."

"I'm game," Fraser said. "It'll be a treat to have some exercise after last night."

Breakfast for five strained the resources of the single Primus somewhat, but Elizabeth turned out a splendidly hot meal of bacon and sausages. David's pumpernickel was not, on the whole, greatly appreciated, but they still had half a loaf of bread bought in Cargreen, and the three policemen topped off their meal with marmalade sandwiches. "Good as a hotel," Martinson said, grinning.

After breakfast, David and Elizabeth went on deck, Elizabeth again making herself as conspicuous as she could. The beach was quite deserted, and there seemed no point in hanging on in the cove any longer. Still feeling disheartened and disappointed, David got the sails up and brought in the anchor. With the offshore northerly wind, *Lily* ran briskly back to sea. When he was satisfied that no watcher from the shore could make out much detail of anything on board, David called the others and they joined him in the cockpit.

"I've only a rough idea of the position of the wreck," he said, "but the divers have buoyed it, and if we can find the buoy we should be all right. It will probably take about an hour to get there, and perhaps a bit more if we have to hunt for the buoy."

"Fine," Martinson said. "We'd have to wait a bit, anyway, after that big breakfast. What you say makes it about right." He smiled at Elizabeth. "And we'll be right hungry for lunch when we come up," he added.

David had taken rough bearings on the buoy when he'd come across it on his first trip out with Elizabeth. That was some time ago, but he'd jotted them down in the notebook in which he kept *Lily*'s working log. He remembered the buoy as not a particularly big one, and he feared that in the broken water it would not be easy to find. It wasn't. After getting to the area in which he believed the buoy to be, it took half an hour of searching on a grid of systematic short tacks before they found it. He was beginning to be really worried that it had perhaps been taken away, when Elizabeth spotted it. She pointed excitedly about two o'clock off the port bow. "Over there," she said, "I'm sure there's something there, David." He sailed closer, and she was right. "Good for you," he said with enormous relief. After the failure of his plan in the cove, it would have been a miserable further blow if he couldn't even find the wreck.

The police divers had not waited for the buoy before getting ready to go down. They had got into their wet suits, adjusted their frogman's gear, and were eager to go over the side. David had a short rope-ladder which he hung from *Lily*'s transom to provide a means of getting back on board—without some sort of boarding ladder it is extremely hard to climb into a boat from the water. The men checked watches and wrist compasses. David would have been happier if they'd gone down on a line, because he was on tenterhooks about spotting them when they wanted to be picked up. But both wanted to be able to work freely—and each carried a set of waterproof flares for emergency use. *Lily* would heave-to fairly well—a tribute to the generations of seamanship that had gone into her lines and her building. David decided to heave-to some way to windward of the buoy, so that she would drift on to it, and not away from it. They fixed a time at which the divers were to reappear, and with a cheerful wave, they went in.

Sergeant Blundell was also nervous. He was responsible for his two officers, and what he was letting them do seemed decidedly unorthodox. It would have been far better, he thought now, for the exploration of the wreck to be carried out openly, with a proper diving tender and a skilled crew. But the arguments against this still had force. There was no evidence that the treasure seekers on the wreck were anything other than they appeared to be, and the failure of the plan to entice anybody to investigate Elizabeth's reappearance rather suggested that they were in the clear as far as anything to do with jewel robberies was concerned. But there was still a lot left unexplained, and if there was any sort of criminal activity going on, open police investigation of the wreck would at once alert everyone concerned. And the divers had gone down, now—it was too late to change the plan of action, unhappy as he was about it.

"I shall be thankful when they're both back on board," he said to David.

"So shall I. But they're highly trained men, and know just what they're doing. They ought to be all right. We've simply got to do our job, and stay put."

"The waiting part is always the hardest part of anything."

Elizabeth, having taken the point about lunch, had gone below to put hot soup in vacuum flasks, and to make a stew of everything that *Lily* could provide. David and Sergeant Blundell stood together in the cockpit, David tense to every movement of *Lily*'s, keyed up to try to take in every yard of her drift. Blundell stared at the buoy as if hypnotised by it, longing to see heads breaking the water as the hands of his watch crawled to the time of their rendezvous.

Keeping *Lily* to windward of the buoy meant, in the northerly wind, that they were inshore of it, with their backs to the land, as it were. Thus it was Elizabeth, coming up from the fo'c'sle to throw potato peelings overboard, who saw the cruiser, working out around the headland. "That looks like the diving boat," she said. "And she's coming towards us."

David and Blundell turned together. The cruiser was still a mile or so away, but she was certainly the diving tender because the crane or gantry she carried stood out clearly. "What the hell do we do now?" Blundell asked.

"Nothing," David said. "We're a fishing-boat, and we're fishing—there's no earthly reason why we shouldn't be. I'll put a line over the side to make it look a bit better. We can't go away, because we've got to stand by to pick up our divers."

"What happens when they come up?"

"God knows. They may not like it, but we're not doing anything wrong."

The cruiser appeared to take no notice of them. As she came nearer David could see two people on board, but whether there were others down below he couldn't know. She passed *Lily* within about a quarter of a mile, and proceeded a little distance beyond the buoy, where she throttled down to just steerage way. She was steered from a wheelhouse amidships. David could see a figure in the wheelhouse, apparently at the wheel,

160

but the wheelhouse was glassed in, and he could not make out through the windows who it was.

A few minutes after throttling down the other figure visible on board came on to the foredeck. It was a man equipped for diving, wearing a wet suit and goggles. He threw over a short rope-ladder, and climbed down into the sea. He used only one hand to climb down—the other was holding what looked like a harpoon gun, and he had various canisters or containers of some sort attached to his belt. The water closed over his head, and he was gone. The cruiser proceeded in a wide, slow circle, which would keep her roughly in position. No one else appeared on deck.

"Ten minutes to go," Blundell said. "If our chaps come up on time we may be able to get away before the other bloke comes back."

"I expect they'll be on time," David said.

They were not. With three minutes still to go an orange flare went up about 200 yards off *Lily*'s starboard bow and a figure broke the surface, swimming desperately towards them. The flare had gone up to leeward of the boat, and the moment he saw it David freed *Lily*'s sheets and as she gathered way stood over towards it. The swimmer had covered perhaps half the distance when *Lily* came up to him. It was Martinson. He grabbed a rung of *Lily*'s boarding ladder and Blundell leaned over to help him into the cockpit. As he came over the side he gasped out, "He's killed Fraser—shot him with a harpoon. I've only got a knife. Give me the long boathook and I'll go down after him."

"No," Blundell said. "He's got to come up himself. We'll get him then."

There wasn't time. While they were getting Martinson back on board, the other diver surfaced near the cruiser, and as Blundell was speaking he was going up the rope-ladder. The cruiser opened up her engine as he clambered over the side. Now she was making straight towards them.

*Lily*, with the strong northerly behind her, was also moving fast. She couldn't compete with the cruiser for speed, but she was considerably more manoeuvrable. David held on until the cruiser was about 50 yards astern, then he put the helm hard

161

over, and swung through 90 degrees, still keeping to windward of the powered boat. His manoeuvre disconcerted whoever was in the wheelhouse, and the cruiser, going flat out, passed astern of them, and was 100 yards away before she could be brought round. She didn't come on again at once. What did happen was that a rifle bullet crashed into *Lily*'s counter. The cruiser came towards them quite slowly, the man in diving dress firing at them from the foredeck.

*Lily*'s fish-hold offered some cover, but her cockpit was horribly exposed. David shouted to Elizabeth, Blundell and Martinson to get down into the fish-hold, and he crouched as low as he could while still being able to steer and sail *Lily*. He didn't see much hope for any of them. It could only be a question of time before he was hit. *Lily* would then be out of control, she would probably broach to, and the cruiser could close them at leisure. The rifleman could then shoot them one by one, come on board, and find some means of sinking *Lily*. He probably had some kind of explosive for use in his diving work, and it would be easy enough to blow a hole in *Lily*'s bottom; if not, he could use the rifle to punch a series of holes in her planking below the water-line. No one would know where *Lily* had sunk, and he could get away with all trace of her vanished. Even if some of her wreckage ultimately fetched up somewhere, it would be some days before it did, and with the cruiser at his disposal he could be in France or Spain with whatever loot he had managed to collect before anyone had any idea of where to look for him. David had hoped that Elizabeth's reappearance might prompt some kind of attack on her, in the course of which their strong police force would be able to arrest the attacker. It had not occurred to him that it would be far simpler—and likely to be much more successful —to attack *Lily* herself at sea. That was an appalling miscalculation—what a mess he'd made of things!

His mind went on working while the man on the cruiser took pot shots at him. The shooting was not very good—*Lily* was a moving target, and the foredeck of a motor cruiser in a fairly tumbled sea is not a good shooting platform. It didn't matter. They had no rifles on board *Lily*, and the rifleman on the cruiser could take his time.

Suddenly a thought struck him—if he could avoid being hit for just a few more minutes, they might have one slim chance.

*Lily* was now on a broad reach, a good point of sailing for her, and she was still to windward of the cruiser. The cruiser was closing them at an angle, making roughly towards her port quarter. With about 75 yards between them, David repeated his previous manoeuvre in reverse—where before he had turned to change a running to a reaching course, he now turned to bring the wind dead astern.

The manoeuvre had one immediate advantage: it swung the cockpit away from the cruiser, and put the rifleman off his aim. It also swung *Lily*'s bow towards the cruiser. Before the helmsman in the wheelhouse had time to realise what was happening, *Lily*, with the full weight of the still strong wind behind her, was bearing down directly on the cruiser.

The cruiser tried to swing away, but Lily had a bone in her teeth and closed the short remaining distance too quickly for the cruiser to escape. She struck just forward of the wheel-house, where the rifleman was standing. Her long bowsprit hit him in the chest with the force of a projectile. There was a dreadful scream, but the man must have screamed a fraction of a second before *Lily* struck, for he could not have survived the blow. David saw what was left of his body tossed contemptuously over the side.

*Lily* went on. Her heavy bow and powerful shoulders, with all the strength that the craftsmanship of David's grandfather could give them, followed the bowsprit. The glass fibre hull of the cruiser was smashed through by the weight of *Lily*'s timbers, and the sea poured into the huge, gaping hole in her side. Within less than a minute of *Lily*'s strike, she was foundering.

The door of the wheelhouse was flung open, and a woman clambered out on to the sinking deck. "You bastard pigs," she screamed. "Take what you've come for—if you can get it!" She flung something that glittered into the sea, and jumped in after it.

David had no recollection afterwards of why he acted as he did: he dived after what the woman had thrown. He saw it half-floating for a second or so before it turned over and began to go down. Just before it sank out of reach he managed to grab it. It was surprisingly heavy, and awkward to hold while swimming. He turned over on his back and made towards *Lily* with the Combe Dean chalice clasped to his breast.

The cruiser, her decks awash, still floated, but only because she was entangled with *Lily*'s bowsprit. As David neared the boats the weight of water in the cruiser became too much for the bowsprit to support, and it broke. The cruiser wallowed for a moment, and then sank like a stone. David felt himself being sucked down, and the heavy gold chalice in his arms did not help. He had a moment of panic, but he was a little too far to be dragged directly into the cruiser's vortex, and he did not go deep. He struggled to the surface, his mouth full of water, and gasping for breath. He was thankful to reach *Lily*'s counter and clutch the boarding ladder. Sergeant Blundell leaned over, took the chalice from him, and helped him on board.

*Lily* was sinking, too. Her sturdy old timbers had vanquished her enemy, but the shock was mortal to her time-worn fastenings and several feet of her planking had been torn open. The breaking bowsprit had snapped her forestay, and the mast leaned drunkenly, still held by the shrouds, but the strain on them was so great that they, or the chain-plates, could not hold much longer. But *Lily* would not give in as easily as the cruiser. She was down by the head, her fo'c'sle already full of water, but the bulkhead aft of the fo'c'sle, although weeping badly, still held. It would go soon, and some of her after planking had also opened, but she would give her people time to think what to do.

Constable Martinson had gone in after the woman, and soon after David was back on board he reappeared at the stern. He had not been able to find her, and he had had to swim clear to avoid being dragged down himself when the cruiser rolled over and sank. The woman, who must have been nearer the cruiser, was presumably sucked down with her. "She may come to the surface again," Martinson said, "but without a lifebelt I doubt if she could stay afloat for long in this sea. It's pretty cold, and even a good swimmer can't survive long without protective clothing."

David was shivering violently. "We're not going to be afloat much longer," he said. "Thank God for the rubber dinghy. Better get it over the side quickly."

Blundell and Martinson launched the dinghy. Elizabeth rubbed David's hands, which were blue with cold. All their spare clothing was under water in the fo'c'sle, but David remembered an old pullover and a torn pair of jeans that he

164

kept for use as rags in one of the cockpit lockers. His own hands were too numb to work. He told Elizabeth where the rags were, and asked her to get them. "They'll be better than nothing," he said.

Elizabeth got the old clothes, and threw them into the dinghy. Then, to David's horror, she ran forward to the waterlogged fo'c'sle, and appeared to dive into it. She crawled back in triumph, with two vacuum flasks. "The hot soup I made," she said. 'It mayn't be very hot now, but the flasks aren't broken, and like your clothes it will be better than nothing."

There was not much time left. Water was lapping over the gunwale into the cockpit. *Lily* lay heavily, her mast swaying more dangerously with every wave that came over her, every movement of the mast straining her timbers and opening more of her planking. She had no longer any freeboard—the dinghy floated level with her deck. They must get clear of her before she went down. Something prompted David to an odd formality —at least they would leave with dignity. "All hands abandon ship," he said. Blundell and Martinson helped Elizabeth into the dinghy, and then Blundell held out a hand to him. David shook his head—he wanted to be the last to leave. "Oars okay?" he asked. "Yes. In you go then, and I'll follow." As he got into the dinghy *Lily* gave a sickening lurch. The dinghy was still held to her by the painter. He didn't try to untie it, but cut the painter with his knife. Martinson was already at the oars, and pulled away as quickly as he could. As soon as they were well clear of *Lily* he stopped rowing—by some unspoken instinct, all felt that they must wait now until *Lily* had gone. She did not keep them waiting. Her mast subsided, quite slowly, and she rolled over as it fell. Gallantly, even at that last moment, she tried to right herself, but with no buoyancy left she could not recover against the leverage exerted by the fallen mast. She gave a sort of gasp as the last air was forced out of her, and went under.

Elizabeth was crying. "Poor good old *Lily*," she said.

"She gave her life for us, and that's that," David said. The sentiment did not strike anyone as at all forced.

They had now to think about themselves. Martinson was the best off, because he was still wearing his wet-suit. The others were all soaked through, David in slightly the worst state because he had been in the sea. The rags he had rescued from the locker were not much use, though they might serve as a sort of blanket. Elizabeth opened her soup. How the flasks had survived in the collision, and how Elizabeth had managed to find them, seemed to David to come into the category of miracle, but they had survived, and the soup in them was still quite hot. They decided to drink the soup in one of them there and then, and to keep the other flask for use later. There was a lidful of soup for all of them, and they felt much better after it had gone down. Martinson had not rowed while they sorted themselves out, and they were still not far from the buoy. "How long do you think we ought to spend looking for the woman? And ought we to try to look for Fraser? We don't really know what happened yet," David said.

"There's nothing we can do for Fraser," Martinson replied. "Of course we must try to recover his body, but that will need a proper diving team to search for it. I could go down again, but my air-bottle is pretty well finished, so I couldn't stay down long. And in this wind it wouldn't be easy to hold the dinghy, and I might have trouble getting back. I'm game to go down if you think it's any use, but in the time I could stay down I doubt very much if I could even find the body."

"No, I'm not letting you go down," Blundell said. "I take full responsibility for that—in fact, I give you a formal order not to go down. But what happened to Fraser?"

"We found the wreck all right, and we began a fairly systematic examination of it. The ship's three-parts buried in sand, but the outline of the hull can still be made out. I started at the bow, and Fraser went to the stern: we intended to work towards each other, to meet about amidships, taking note of anything we could. I got along quicker than Fraser. There isn't much left of the deck, but the side timbers seem more or less in place. There'd be great holds, and presumably the remains of the crew's quarters, buried in the sand, but it would need a lot of equipment to excavate them. There was nothing I could do except make a mental picture of the shape of the vessel.

"I'd worked my way amidships while Fraser was still on the poop, or where the poop would have been, I suppose. I couldn't see very well, but he seemed to have found some place he could get down into—I expect that's where the other divers had been working. I was going towards him when I saw this other man in a frogman's outfit swimming towards him. Fraser must have sensed something, for he turned to meet him. The man had some sort of harpoon-gun, and he let it off at Fraser at almost point-blank range. I saw the harpoon strike—it must have pretty well gone through him. I saw Fraser collapse, and the man then pulled a knife and slashed at Fraser's harness, cutting away his air-bottle, I think, so that even if Fraser wasn't quite dead, he wouldn't have a chance.

"All this happened in a few seconds; maybe I ought to have acted quicker, but it was all so extraordinary that I suppose it took me a bit of time to realise what was happening. Anyway, I started to go towards Fraser when the man got out another harpoon and began coming at me. If I'd had a lance, or anything longer than my knife, I think I'd have tried to tackle him, but I had no chance at all against his harpoon. All I could do was to dodge away, and get back upstairs as fast as I could. I thought if I could get hold of a boathook I'd go down again after the murdering swine."

"Just as well you didn't. It was a good effort, Martinson, there was nothing else you could do. Anyway, he didn't stay down for you to come after him, but came after us instead. And killing Fraser didn't do him any good—or the woman. I wonder who the hell she is—or was, I suppose I should say."

They had been blown some distance from the buoy while Martinson was talking, and already it was impossible to be sure just where *Lily* and the cruiser had gone down. They were so low in the water that they could not make out anything beyond the tumbled seas immediately around them. David thought that there might be some floating wreckage from *Lily* but there was nothing they could see. It was pointless to hang about on the faint chance that the woman's body might come up again—even if it did, the odds against its reappearance anywhere within reach were many millions to one. David considered what to do.

"We're not more than two or three miles offshore," he said, "but we can't row ashore against this wind, though we can use the oars to check our drift to sea. The tide will be making soon, and with any luck the flood will help us—if the wind drops, it will carry us inshore, and even if it doesn't it will give us a chance to hold our own with the oars. It may be hours before

167

we get anywhere, but there's always a chance that we may be picked up. It will be damned uncomfortable, but the rubber dinghy's safe enough. The main thing is to try to keep warm. We can take it in turns to row, and when we're not rowing we'd better rub our limbs and clap our arms to keep the circulation going."

Elizabeth and Blundell were seasick again, but this was partly reaction to the strain of events. The dinghy's motion in the choppy sea was at first unpleasant, but they found themselves getting used to it: with no power to drive her into a sea she rode the waves like a gull sitting on the water, yielding to everything, but taking very little spray on board. Martinson rowed, but he could do little more than hold the dinghy's head to the wind. The distant line of the coast got no nearer, but it didn't seem to get much farther off. The tide, David reckoned, must have turned.

Blundell fiddled with the little police radio he still had in his pocket. It had been agreed that no radio was to be used from *Lily*, in case anyone on shore who might be interested in them was capable of listening in. 'I wish I'd had the sense to radio for help when he started shooting at us," he said, "but everything happened so quickly that I didn't think of it—it wouldn't have done much good, anyway, because no one could have got to us in time. Now the damned thing's soaking wet, and doesn't seem to work. Apart from anything else, I'd like to be able to report that we've got the Combe Dean chalice—I suppose that's something on the credit side."

David was thinking of Fraser, and *Lily*. "I suppose so," he said. "But, God knows, we've had to pay for it."

"Was Constable Fraser married?" Elizabeth asked.

"No," Martinson replied. "He lived with his mother—it'll be a bad blow to her. But he had a younger brother, and a married sister, so it's not like as if he was an only son. It's odd how practically everything bad could be a bit worse."

"It's bad enough," Elizabeth said. "He was so nice."

"He couldn't have known much about what happened."

"Perhaps not. But why kill a man like that? Why go straight down and kill somebody?" Blundell asked.

"I don't know what he saw in his part of the wreck,"

168

Martinson said. "He must have seen something which the other man thought was so dangerous that he had to be killed."

"Maybe we shall find out about that later. But he took his harpoon-gun down with him. Obviously he went down ready to use it."

"Whoever they were, I think they came out meaning to do in Elizabeth and me," David said. "They could have caught up with *Lily* easily enough, and with that rifle they could have settled us, and then come on board to sink *Lily*. Or they could have chucked us over the side and just left *Lily* to drift—when she was found it would be presumed that we must somehow have fallen overboard. What upset them, I think, was finding *Lily* hove-to near the wreck. They had to assume either that one of us was a diver and had gone down, or that we had a diver on board with us. So the man had to go down to find out what was happening. What he did find obviously seemed to threaten them so much that he killed Fraser on the spot and then came back to deal with us. Why did they have the chalice with them? Do you think they meant to plant it in the wreck and find it today?"

Blundell thought a bit before answering. Then he said, "It looks a bit like it, but I don't see how we can know. There are two main possibilities. The first is the obvious one that they simply kept the chalice on board the cruiser. They had to keep it somewhere, and the cruiser would be as good a place as any. Then when the cruiser was sinking and the man was dead, the woman chucked it overboard in a final fit of rage. She didn't know that *Lily* was sinking too, and she didn't have a chance any longer against all of us. But it may be that they did intend to plant it today. We don't know what was really worrying them, but something must have been worrying them very much indeed, or they wouldn't have taken such desperate measures against us. Perhaps they thought that we were getting wise to the wreck, and that they'd got to find the chalice there pretty quickly."

"It's maddening not to know," David said. "We don't even know who they were. The man was dressed up in diving gear with a rubber cap—it might or might not have been the Layton man, but I certainly couldn't recognise him. As for the woman —until she rushed out at the last moment we only saw her through the window of the wheelhouse, and I didn't even know

169

that it was a woman. And when she rushed out she was wearing an oilskin jacket with a hood. She might have been anybody."

"She might have been the girl we met in the pub," Elizabeth said.

"She might. She might equally well have been the waitress in the hotel where we had lunch. Or my cousin in Scotland. I wonder if we shall ever know?"

In spite of clapping his arms, David was still shivering. He took over the oars from Martinson for a spell of rowing, and this gradually brought some warmth back into his body. After half an hour of rowing he gave Blundell a turn, and then made Elizabeth have a go. It was during Elizabeth's spell that they noticed a slightly different motion in the dinghy—she was actually beginning to move through the water, instead of just being tossed up and down more or less where she was.

"Wind's dropping!" Martinson exclaimed.

It was. It was also getting dark, and the line of the land they had been able to make out was merging into a blur of sea and sky. Martinson was the strongest of the party, and David asked him to take the oars again. With his powerful stroke the dinghy was soon moving quite quickly. He still had his wrist compass, and David asked him to keep an eye on it. "When it's properly dark we may be able to see some shore lights," he said, "but it's just as well to keep going in the right direction. Try to hold her a shade west of north. The current is probably setting a bit east—we don't want to be carried too far down the coast. And we don't want to fetch up at the foot of the cliffs. If we head a little west, with luck we'll be carried back towards the cove we left this morning."

Blundell gave a grunt of triumph. "I think I've got the radio to work," he said. He spoke into it. "Sergeant Blundell here, Sergeant Blundell, calling Police Control. Can you read me? Can you read me?"

The others could hear a voice coming back. "You're very faint, but I can just about make you out. Carry on."

"I can hear you okay but I'm sending under difficulty. I don't think the battery will last long."

"Understood. Carry on, then."

"Constable Fraser is dead. Constable Martinson, Miss Danvers, Mr Grendon and I have been shipwrecked. We have recovered the Combe Dean chalice. I repeat, we have recovered the Combe Dean chalice. We are now in a rubber dinghy rowing towards the shore."

"Where are you? Can you send up a flare?"

"Just where would you say we are?" Blundell asked David. "And have we got any flares?"

"I have one flare," David said, "but there's no point in sending it up at the moment. There's no ship in sight, and while a coastguard might see it from the shore there's not much he could do because we haven't any other light to guide any boat he might send out to us. We're in no immediate danger. As for where we are, I don't know exactly, but I'm hoping that we're making towards the western end of Bigbury Bay. Ask him if he can get a police car to patrol the cliff road, say in a couple of hours' time. If we can keep going as we are now we should be ashore in about three hours, and if we can land somewhere near the cove we can get up to the road. If there could be a car on the road above the cove with lights shining out to sea, it would be a big help."

Blundell passed on this information, but as he was finishing the radio went dead. "That's that," he said. "I think he got most of it, though."

"What about the rest of the soup?" Elizabeth asked. "We might as well have it before it's stone cold."

"I'm horribly thirsty," Blundell said.

David was sitting aft, Blundell was in the bow. "Just ahead of where you're sitting," David told him, "there's a sort of little apron. I keep one or two things there, and there should be a plastic jar—it's an old orange juice jar—full of water. It won't be all that fresh, but it's all right."

Blundell felt around. "Yes, there is," he said.

"Well, here's the cup from the flask of soup we had before." David passed it up to him. "Give yourself a drink, and then send the jar and cup back to us. We could all do with a drink. Then we'll have the remains of Elizabeth's soup."

Stale as it was, the water seemed delicious, and they all felt better for it. The soup was still warm, and that was another good reviver. David relieved Martinson at the oars. "We'll do half-hour spells," he said. "The oarsman better have the compass. You can't row a rubber dinghy very accurately, but if we try to keep about north-north-west we should be all right."

Elizabeth insisted on taking her turn at the oars, but they wanted to row hard now, so they limited her spell to fifteen minutes. In the middle of David's second spell, Blundell, who was looking out in the bow, said, "I can see car lights." David rested for a moment, and looked round. "No doubt about that," he said. He took a quick compass bearing on the lights. "We should be in quite soon now. I reckon we're close enough inshore now to head straight for the lights. If we're carried a little past them it won't matter, for we can easily row back." He bent again to the oars.

When his half-hour was up Blundell offered to relieve him, but David said he'd carry on. "We can see the line of the beach now, no sense in losing time by changing over."

A few minutes later a wave carried them up the beach and the dinghy grounded. David stowed his oars and jumped out. "We've lost the painter because I had to cut it," he said, "but I've got a spare line on the grapnel." He held the dinghy's bow while the others got out. Then he got the grapnel and hitched the line to the cut end of the painter. Martinson helped him to haul the dinghy up the beach. "At least I've still got a dinghy," David reflected. "And we're alive, and Fraser isn't." They began to walk up the beach when he remembered that the chalice was still in the boat. "Lord, we've forgotten the chalice," he said, and ran back for it.

# XI

## *Chain of Circumstance*

THERE WERE THREE police cars on the cliff road, and the reception party included Chief Inspector Evans, Inspector Cornish and the police doctor who had attended David and Elizabeth after their car accident. "You two again!" he said cheerfully. "I shall really have to send you to hospital this time—and get them to keep you there."

"We're not going to hospital," David said. "We want some dry clothes."

Chief Inspector Evans saw that David was carrying the chalice. He took it from him gently, and held it in one of the car headlamps. The heavy gold glowed almost as if it had a light of its own. "It seems quite undamaged," the Chief Inspector said. "I don't know how you managed it, but it was a wonderful piece of work to get it back."

"For God's sake put it somewhere safe. It's caused enough trouble."

Martinson was still in his wet-suit. It had been useful wear in the dinghy, but was uncomfortable on land. Blundell, Elizabeth and David were all wet through, though their clothes had dried on them to some extent. "Is there any reason why we shouldn't go home to the rectory now?" Elizabeth asked.

There didn't seem to be any reason, so it was arranged that one of the cars should take Elizabeth and David to Combe Dean. The doctor went with them. Blundell went home in one of the other cars, the two senior officers accompanying him. "I'll give you a report as soon as I've changed," he said.

"There have been some developments here, too," said the Chief Inspector.

Martinson went off in the third car. "There's nothing more that you can do tonight, but I'd like you to come to headquarters in the morning," Inspector Cornish said to him. "We

173

must make a thorough search of that wreck as soon as we can, and we'll need your help. But that's for the morning. The main thing now is for you to get a decent meal and have a rest."

"It's like coming home from school," Elizabeth said, as their car drove up to the rectory.

"Or waking up after a bad dream." David felt drained of all feeling. One thoroughly decent man had gone to his death, two other people, who were probably not very nice, but who had been alive and full of hopes and plans a few hours ago, were also dead. He had lost *Lily*. He was overwhelmingly tired.

Elizabeth was excited. There were some letters on the mat as she opened the door, and she picked them up. "A telephone bill, a circular from the diocese, a letter from the rural dean—it's hard to believe that ordinary life has been going on all the time," she said. "Oh, and there's one for you, David."

He put the envelope in his pocket without looking at it. "Don't let's bother with them now," he said. "Can we raise hot water for a bath?"

"Well, the boiler will be out. But we've got an immersion heater, though we try not to use it because electricity is so expensive."

"Let's be spendthrifts and get it going. I desperately need a bath, and a hot bath will be good for you, too. While you're dealing with the immersion heater I'll get the boiler lighted—I know where the things are."

They'd forgotten that the doctor was still with them. "I don't want to interfere with domesticity," he said, "but I'm not at all sure that either of you is fit for carrying on like this tonight. You, Mr Grendon, had quite a severe wound in your thigh only a few nights ago, and Miss Danvers was badly bruised. Goodness knows what you have gone through in your ship-wreck. I think you must let me examine you—and I hope you will take my advice."

"Oh, Lord," David said. Then he was ashamed of himself for appearing rude, and went on, "I'm sorry, doctor. It's awfully good of you to come home with us, but we've a hell of a lot to think about, and we really must get into some dry clothes."

"Well, I can have a look at you while you're changing. Perhaps I can go up with Miss Danvers now, and if you feel

174

you really must light the boiler straight away, I'll examine you when you're through with it."

David would have preferred to have a bath before changing but the doctor seemed such a decent chap that he just nodded agreement. Elizabeth, whose bruises were much better, was given a fair bill of health, though the doctor urged her to try to take things quietly over the next few days. He was less pleased with David. "That cut of yours has opened up again, and you have lost a good deal of blood."

"Probably happened when I was swimming."

"That seems quite likely. And the wet clothes helped you a bit by clinging to the wound and reducing bleeding somewhat."

"Salt water is supposed to be a good antiseptic."

"I'm not greatly worried about infection, though I'll give you another injection, and I'd like you to take one of these tablets every four hours for the next three days. But you have lost more blood than is good for you, and you really ought to go to hospital for a bit."

"I am not going to hospital. I've lost my boat, and that means I've lost my job, and most of what I possessed has gone down with her. I've just got to get on with trying to sort out things."

"David, please do what the doctor says. I shall be perfectly all right here—and I expect Daddy will come back soon."

"No, Elizabeth, I'll take the tablets, and I'll be as sensible as I can, but I have a fearful lot to do. I must talk to Jess Grimble as soon as possible, for one thing."

The doctor shook his head. "Very well, then, I give up," he said. "You've got youth and general fitness on your side, and we'll hope for the best. But I shall have to put some stitches in your wound, and I'd rather you didn't have a bath for the next twenty-four hours to give the thing a chance to knit. And don't go swimming again for two or three weeks. You have my telephone number—if you haven't a regular doctor of your own, get in touch with me at once if anything seems to be going wrong. And if you're still in this part of the world next week, let me know, and I'll arrange to take out the stitches."

"All right. Please don't think I'm ungrateful, I'm really not. It's simply that I've got so much else to do; I'll swap my bath for not going to hospital, anyway—much as I want a hot bath."

The doctor laughed. "You're an obstinate young man, but you've got a certain amount of pluck. I can give you a local anaesthetic from what I've got with me, but I'm afraid the stitches may hurt a bit. They'd do the job much better in hospital, but there it is."

The stiches did hurt, but David was beyond caring. He was thankful when the doctor went away.

Elizabeth was much concerned about David, but he refused to be fussed over. "Having gone to all this trouble to get hot water, you might as well have a bath," he said. "I can at least find some dry clothes in my room. While you're having a bath I'll see if I can rustle up some supper."

There wasn't much food in the house, but he found a few eggs in the refrigerator, and there was a tin of biscuits. Elizabeth came down to find a meal of scrambled eggs and coffee on the kitchen table. "I don't know why I let you order me around like this," she said, "and after tonight I'm not going to. But it's been such a bewildering day that I scarcely know where I am."

"Well, I expect you're pretty hungry. I certainly am. Let's eat what we've got and go to bed. We'll face tomorrow when it comes."

Over their meal Elizabeth said, "There's one thing I must do before I go to bed—I must tell Daddy that the chalice has been found. But I'm not at all sure how to do it."

"There's the telephone—even All Saints at Oxford must have a telephone by now."

"That's just it. They do have a telephone because I tried to ring Daddy when he was staying there once before. But I think they keep it hidden under the stairs, or something. And I don't think anybody answers it after six o'clock."

David laughed. "I'm a Cambridge man, and I don't know anything about these Oxford customs. Why not ring Sir George Dorrance? He'll be nearly as pleased as your father, and he can dig him out and tell him."

"That's a good idea. I'll go and do it now." She went off to telephone, and was away for what seemed to David a long time. She came back looking excited. "I told him," she said, "and he asked a lot of questions about how we found it. He

176

says that as far as he can see you're entitled to the £10,000 reward."

"Then he can have another think," David said. "I'm going to bed."

On the bed he found his letter, lying where he had thrown it when he had taken it out of the pocket of his wet clothes. He was not expecting any letter, and not much interested in it, but he thought he'd better see what it was about. It was a communication from Messrs Bray, Bray, Bickersnatch and Bray informing him that a petition for divorce by Mrs Louise Grendon, having been undefended, had been duly granted, with costs against Mr David Grendon. Messrs Bray, Bray, etc. had pleasure in enclosing their bill, and would be grateful to receive payment at Mr Grendon's earliest convenience.

He threw it on the floor, and without even bothering to undress lay down on the bed and went to sleep.

He was woken up by Elizabeth. "I'm awfully sorry," she said, "but there's a newspaper reporter—I think there are actually about four newspaper reporters—and a man from Television News and a man from the radio. There are a lot of photographers, too, and they are all asking for you."

"But it's not yet eight o'clock!"

"I know, David—it's awful. But I didn't ask them to come. And how do we get them to go away?"

"Well, I'm dressed, anyway. I suppose we'll have to see them. I wish I knew what the police have said, or what they're expecting us to say. Look, while I'm talking to them, can you ring Blundell and ask for his advice?"

Reluctant as he was to be interviewed, David accepted that the recovery of the chalice was important news, and that the reporters had to do their job. The main facts of the story had been given in an official statement by the police, and in some respects the reporters knew more than he did. They knew, for instance, that Mr Philip Layton and Miss Sheila Davies had been missing from the diving camp since yesterday morning, that the cruiser apparently belonged to Mr Layton, and that if Mr Layton and Miss Davies were not the man and woman lost at sea, the police were extremely anxious to get in touch with them. David could add nothing to this. The police

177

statement simply said that three officers, acting on information received, had been on board Mr Grendon's fishing-boat *Lily*, and continued with a brief factual account of the events that led to the recovery of the chalice. David refused to be drawn into any discussion of why he and the police had been out in *Lily*, but he gave a straightforward account of how they had been fired on from the cruiser, of the collision, of his dive to recover the chalice, and of the sinking of the two boats. That was a good enough story for the moment. But the reporters wanted Elizabeth, too. "I'll see if I can find her," David said, knowing that she was telephoning Blundell.

She was putting down the phone as he got to her, and they had a few hurried words together before going back to face the news men. "I got hold of him all right," she said, "and he's coming out to see us later in the morning. He says there isn't much doubt that the man was Layton and the woman the girl we met in the pub—that she was older than she looked, and that the police now know a good deal about her. He says that she was going to be arrested anyway yesterday morning, if she hadn't gone off in the cruiser. He says it's such a big news story that there isn't much we can do but answer the reporters' questions, but that we must try to keep off making statements about Mr Layton and the girl, since they can't be charged with anything if they're dead. Oh, David, what a horried muddle it all is. I wish we knew more about it."

He patted her shoulder. "Well, we don't," he said. "Come and face the music—these chaps seem quite a decent lot, and they haven't been too bad so far."

After Elizabeth had given her account of the events on *Lily*, and much photographing of both her and David, one of the reporters asked, "What about the reward, Mr Grendon? It certainly looks as if it ought to go to you. Are you going to claim it?"

"No," David said firmly.

The news party was somewhat startled.

"Do you really mean that? Aren't you even going to claim £10,000?"

"I'm claiming nothing, except that I have got some insurance on my boat, and naturally I want that paid if possible. If there is a reward for getting back the chalice, it ought to go to

178

Constable Fraser's family. It's nothing to do with me, and I want nothing to do with it."

"Can we quote you as saying that, Mr Grendon?"

"Yes."

At last the Press party went away, and then the phone started ringing. It was more newspapers and radio and TV programmes from London. After Elizabeth had answered the telephone for the sixth time in just over half an hour David said, "I don't care what the Post Office says—take the thing off the hook. We haven't had any breakfast yet."

While they were having breakfast, a police car brought Sergeant Blundell. He accepted a cup of coffee and talked to them in the kitchen. He had been up most of the night and looked tired, but he was decidedly cheerful. "Thanks to you," he said, "I seem to have been given a good mark. The high-ups are cock-a-hoop that we've got back the chalice, and since I'm the nearest policeman involved they're pleased with me. Not that I had much to do with it."

"You had a great deal to do with it," David said. "You didn't laugh at my theories, you took our car accident seriously, and you came with us on *Lily*. I don't see what more any policeman could have done."

"I might have thought up the theories."

"You're not a fisherman, and you didn't go to the pub. Come off it. But you haven't told us about the woman. We know nothing about that side of things. Who was she?"

"Quite a lot happened while we were at sea—it was really due to Miss Danvers, I think," Blundell added inconsequentially. He went on, "I didn't tell you, because it was departmental work, and there was no reason why I should, but before I met you at Plymouth Inspector Cornish and I had a long meeting with Commander Furness, who is head of the special Fine Art Squad of the Metropolitan Police. He had a jewellery expert with him, and they were both very interested in one of the pieces that newspaper story was about—the ones alleged to have been recovered from the *Madras* and handed to the Receiver of Wreck at Plymouth. The piece that particularly interested them was a ruby, bearing some resemblance to a stone reported stolen a year or so ago, in a setting apparently by an eighteenth-century French goldsmith, that might have come from another big jewel robbery. The police put in a lot of work on both robberies, but got nowhere, except to find out that a girl answering to much the same description had worked in both the country houses robbed, in one case as a secretary, in the other as a lady's maid. She had different names—the secretary was called Emily Benson, the lady's maid Josephine Edwards. Neither seemed to have any relations, and though they both had references, which were duly checked, they were the kind of references that didn't mean much—they gave the names of various employers, and the girls—or girl, if it was the same girl—had certainly worked there, though never for more than a few months, giving up the jobs for apparently quite good reasons, which, it turned out, couldn't be checked. Both girls had left the country houses concerned in the robberies shortly before the robberies took place. Naturally the police tried to trace them, but in neither case did they have any luck. One problem was that nobody seemed to have a photograph of Josephine Edwards, and the only picture of Emily Benson was in a fairly large group of spectators at a cricket match in the grounds of the place where she worked.

"There was no sort of evidence against the girls, but their disappearance—for neither ever has been traced—was certainly a bit odd, though it's not uncommon nowadays for young women to do a job for a bit, then drift off into some casual relationship, and when that breaks up, to take a job again. They may even change their names if they're living with a man, which makes things all the harder. None of this is in the least criminal and though the police do what they can to find missing young women it can be a next to impossible job to find them if they never come before a court.

"Anyway, nothing more was heard of either Miss Benson or Miss Edwards—until Commander Furness heard of the MEW registration that Miss Danvers noticed on Mr Platt's car. Now EW is a Huntingdonshire mark, and the French setting among the objects deposited with the Receiver of Wreck at Plymouth was similar to one of the pieces of jewellery stolen from a certain Mrs Sighurst of Star Place, Huntingdon.

"Commander Furness put some men on a new line of inquiry, to see if Miss Benson had a car while she worked at Star Place. It turned out that she had, a small Fiat, and she had bought it new from a garage in Huntingdon. The police soon found the garage, and they had details of the transaction—and the registration of Miss Benson's car was MEW.

"Commander Furness at once got on to the police in Yorkshire to see if the Miss Edwards, who had worked at Holmfirth Castle, where the other jewel robbery was, had had a car. The staff there remembered that she had—there was nothing unusual about it, because several of the staff have their own cars—but two people remembered that Miss Edwards's car was a Fiat, and one thought that the registration might have been MEW—it had stayed in her mind because it made her think of cats, just as the MEW that Miss Danvers saw made her think of gulls.

"Nothing succeeds like success—or you might say that when a log-jam is broken, all the logs in the river begin to move. The next thing was that Commander Furness showed the group photograph with Miss Benson in it to the leading Fine Art auctioneers in London, and one of them thought that Miss Benson's picture resembled a girl who had once worked for his firm, although *she* was called Deborah Smith. The really big stroke of luck, though, came to our own Devonshire police who made inquiries at the pub near the diving camp and discovered that the girl you met there—who often came down to the camp—used to have a Fiat with a MEW mark. They remembered it because of the publicity given to MEW at the time of the hunt for Mr Platt's car, but nobody had said anything about it because the car the police were looking for was a big estate car, and the girl's car was a little Fiat. She didn't have it on her last visit; she told the barman, whom she knew quite well because she was often in the pub, that an aunt had left her a bit of money and that she'd sold the Fiat and bought an M.G.

"We didn't have all this information until about the middle of yesterday morning. The girl you knew as Sheila had a lot of explaining to do, and it was decided that she'd have to be brought in for questioning. But by the time Inspector Cornish got to the camp, she and the Layton man—at least, we must assume it was them—were at sea."

"What an extraordinary story!" Elizabeth said.

181

"It's an extraordinarily unsatisfactory one," said David. "How did the Layton man come into it?"

"At the moment I just don't know," Blundell replied. "But Inspector Cornish is at the camp now, and a man from the Metropolitan Police is on his way to join him. We can make a really thorough investigation of Mr Layton now, and although everything may not come to light, a good deal will. My own feeling is that the woman was the brains of the outfit, and that the plan for using wrecks to dispose of stolen jewellery was hers. She had worked for a big firm of auctioneers, and she knew her way about the Fine Art world. I think she was probably suspicious of you from your first appearance at the pub."

"Why of me? I was just a chance visiting yachtsman."

"Well, that's just what you weren't. They saw your boat come in, and she had her Fishing Boat Registration—F.17—in big letters on her bows. When you didn't say that you were a fisherman and rather implied that you were a yachtsman it must have made her suspicious at once. There was no need for her to tell you that story about how she'd been present at the finding of the jewels. I've been thinking a lot about it, and it strikes me as curious now that she should have gone into such detail to a chance-met stranger in a pub. It was quite a clever story, though."

"As far as she herself was concerned, maybe it was. It certainly gave me the impression of her as an office-girl or something on holiday, keen on underwater swimming and terrifically excited about the wreck. But what a fool I was to forget about *Lily*'s fishing marks. I never thought of them until you mentioned it. Lord, what mistakes I made!"

"She made mistakes, too. It was foolish of her to keep her car—and perhaps even more foolish to sell it after the chalice had been stolen. But I suppose, like you with *Lily*'s fishing marks, she never thought about it."

"Do you think she engineered our accident on the cliff road?"

"I don't know—probably we shall never know. But I'd think it probable. Everything goes to show that she had a hard, clear mind, did the planning, and was apparently quite unscrupulous. When you turned up again with Miss Danvers she knew she had to act quickly. I think the Layton man certainly recognised Miss Danvers, and I daresay she did, too. She may have put in

182

a lot of reconnaissance work at Combe Dean—she could have visited the place a dozen times as a holiday visitor, and she may have made it her job to learn about Miss Danvers, and her car. The fact that a woman turned up to look for wreckage from the cliff-top, and that the intruder in the rectory was probably a woman, both rather suggest her work. Don't forget that she was pretty familiar with rambling country houses."

"Do you think she would have harmed Daddy?" Elizabeth asked.

"I think it just as well that your father was not there."

David could get no further with speculation about the Layton-Sheila partnership because he had no facts of any sort to go on, so, for the moment, he stopped thinking about it. He was very much bothered about his own affairs. There was what seemed to him a huge bill from the Bray, Bray confederation to be met, he had to see Grimble about paying for *Lily*, and he had to find some sort of job for himself—and with Elizabeth's car a complete write-off he was without transport out of Combe Dean. True, he still had his bicycle, but he did not feel like bicycling—there was too much to do. At least he still had a few reserves, and he knew how to deal with banks. He asked Blundell to give him a lift to Finmouth. Elizabeth stayed to hold the fort at the rectory.

There was a branch of his own bank in Finmouth. He went there first, became again an efficient professional accountant, and after some telephoning arranged his immediate affairs. He didn't want anything to do with Bray and company, so he instructed the bank to send them a draft in full settlement of their bill. He also drew £800 in cash. He next went to a garage, and bought a secondhand Mini in what seemed reasonable condition. It was priced at £700, but his offer of cash on the spot brought the price down to £600. This left him £200 in hand, enough, he felt, to replace some of the clothes he had lost with *Lily*, and to see him through the next few weeks. He had now to find Grimble, who would almost certainly be in the pub.

His various transactions had taken the whole morning, and when he got to the pub it was crowded, with everyone listening to the one o'clock radio news. It all seemed to be about him, and Elizabeth, and the chalice.

"Why, here's Dave himself!" Grimble said as he walked in. Grimble, and at least half a dozen of the other fishermen there, all wanted to buy him a drink. He was glad enough of the drink, which rapidly became drinks, but who paid for them he never discovered: he was allowed to pay for nothing himself. "Tell us, Dave," said one of the men, "was it just a bit beyond your new Grendon's ground?"

Grimble hit him in the ribs. "Hear that, Dave?" he said. "Grendon's ground—that means you're proper one of us."

David told his story over again. Being seamen, the men were chiefly interested in his manoeuvres with *Lily*, and in the way she sank her enemy and foundered. They also regarded it as a personal triumph that a Finmouth fisherman should have put paid to the scheming of "them lobster-poaching bastards". Everyone wanted to do something to help. "Look, Dave, I've got some spare gear you can have," said one man. "And you can borrow my boat for a week or two—I was thinking of taking a bit of holiday," said another. David found himself wanting to cry. He was thankful when it was closing time, and he walked with Grimble to the quay.

"What are you going to do about *Lily*?" Grimble asked.

"Don't worry—you'll be paid in full. I had her insured for as much as I owe you, and I don't forget to pay my debts. I may have to ask you to wait, though, until I get the insurance money."

"There you go, Dave, always jumping to conclusions. I didn't mean that—I meant, what are you going to do about a boat?"

"God knows."

"Well, look. I know a man over to Dartmouth who has another of your grand-dad's boats. She's a year or two older than *Lily*, maybe, and a mite bigger, but she's a good boat. I reckon he'd sell her to me if I asked him. Then I could sell her to you, like, same as I was selling *Lily*, the money to come out of shares from the catch. Then you wouldn't have to find a lot of money for a new boat."

"Jess, why are you all being so damned good to me?"

"You've played straight with us, Dave. And although we all use engines now, and I daresay you will one day, we've all got a bit of sail in our hearts. The lads like the way you handled *Lily*. As for money—maybe my dad once owed your grand-dad some money, and your grand-dad didn't press for payment.

Fishing-folk's got long memories. I like the sound of Grendon's ground. Seems to fit in, somehow."

"You're a real partner, Jess. Yes, of course, if you can get the Dartmouth boat, I'd love to have her."

"There's another thing, Dave. How long are you going on living at that rectory?"

"Again, God knows. I've nowhere else to go."

"Well, I've got an old cottage, not far from the quay. Belonged to an uncle of mine, and it came to me when he died without leaving a widow, because she died first, and they had no children, see? We've been letting it to summer visitors, but they mean a lot of work, and with my daughters all married and away, it's getting too much for my wife. I was wondering if you'd like to take it on—raise a mortgage or something, or pay for it through the catch, somehow. It's not a bad little house. Would you like to look at it sometime?"

"I don't know what to say, Jess. Yes, of course I would. But not now—I've got to get back and see what those bloody newspaper people have been doing to Elizabeth."

Elizabeth was greatly relieved at David's return, but puzzled to see him drive up in a car. "How did you get hold of it? Whose is it?" she asked.

"It's for you," David said. "You can't live in Combe without transport, and while I daresay you'll get something out of insurance on the old Mini, it may be ages before you do. This one's insured for you as well as me—I saw to that when I fixed up the insurance. So you can drive it with a clear conscience."

"But David, you can't go buying cars like this!"

"Well, I have. I'm not married any longer, I paid the bill for Louise's divorce this morning, and I can do what I like. What's more, I've got the chance of a new boat, and I've even been offered a house in Finmouth, which will be much more convenient."

Elizabeth felt her world falling away from her. "Of course, I always knew you'd have to go away," she said. "Only—only I didn't think it would be quite so soon. I shall miss you terribly."

David put his arms round her. "You need old Jess Grimble, to tick you off about jumping to conclusions," he said. "I'm not going away unless you want me to. What do you think I

185

want a boat and a house for? To earn a living and have somewhere to live—for us."

"David—are you asking me to marry you?"

"You could put it like that."

"Well, you'd better be careful, because if you do I shall say Yes."

The telephone rang. It was yet another newspaper. "I'm sorry," Elizabeth said. "I used the telephone to speak to Daddy—I rang up Sir George Dorrance again, and Daddy was at his house. I forgot to leave the receiver off when I'd finished. Daddy is coming home this evening—he's getting to Totnes just after eight o'clock. I was wondering how on earth to meet him without a car. Oh, David, I'm so mixed up. I can't help thinking about that nice Mr Fraser's mother—but everything is working out like a kind of fairy story for me. It seems so unfair, somehow." And she burst into tears.

David kissed her. "I don't understand things any more than you do," he said. "But I'm quite sure that Fraser himself—and his mother—wouldn't want you to be unhappy. He was like a soldier killed in action: it's desperately sad, but he died doing a job for the protection of other people—that's what police work really is. I won't say, 'Try not to think of him'. I do say, 'Try to think of him with understanding'. I don't know about you, but I haven't had any lunch. I was given a lot to drink in the fishermen's pub at Finmouth, but I haven't had anything to eat."

"I haven't either. I just didn't feel like it with you away. But I did bake some bread. So we could have a tea-meal if you like."

"I do like. But let's take the receiver off that phone again."

They had a lot to discuss. David said, "It seems pretty awful to rush from one marriage into another. I thought I'd never want to marry anyone again—but that was before I met you. I don't even know when we can get married—Louise has got her divorce decree, but I don't know how long we have to wait before I can legally be married again. You're taking a horribly big risk—I won't try to hold you to a remark made under considerable emotional strain."

"Well, it's a risk that I'm going to take. But there are one or two difficulties, my darling David. Daddy is not a bit sanctimonious, but he is a priest, and naturally he'd like me to be married

186

in church. As far as that goes, the parish would expect me to be married in Combe Dean church. That won't be possible. Daddy likes you, I think he likes you very much, but it might be better not to say anything about us to him at present. I don't want to hurt him—I absolutely dread hurting him."

"You were wrong before in not wanting to explain things to your father. I think you are wrong now. Will you let me talk to him? You needn't try to say anything to him until I have."

"I don't know, David—I'm not trying to dodge anything, I just don't want to hurt him. Yes, if you like. I'm still so mixed up. Who's going to look after Daddy? If I had to choose between Daddy and you, I'm afraid I'd choose you. But I don't want it to be like that."

"It won't be."

And it wasn't. There was no chance of talking about anything that evening, because the rector was so nervous and exhausted that when Elizabeth met him at Totnes he did not even notice that she was driving a different car. But he appeared unexpectedly next morning when Elizabeth and David were having breakfast. Normally, Elizabeth took coffee and toast to his room, but he had seemed so tired last night that she had said that she wouldn't disturb him until he called. Now he was up and dressed, much earlier than his usual time. "I couldn't sleep, I have very much on my mind," he said. "I have been subject to a great temptation. I must tell you about it, Elizabeth."

David got up to go, but Elizabeth said, "Can David stay, please, Daddy? We are close friends now, and I wouldn't want him to think we had any secrets from him."

"Of course," the rector answered courteously. "He knows our household, and I should, indeed, welcome his advice." He paused, and went on, "I have been remiss, as you know, I have been criminally remiss over the custody of our chalice. Had it not been restored to us, my path was clear—to continue working in the parish, for as little of my stipend as we could live on, using everything else to try to pay my debt. Miraculously, or so it seems to me, the chalice has been restored, and here is my temptation. All Saints has recently been left a substantial legacy for the special purpose of furthering research into Hittite studies. The Warden has discussed the matter with the Fellows, and he intimated to me yesterday before I left that the College would like to give me a Residential Fellowship to enable me to pursue these studies. It is my own field—it is work very near my heart. To my shame, I did not reject the offer there and then. I felt I needed time to think about it. Now, of course, I know my duty—I must write today to say that I cannot accept the proposed Fellowship."

"Why?" David asked.

"There are many reasons. Partly, I feel that I must punish myself for my carelessness over the chalice. Mainly, I must continue to provide a home for Elizabeth, and residence at All Saints would not, alas, permit me to do that."

"I am not much of a churchgoer," David said, "but I was brought up to be a Christian, and I hope that I still am. I was taught that punishment belongs to God—that is my answer to your first point. On your second, you need have no fear for Elizabeth's future. By the law of England, if not of the Church, I am free to marry again, and Elizabeth has agreed to be my wife. We have—or shall have soon—a house in Finmouth. Our anxiety until now has been for you—Elizabeth's major worry has been concern for looking after you."

The rector sat down at the kitchen table, and put his head in his hands. Then he looked up and said, "It is unfashionable to believe in the efficacy of prayer, but who shall say now? I prayed for the recovery of the chalice—and it has been restored. I prayed for guidance in my temptation, both to God, and with a special prayer to Saint Edmund of Abingdon, one of the first great teachers at Oxford, to whom I have always felt strongly drawn. I thought this morning that my prayers had been answered, in that I knew where my duty lay. What you have just told me proves that God is merciful as well as just.

"My children, I am of my generation in the Church, and it would not be honest to pretend that I welcome remarriage after divorce. But I am human and fallible, and in my pastoral life I have always counselled faith in the compassion of God to those whose marriages have broken. I cannot do less for my own daughter. You have been living in our home, David, and I know you, I suppose, a good deal better than most fathers know their prospective sons-in-law. Everything I know, I like—and it would seem that the recovery of the chalice owes much to you. I am sad that I shall not be able to marry you in

Elizabeth's own parish church. But our Church does provide for the blessing of all marriages sincerely undertaken, and that blessing I give to both of you, without reserve. Elizabeth, my darling, I have been, I fear, a very selfish father, in that I have permitted you to shoulder all the work of the rectory without much opportunity of having a life of your own. This has often worried me, but the parish always had to come first, and without you I do not see how I could have continued working for the parish. Now God has intervened to rescue you from my neglect. If I may speak as a man and not as a priest—yes, and as a priest too, conscious of God's mercy—I am utterly and absolutely delighted."

"Daddy, you have never neglected me. Life has just been horribly difficult," Elizabeth said.

Nearly two years later, David and Elizabeth's infant son was christened in Combe Dean church. His godfathers were Jess Grimble and Inspector Blundell, promoted to succeed Inspector Cornish when he retired.

Grimble was especially delighted. "It's the next best thing to the son I never had," he said. "We'll bring him up between us to handle a boat proper."

Canon Danvers travelled down from Oxford to assist the new rector at the service, and Sir George Dorrance came with him. Afterwards they all drove to the house in Finmouth for a small christening party. With the party meal over, and the baby safely asleep in his cot, they had about an hour to wait before Sir George and the Canon needed to leave for their train back to Oxford.

"What a happy occasion it has been," Sir George said. "But I can't help reflecting what an extraordinary chain of circumstance brought us all together."

"But where did the chain start?" David asked. "With Drake's plunder of a Spanish treasure ship? With the wreck of the *Madras*?"

"Those are all merely links—we should go back to the Spanish conquest of Peru, perhaps. To my mind the most extraordinary circumstance of all is the evidence that the archaeologists working on the *Madras* have brought to light— that she seems to have been wrecked by an explosion of gunpowder, and that the story of her scuttling by pirates was probably true."

"One evil followed by another, and another, and another," observed the Canon.

"And yet some good came of it in the end," Inspector Blundell said. "It broke up a particularly nasty bunch of jewel thieves—and blocked a horribly ingenious way of disposing of their loot."

"I still feel a bit sorry for the Layton man," David said. "He was just used by some much nastier people. I thought at first that using his own name for his maternal ancestors was a clever piece of work. I suppose it was, in a way, but the real reason must have been that they wanted to tighten the screws on him—it left him hopelessly incriminated—an anonymous telephone call could have put him out of the way at any time. They needed his particular skill, but it doesn't look as if he would ever have got much out of things for himself."

"I don't think you need feel all that sorry for him—at least, no sorrier than for the human tragedy behind any crook. When Fraser saw the chest prepared for the chalice—on a sling over the after hold, waiting to be let *down* into the half-excavated hold, not hauled *up* from it—Layton was quite ready to kill him on the spot. It was a merciful thing that the woman's body came ashore as it did. Fraser and Layton were never found—without the woman's body we could never have identified her, or broken up the gang."

"I've never been quite clear how you did identify her," Sir George said. "It struck me as a wonderful bit of police work after a body had been in the sea for a week."

"It was routine work mainly, luck partly," Blundell said. "It was luck that she'd had trouble with her teeth, and been to two dentists under two different names. The first time she was Deborah Smith, when she was working in London for the firm of auctioneers. That gave us a London address, and a starting point. Then she had to go to a dentist again in Huntingdon, as Emily Benson. The dental work proved that Deborah Smith and Emily Benson were the same. We managed to find some acquaintances of Deborah Smith, and got a good snapshot of her from one of them. That identified her as the Josephine Edwards who'd worked at Holmfirth Castle. It was while investigating Deborah Smith that we found the first links with Layton. He'd just come out of the Navy, and was instructing at a sub-aqua club to which she belonged—she was keen on underwater swimming genuinely enough, and I suppose that gave her the whole idea. Layton was very much attracted to her, and after that she could do anything with him."

"She was certainly attractive," David said. "Why did she want to be a crook?"

"Why does any crook? To have power over other people—to have money. . . . She was a very gifted woman. Before going to the auctioneers she'd been at an art school, and taken a course in goldsmith's work. We found one of her teachers—he said she was the best pupil he'd ever had, and he thought she'd have a great career as a designer. She did all the re-setting to disguise the various jewels stolen. Perhaps she couldn't get on as fast as she wanted by sticking to honest work. Even in these days some firms are pretty slow to give much responsibility to a girl. I don't know what happened. She became utterly ruthless and unscrupulous—I don't know what made her so. For all I know she was just born like that—in spite of what all the do-gooders say, there are evil people in the world."

Coming back from taking Sir George and the Canon to their train at Totnes, David and Elizabeth lingered on the quay for a moment before going into their house. *Dartmouth Lass*, David's new, or rather, slightly older, boat was on *Lily*'s old mooring, but he had little time to go out in her much now-adays. He'd formed his co-operative marketing organisation, and Finmouth Fish Enterprises was a thriving business. If the Breton fishermen find it worth while to come over and poach our lobsters, why don't we send lobsters to France? he had asked himself. Now a chartered aeroplane flew from Plymouth daily throughout the season with a cargo of Finmouth lobsters for restaurants in Paris. And why not mussels, too? There might not be much market locally for mussels, but the French seemed to have an insatiable appetite for them. So a new inshore fishing industry had been added to the rest.

Elizabeth's hand was in his. "I'm glad Louise married again," she said. "I've never understood why she wanted to be unmarried to you, but naturally I'm very grateful to her."

"Well, I couldn't make her Lady Louise, and her new husband is Sir Eric. I used to know him slightly. He's twice her age, but he's got pots of money, and a title. By my reckoning he's a pompous ass, but he can give Louise what she wants. I couldn't. The thing is, my darling, can I give anything to you?"

"Just everything," she said.

"What bothers me sometimes is that I started out to be a fisherman, and have almost gone back to being an accountant. Do you think that's bad?"

"You're helping a lot of other fishermen to make a better living. You're giving me—oh, David, I can never hope to tell you what you're giving me."

"So you don't think it's just another paper-money chase?"

"I don't think Grendon's ground is made of paper. Nor do you. What you've really done is to come home."

تمام شد